The StArchetypal Theater provides practical periencing your birthchart. Planets, Signs, House mental analysis and instead transform into a vib ied through movement, contemplated through meditation, and acted out through drama.

Planets are explored as evolutionary forces within our soul, seeking to be awakened and realized at certain regular intervals. Utilizing famous biographies and tools of practical magic, VerDarLuz paints a mythical map of the entirety of the human journey through planetary rites of passage, offering hands-on tools to individuals, parents, and lovers for the best ways to harmonize with all of life's initiations.

Student and Client Testimonials

VerDarLuz has given us a world of insight into our 2 year old. His readings have given us knowledge that our little one could never have verbalized—about his learning style, strengths and weaknesses, and ways to help him thrive in partnership with us. I often refer back to the readings. This awareness is invaluable, and I would encourage anyone interested to begin this precious journey with Ver.

—Jamie Burke, Denver

VerDarLuz is a fantastically gifted communicator and teacher with perceptibly light-filled intention.

—Rebecca Lerner, Portland; Journalist and Urban Foraging

VerDarLuz' teaching was concise and easy to follow—it was really positive and a great perspective on astrology and life.

—Gabrielle Earls, Australia; Yoga Instructor

I loved the multidisciplinary approach. Visually, the class was excellent, and I found his way of communicating to be thorough and intuitive.

—Amanda Moreno, Seattle; Depth Psychology Student

I was incredibly amazed at VerDarLuz' intuitiveness, compassion, and ability to ground the language of astrology to resonate with my process. He is an amazing healer, a true embodiment of a 21st century alchemist.

—Rashin D'Angelo, Denver, CO, Psychotherapist

EMBLEMA 5.
AVRI POTABILIS CHIMICE
PRÆPARATI

Codex of The Soul:

Astrology As a Spiritual Practice

Volume I:
The StArchetypal Theater

✶

VerDarLuz

Coming in 2011:
Codex of the Soul,
Astrology as a Spiritual Practice, vol. 2

Follow VerDarLuz on astralshaman.com

Codex of the Soul: Astrology as a Spiritual Practice,
Vol. 1: The StArchetypal Theater
Copyright 2010, VerDarLuz
Theophany Publishing

Cover Art by VerDarLuz and Hubble
Image of Pleiadian Star System and Chakras

Published by Theophany Publishing
First Edition, May 2010
10 9 8 7 6 5 4 3 2 1 0

Dedication

To my father, a living saint. You always said that each generation should improve upon the previous. This is my offering.

Acknowledgments

I would like to thank all of my teachers and mentors, those met and those still to meet on the path.

I wish to honor the lineage of sages, magi, stargazers, priests, and mystics—all who have received the flame of gnosis from the heavens and passed the torch of wisdom to future generations.

Thank you to Barbara Schermer for use of her elegant astrological cheat sheet.

I would like to give thanks to my editor Tara Shakti, for her tireless efforts, discerning eye, and warm heart. Om Tara Tuttare Ture Soha!

Thank you to my friend and designer Chelsey Lehl, for giving this book texture, shape, and contour.

I would like to give special thanks to Peter Wacks for his mentorship and guidance through the delicate process of self-publishing. Your generosity has helped to bring this book into embodiment.

I offer my sincerest gratitude to the helping spirits from other dimensions, who have been the true composers of this material. I especially honor Saraswati, Gabriel, Jeremiel, Urania, Mercury, and Jupiter.

And I wish to thank every reader for opening this book, for answering an invitation from beyond to step into the mirror and meet your higher self with the language of the stars.

Special Dedication

To the true authors of this book:

Gabriel - Archangel who assists messengers, artists, writers, and communicators.

Saraswati - Hindu goddess of wisdom, learning, music, and the arts.

Urania - Greek muse of astronomy and astrology.

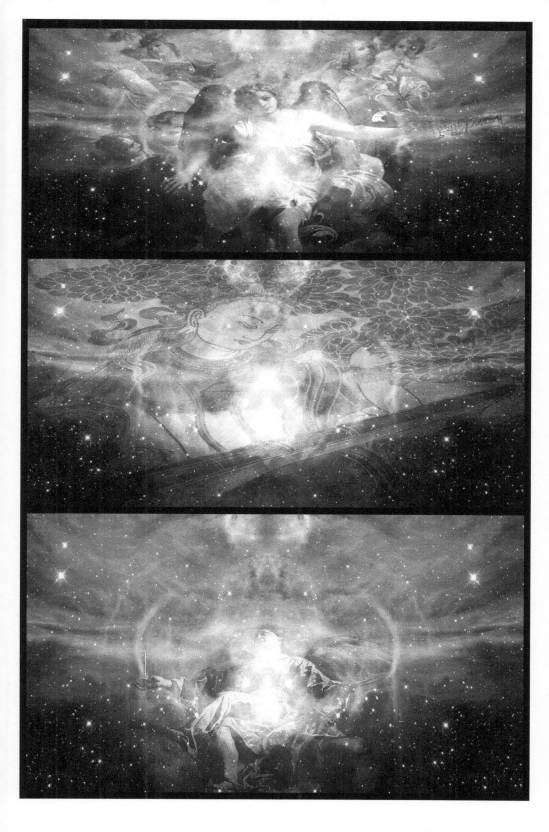

Contents

The Precious Gift

From the Source of Consciousness
Your birth erupts
an evolutionary intention.

Each breath initiates you,
into the prismatic Theater of Light
Your body is a rite of passage,
And you have come to translate the celestial map:
You have come to proclaim
the Zodiac,
the Codex of the Soul

You are the director, the soul-memory
You are the audience, the watcher
And you play every role

The Houses are the stages and scenes, the fields of life experience,
The Planets are the players within these scenes,
The Signs the roles they play,
And the Aspects are the wondrous dialogue,
the cosmic narrative of the tragicomic drama
where display the technicolor dreamscape
of spiritsong
and incarnation's passionplay.

So embark
upon this RelationShip
As souls entwined in density
still you sail
the sacred angles of intimacy
While the Fates who weave the fabric
of Humanifestation
sing out
your Destiny.

Your birth is a precious gift.
Your birth is the ultimate
Present.
Open it.

Introduction

As long as you consider the stars as something above the head, you will lack the eye of knowledge.

—Friedrich Nietzsche

In late 2005, I visited Guatemala for multiple reasons: to further understand the long count and day count of the Mayan calendar by working with Mayan elders, to participate in the Maya Activation ceremonies over the winter solstice at the ceremonial center of Tikal, and to help the survivors of the horribly destructive Hurricane Stan, which decimated villages near the sacred lake, Lago Atitlan. I planned to assist them in recovery, to document their struggle, and to share their story and their rich, cultural heritage upon my return to the United States.

I arrived amidst the post-earthquake rubble in my own internal state of crumbling. Just days before I arrived at Lake Atitlan, I had nicked my camera on a stone in a cave I had been exploring. Over the week that followed, the camera would not turn off, and eventually, would never turn on again. This fated event would transform my life and serve to teach me certain astrological truths over the years which followed, helping to heal the wounds inflicted in the ensuing months in Guatemala.

In my zeal to experience a culture I felt so kindred with, I did not understand then that I was about to experience the threshold of the most formidable planetary rites of passage in the entire life cycle—a triple initiation that occurs around the tender age of 27-28—the Lunar Return, the Nodal Reversal, and the early stages of the Saturn Return.

I was also unaware that I had traveled to an area on the Earth where the evolutionary forces of Mercury and Pluto crossed. There, the messenger, communicator, traveler, and storyteller Mercury would be forced into a Plutonian initiation of surrender, loss, grief, despair, and transformation.

Quite literally, the Plutonian symbol of destruction surrounded me. The rubble from the earthquake was slowly, but steadily being cleared from various buildings in the village of San Marcos, where I rented a small house. At 6:30 a.m. each morning except Sunday, I would hear the young Mayan workers banter and laugh in an ancient language, and then suddenly I would hear their sledgehammers plunge into the piles of stone.

During the months that followed, I felt my own soul pummeled as well. I watched as I became obsessed with my "role." How could I "identify" myself as a photographer and a documentary storyteller without my camera? Without my technology or tools, I was stuck and unable to fulfill this role. And the more attached I was to this identity, the purpose for which I thought I was there, the more I seemed to suffer.

✳ ✳ ✳

While I waited to see if my camera could get fixed so I could begin my documentary journey, I let myself connect with the heavens in a way I never had. I began to tell time by the position of Orion, aware that when the Hunter was directly overhead, it was roughly 8 p.m. I could also "clock" the nearby dance of the Pleiades, those "Seven Weeping Sisters," to the Greeks, the "400 Boys" to the Mayans, more commonly experienced by the average American as the Subaru logo.

At that time, I was unaware of the depth of astrology's history, its ubiquitous use in the world of the Renaissance and heights of the Islamic Empire, its beginnings with early man recording menstrual cycles by carving notches onto stones, and the depth and breadth of the monolithic monuments anchored around the planet— testaments to our ancestors' sacred relationship with the patterns and revolutions of the heavens.

I did not know that my ability to tell time by Orion had been mirrored on a famous journey by a man who had taken a last name which translated to "the dove." This man's name was Christopher Columbus, and on his journey across the Atlantic, he would tell time by studying Ursa Major, the constellation of the Great Bear. His name, "Columbus," was taken from the Italian "colombo" translated to "the dove," another name the ancient Greeks often used to refer to the Pleiades. On his journey, Columbus would take with him an astrolabe and an ephemeris, both essential tools to discern the planetary positions, to guide his journey across the seas. In fact, Columbus was just one of many oceanic explorers, all of whom navigated the vast oceans by the map in the stars above. (Bobrick 2005)

In that period of 12 weeks I stayed at the Lake, I learned roughly 12-15 constellations, and many of the stars within each celestial being, including some of the world myths for each of the constellations. I prided myself on learning the names of every star in Orion. I would create meditations where I would form a telescope with my hands and block off all sky but a single star. I would then inhale the light-energy and ask for the blessing from those star-tribes. With each exhalation, I would chant the name of the star and send my consciousness out to that system of entities.

I was not told or taught to do this. Rather, I was compelled. I was called by the luminous pulse of the stars themselves. Without TV, radio waves, or the global internet to distract me, I thought of the ancestors as they must have communed with the night. As Plato so eloquently communicated in The Republic, "It is clear to everyone that astronomy at all events compels the soul to look upwards, and draws it from the things of this world to the other."

The following poem was delivered by a celestial angel to me in those moments:

The Journey of your Soul

Once upon a night, you were mountaintop,
a child of awe,
humbled by the majesty
of innumerable pulsing light-beings,
frolicking in the forever-echo
of infinite star-songs.
You gazed upon a celestial theater.
Some lights shimmered fiery red incandescence,
some cool blue contemplation.
Some huddled together in packs,
others followed their own path.
Each was a candle and a character,
a story to illuminate the mysterious feelings within.
You were alone, but with 100 billion mirrors,
you wove a song of sacred magic
that would persist the whole night through.
And that song would continue
as long as you climbed to the mountaintop,
as long as turned your pensive gaze upward
and tuned your open heart heavenward,
and allowed your imagination to meet its maker.
The divine encounter,
remember?
Unplug!
Unplug your frail, electric umbilical cord.
No television, no computer, no sound system,
no environment to mediate
between you
and the dimensions beyond.
Simply the quiet, vast, unfathomable sky,
the holy star family,
the luminous tribes of the Night...

I wondered how I could grow up in a culture where I could name every character from Friday night's sitcoms or could have an infinite amount of sappy songs from the 80's etched into my memory banks, yet I had no awareness whatsoever of the stars and their meanings throughout time, nor the profound significance of their motions upon my own life.

And for some reason, the astrological bases of Columbus and other world explorer's vast journeys did not make it into the history books from which I was taught in my Catholic schools—nor did the fact that the Vatican owns the largest collection of astrological books on the planet.

What information could be so personally empowering that it must be hidden away? What language could be so expansive as to guide explorers across oceans to new lands? What perceptual medicine could compel shaman-kings to ascend to pyramid tops to perform sacred ceremonies that would guide their people for generations to come?

Initiation

For a man to conquer himself is the first and noblest of all victories.

—Plato

As I contemplated my connection to the heavens, I anxiously awaited news of my broken camera. I had given it to a native Guatemalan who said she could ask her friend in Gauatemala City to repair it. I waited for a month for the woman to return from Guatemala City, only to find out that the parts did not even exist in the country.

As the nodes in the sky reversed their position in my birth chart, my soul felt defeated, almost punished. I had wanted to travel to further develop my creative gifts. My soul longed to fulfill its spiritual quest, the North Node in Libra, the sign of the artist, in the fifth house of personal expression and creativity. But even as the soul becomes aware of its North Node potential at this time, often situations arise to tether it back to its South Node karmic attachments. Thus, instead of finding other means of creatively expressing myself at this time of disappointment, I returned to my soul's place of familiarity—my South Node Aries in the eleventh house. I forced the issue, with headstrong Aries determination and resilient will. I felt like a warrior on the battlefield. I distinctly recall my voracious online searching for a similar camera, my way of asking a friend to meet up with my parents and grab the new camera on her return trip back down to Lake Atitlan.

It seemed to be a synchronistic miracle that a friend would be coming down at the time that I needed this tool. Yet, her return was delayed, and I was forced to continue to wait.

It was at this Nodal reversal and the simultaneous emotional rebirth of the Lunar Return initiation when I most poetically and tragically experienced the Buddhist realization of anicca— impermanence and the First Noble Truth of suf-

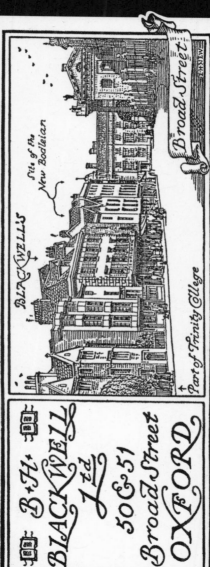

B·H· BLACKWELL Ltd
50 & 51 Broad Street OXFORD

BLACKWELL'S
Site of the New Bodleian
Broad Street
Part of Trinity College

fering. Each day, I would cleanse myself with tears in the purifying waters of Lago Atitlan, surrounded by volcanoes, a Plutonian symbol of the potent, unconscious forces bubbling up like destructive magma inside our hidden cores.

Meanwhile, I would not allow myself to leave the lake, because I did not have my photographic tool to "create memories or art." I also refused to visit the village that had been excessively damaged by the hurricane, since again, I did not have my tool to document their story.

The Interface of Eastern Spirituality and Shamanism

The feeling of entrapment that consumed me during these initiatory trials felt predestined. My soul seemed tethered, bound, and suffocated. In that miserable uncertainty, paralysis overwhelmed me. What was I doing there if I did not have my camera? And more importantly, why was I so damn attached to this identity mask?

I watched as I became exceedingly critical of myself, witnessing the absurdity of my situation and feeling imprisoned in my own story. I did not know that I was experiencing the Lunar Return, a universal occurrence around the age of 27. My Moon had returned to its birth position in the sign of Virgo, the most critical and analytical sign in the zodiac. I suffered the shadow of the Virgo archetype as I recognized only the lack, only the imperfection of what was happening.

My mind wanted to understand these processes so that my spirit could cooperate with forces that seemed so powerful and beyond my limited understanding. I knew meditation could help me return to the essence of simple being, beyond form and definition, and shamanic practice could connect me with the spirit world and the body of the earth in a sacred dialogue. But my emotional intelligence yearned for a language to truly comprehend my experiences as personally meaningful within a cosmic context. I was too young in my awareness of the astrological language to fully grasp its role as the healing bridge from my yogic and mystical disciplines to my transformational shamanic practices.

After six weeks of waiting, I at last received the new camera. I urgently tore it from its package and began to take pictures of the beautiful lake out in the distance. Finally, I could begin what I had intended to do: I could document the hurricane survivors and continue my own travels to other sacred sites.

And then, the lessons intensified.

Within just moments of taking my first pictures with my new camera, I dropped it. When I picked it back up, I fell into a state of shock as the camera only communicated back to me the phrase "Lens Error." For the next few days, I tried, repeatedly to turn the camera on, but it would not work.

My South Node in Aries flew off in angry fury, and my Moon relentlessly blamed myself for my careless irresponsibility. Pluto had once again swallowed the Mercury in me—the communicator, the recorder, the messenger—and tossed it into the volcano.

Dragging through the moments days later, I found myself magnetized to a book in a local guesthouse library. The book was called *Journey of Souls*, by hypnotherapist Dr. Michael Newton. It described his work with clients, guiding them through the spiritual passages of the *interlife*, the life between lives. Never had I read a cosmology that seemed to resonate so deeply within me. The descriptions of the Akashic records, the life review, soul clusters, levels of soul-development, guides, body and life selection—all of these transported my awareness into realms of such depth that each page I read seemed to transform my entire vibration. I experienced the positive aspects of the Mercury and Pluto crossing at that location on the globe—deep, penetrating information; a mind absorbed in the mysteries of birth, death, and rebirth; a cultivation and development of soul-linguistics. The more I read, the more clarity and peace I experienced.

I felt that the extreme nature of my situation had to be karmically related. Perhaps I had been a messenger in a past life, unable to deliver my message. Now I was becoming acutely aware of that deep wound, and repeating it, so that I could choose to react in a different way. Perhaps, I needed to learn the lessons of absolute presence, of appreciating the sanctity of the moment and its offerings, without the agenda to record it, to possess it, to etch it into some form for later study.

Each day, after my morning cleansing and crying in the lake, I would read Dr. Newton's book and allow my soul to consider the breadth and sanctity of its journey. For some reason, I had asked for this experience. Now, in hindsight, I understand the importance of the reversal of the Moon's nodes at that time. Long before incarnation, I had chosen these experiences to reflect the holding patterns within my soul. This choice allowed me to undergo such a level of suffering so that I could actually awaken to the intensity of my karmic journey. In addition, the return of the Moon to its natal placement forced me to submerge in the watery abyss of the fourth house, where my Moon is located. The fourth house invites one back into their soul-vision. This realm is associated with our family of origin, our early upbringing, possible past life imprints, and the stories we tell ourselves about who we are. The Virgo archetype of my Moon was able to weave together the disparate aspects of the apparent chaos around me, in order to understand their interdependent nature in a sacred context, as a turning point in the web of my multidimensional soul.

Rebirth of the Astral Shaman

Upon these revelations, I entered an important, transformational period, surrounding the event of a Full Moon. I had been gifted a very special drawing by a fellow Californian and visionary artist. He had drawn a beautiful image of the legendary Mayan shaman-king Pacal Votan. The drawing had been blessed in a shower of holy water: it had been dosed with LSD.

In my studies of the Mayan shamans as well as indigenous shamans from around the world, I had learned that to commune with the heavens in an altered state of consciousness was an essential component of spiritual practice. It was necessary—through meditation, psychotropic plants, ceremony, and ritual movement—to transcend the ordinary mind in order to grasp the vast expanse of the cosmos in a sacred dialogue with the star nations.

On this special Full Moon, I spent much of the night dancing at the peak of a beautiful mountain, bathed in the light of the Moon goddess, named Ix Chel in the Mayan tradition. As I danced, I prayed to Luna with the mantra I had learned in India: *Om hreem chandraye namah.* Her silvery kisses caressed the entirety of Lake Atitlan, as if she were dipping her royal gown into the majestic waters.

Through the eternal night, She traversed the sky, casting her glow. Then, as the few visible stars began to fade, the dawn of a new day slowly ascended, and friends from around the world gathered to behold the rising Sun on an outcrop of the cliff.

The bestower of life, the Solar Source rose above the distant volcanic peak, and began to radiate His divine heat and light onto me. Something ancient, primal, and preverbal stirred in me as Ahau, the Mayan Sun god, seemed to tiptoe along the wrinkled sparkles of the morning waters. A solitary fisherman sent his canoe out into the heart of the vast lake, and I once more transfixed my gaze on the rising Sun.

I realized then, in that holy moment, that the "second coming" of the "savior of the world," occurred each morning with the solar kiss of first light. The words of the Bible became suddenly illuminated as never before:

> And God said, 'Let there be lights in the firmament of the heaven to divide the day from the night; and let them be for signs, and for seasons, and for days, and years. And let them be for lights in the firmament of the heaven to give light upon the earth,' and it was so. And God made two great lights; the greater light to rule the day, and the lesser light to rule the night: He made the stars also... And evening passed and morning came.... (Genesis 1:15-1:19)

Cosmic Coincidence and Primary Duality

I suddenly understood the most simple and most profound truth—that there was only ever one time, split into a body of two: day and night, wakefulness and sleep, heaven and earth. All of apparent duality dissolved as a mirage, with the deeper awareness of the infinite and single thread weaving life together in an endless and eternal knot.

I could not help but recognizing once again the ultimate experience of cosmic coincidence or what I've come to feel as an awesome display of divine design. Behold the size of the Sun and the Moon as they appear in the sky. Now allow your mind to grasp that the Moon is 400 times smaller than the Sun, but 400 times closer to us, which gives the two heavenly luminaries the appearance of the same size in the sky, allowing for the majesty and awe of the eclipse. How could this be?

And then, as I sat with this awareness, letting it sink into me as the Sun showered me with its radiant heartbeat, I understood: how could this not be?

We are a mirror of the cosmos. "God created man in His own image, in the image of God He created him; male and female He created them." We are symmetrical beings, composed of X and Y chromsomes, resulting in one of two genders. This was the idea that Plato, the Pythagoreans, the Neoplatonists, the Gnostics, the Chaldean magi, the mystery school initiates, and the mystics of all traditions had understood: As above, so below. The heavens impart a knowledge, as Jesus said, "for those with ears to hear."

One of my first astrology teachers, the creator of Shamanic Astrology, Daniel Giamario, had stressed to me the importance of being with the heavens, beholding the mystery of the skies in order to receive their wisdom. This was the way of the ancients on the path to the anceStars.

I had only the summer before began to understand myself more con-sciously as a collection of archetypal energies—gods and goddesses surging, sing-ing, fighting, psychological forces intrinsic to creation, playing at love and war within me.

At Lake Atitlan in Guatemala, during that delicate passage of the Lunar Return and Nodal Reversal, I felt those gods battle in me. Like the shamans of old, I was carved from the inside out, dismembered so that I could shed the tired layers which cloaked my perception. Beneath these, a sacred myth unfolded, the origins reverberated, the divine design began to emanate; I was slowly becoming conscious of the Codex of the Soul.

Then the lamp of wisdom is lit by itself. How can it remain unlit when the light of Allah's secrets shines over it? If only the light of divine secrets shines upon it, the night sky of secrets will be lit with thousands of stars,

and by the stars [you] find [your] way
(*Nahl* 16)

It is not the stars that guide us, but the divine light. For Allah has

decked the lower heaven
with beauty [in] the stars.
(*Ya Sin* 6)

If only the lamp of divine secrets is kindled in your inner self, the rest will come, either all at once or little by little. Some you already know, some we will tell you here. Read, listen, try to understand. The dark skies of unconsciousness will be lit by divine presence and the peace and beauty of the full moon, which will rise from the horizon, shedding

> Light upon Light
> (*Nur* 35)

ever rising in the sky, passing through its appointed stage as Allah

> has ordained for it stages, till it
> (*Ya Sin* 39)

shines in glory in the center of the sky, dispersing the darkness of heedlessness.

> (I swear) by the night when it is still.
> (*Dhuha* 2)

> By the glorious morning light,
> (*Dhuha* 1)

your night of unconsciousness will see the brightness of the day. Then you will inhale the perfume of remembrance....And you will understand the secret that

> It is not permitted to the sun to catch up
> to the moon, nor can the night outstrip the day.
> Each swims along in (its appointed) orbit
> (*Ya Sin* 40)

...and the veils will lift and shells will shatter, showing the fine under the coarse; the truth will uncover her face. All this will start when the mirror of your heart is cleansed. The light of the divine secrets will fall upon it if you wish and ask for Him, from Him, with Him.

—From a letter by Hadrat 'Abdul-Qadir al-Jilani
(Bayrak 1998)

Preface

Astrology is astronomy brought down to earth and applied to the affairs of men.

—Ralph Waldo Emerson

Astrology derives from experience which can be denied only by people who have not examined it.

—Kepler

In a teleconference seminar I held in the winter of 2010, one student was very concerned with "waking up" a significant number of people before 2012. He asked what we should do about this urgency. I responded with an aphorism, combining the wisdom of Jesus and the ancient Greek world: "Know thyself that you may heal thyself."

Today, this quest for self-knowledge and the importance of righteous livelihood is expressed in Gandhi's phrase "Be the change you want to see in the world." Indeed, we must learn to act as our own physician, shaman, and agent of change. The Astral Shaman utilizes the medicine of the stars as a healing and instructional tool for the soul to grow. Who is the Astral Shaman? You are. You tunneled through wormholes, you slid through celestial dimensions, you crossed over, and you arrived here, now.

But astrology? Really? You're skeptical. And that's a good thing.

Thank the Stars for Skepticism: A Correction of Pop Astrology

After pornography, astrology websites are the most visited online sites. Hmm. So we know it's a popular subject, but isn't astrology just those silly sun-sign columns?

We all recognize Sun-sign columns as that infamous version of pop astrology. Pop astrology is a bit like pop music, and both are a bit like lollipops—they may taste good, but there's not much nutritious substance beyond the immediate gratification of their sugary coat. If one listened only to the radio, music would cease to be an interesting, enlightening, or spiritual experience relatively quickly. Likewise, if astrology was limited to simply what is found in weekly Sun-sign columns, there would be good reason to hesitate with this information.

Sun-sign columns are both helpful and dangerous to astrology. They invite many of us into the language of the stars, and there is some guidance there. However, by its nature, it must be highly generalized, applying to one in twelve people.

How did Sun-sign columns become so popular? They began in 1930 as the editor of the Sunday Express wished to do a story about the birth of the Princess Margaret. He wanted to do a piece about what the stars foretold for the princess and so wished to work with Cheiro, a famous astrologer at the time. Cheiro was unavailable, so the job went to R. H. Naylor, one of Cheiro's assistants.

The story listed certain key factors of the princess' chart beyond her Sun-sign, such as the nature of her midheaven, the vocational path. It also predicted powerfully important events in her life around age seven, which later came true. In a side note, Naylor mentioned some key world forecasts to watch for and forecasts for each birthday in the coming week.

Naylor's article aroused a huge response with requests for more forecasts. Naturally, the Sunday Express saw a huge potential here for increasing their readership, and so within a month, began a weekly column that according to the editor, would "interpret the astrological portents likely to influence national and world affairs each week. He will give warning advice to City men, racing men, and politicians, and will, in addition, tell you what fate may have in store for you if your birthday should fall during the week."

The article ran into the 1940s and was religiously followed by many. It included such tips as the best days for buying, selling, entertaining, and playing sports and games. Naylor's forecasts were by birth date, not by the generalized Sun-sign. However, the article's instant popularity led to pressure to create a simplified system of astrology suitable for a newspaper column. The only type of highly generalized, simple astrology Naylor could come up with was a Sun-sign analysis. Immediately, the Sun-sign column was picked up by newspapers around the country, and has been popular ever since. (Dean and Mather 1996)

The Solar Hero and Western Individualism

We may argue that the same force which has created a fear of pre-destination in the Western mind is the same force which compels so many people to attach importance to Sun-sign columns. As mythologist Joseph Campbell has made abundantly clear in the body of his works, the fundamental mythos of the western mind revolves around the symbol of the Solar Hero.

Sun worship has been a primary component of western culture since before its heights in pharaonic Egypt. The Sun is our life-giver, the sustainer of our vitality, and so was worshipped as a primary deity in almost every known culture.

The emperor or king, as the pinnacle of the life of the nation, was always an extension of the solar principle. In Rome, for instance, Sol Invictus was worshipped as the "unconquerable Sun," and represents that principle of the undying hero.

We in Western cultures have adopted this notion that we are the sole or "sol" (Spanish for sun) source of radiance for the achievement of our life purpose. We are the creators of our own destiny; therefore, we attach the greatest of symbolic importance to the life-sustainer, the Sun.

But this is why the mystical traditions and even certain aspects of the Koran and the Bible admonish those who worship the sun, moon, and stars as deities, instead of as symbols of God's love. They remind us that the Sun receives its ability to give life and light from a much more fundamental Source.

Life continuously reminds us that although we have many purposes, we are not in charge. We are instead a collection of various psychological urges dynamically exchanging with each other.

In astrology, each planet represents a different, but equally important, primal psychological and evolutionary forces within us. Once one steps beyond the narrow confines of the entertaining Sun-sign columns, a kaleidoscopic vision of the self emerges, a multidimensional mandala of the life process.

In its simplest form, astrology is a manual for living life that works. On the individual level, astrology can act as an x-ray into the psyche. According to stariq.com author Jeff Jawer, it is the "clearest, most concise and well-developed system of personality analysis ever created—a twelve-fold typology with overlapping elements and modes that both makes practical sense and tells an elaborate and comprehensible story of the individual." (Phipps 2008)

When you begin to study astrology, a profound realization occurs. In the simplest sense, an evolutionary urge within you can express itself in one of twelve energetic styles, one of twelve realms of life experience. Immediately, you discover 144 possible costumes for a single evolutionary force within you. The texture of this psychological force is further augmented and developed by its relationships to other planets, those other characters in the drama. The amount of diversity in the human experience is a testament to the myriad expressions possible with so many evolutionary forces dancing and playing with each other.

And yet experiences, relationships, stories repeat in our lives. We can watch a film or read a story and feel the resonance within us. The stacking of similarity on top of the unique helps us to understand the primacy of twelve fundamental archetypes—shaded, shaped, and sculpted in different proportions, poetically prescribed to us in our passage through the dimensions into this sacred experience called life.

As Our Languages Evolve, So Do We

The majority of astrologers begin their work as skeptics, attempting to disprove what seems initially like the silliest of concepts—that the skies somehow tell me who I am. But, as astrologer Nick Dagan Best says, "I wake up every day with the exclusive intent of disproving astrology, and I go to bed each night having utterly failed." (Phipps 2008)

However, those former skeptics don't actually become "believers" in astrology. The word astrology can be broken down into *astro* (star) and *logos* (language/study of). So, astrology is a language, and a language is a form of perception. One does not 'believe" in Spanish or English, but one can use its vocabulary, grammar, and verse as a perceptual lens through which to experience the world. Astrologer and talk-show host Carolyn Casey says "Remember, we don't believe in astrology, we just notice that it works." (Phipps 2008) Well, we might as well use what works, and get passionate about it in the process.

I consider myself a pragmatic person—I'm interested in languages I can use that help me to more efficiently live, love, serve, and evolve. Along with millions of other astrology students, I have found the language of the heavens has the potential to guide us to an extent beyond any individual's comprehension.

Naturally, we might ask, "*Why* does astrology work? Perhaps it works because it is both a science and an art, and so synthesizes the left and right brains, the modes of masculine and feminine perception. The art is practiced through the astrologer's role as counselor, coach, and translator. The astrologer, also, is a technician, adept at combining an applied, exact, and empirical science. As Benson Bobrick writes, [Astrology] is an *applied science*, insofar as it is based on astronomy; an *exact science*, insofar as its judgments are based on mathematical calculations; and an *empirical science*, insofar as its deductions are based on data gathered over the course of time." (2005, 5)

Indeed, there is nothing more "scientific," in the pure sense than an ephemeris, which is a table of planetary positions. By observing the regular motions of the planets around the Sun, and through thousands of years of correlating the meaning of the planet's position by constellation sign and by geometrical angle to other planetary bodies, astrologers have developed a system for synchronistic meaning and symbolic understanding. Astrologers study an ephemeris in order to learn where the planets were last year or a thousand years ago, as well as next year or one hundred years from now. Simultaneously, the ephemeris, as Nick Dagan Best states, is the "combined biography of billions of souls." (Phipps 2008)

And whether or not we can fully grok the mystic roots of its mechanisms, we need not know how astrology works in order to utilize it as a tool for personal growth and collective evolution. Practice astrology, first, because it works, and because efficiency in life is a great attractor at this momentous time of cultural transition and spiritual transformation. As scientific findings continue to confirm a quantum reality, our old mechanistic models of the universe keep decaying, our limiting ways of viewing ourselves and the world keep fading, giving rise instead to descriptions of life and reality based on inspiration, meaning, and purpose.

One of my goals as an astrologer, writer, and teacher is to demonstrate how astrology is one of the most "practical" of spiritual practices, once it is understood as a system of archetypal linguistics which pulses in, through, and around you in every moment.

As Terence McKenna theorized, the unique condition of humanity is that we are a language-creating species. As our environments change, we fashion stories to adapt and evolve with them. And we cannot evolve until our languages evolve. (1994)

Since astrology is a language composed of archetypes—the primal components of creation—there is really no realm of life which could not benefit from its application. This is the very reason why there are so many branches sprouting from the roots of the astrological Tree of Knowledge.

The Fields of heaven: Types of Astrology

Before we dive into the language, I want to give you a brief but comprehensive overview of the vast applications of the heavenly language.

Every culture in history has utilized a language of the heavens. It is the single, unifying intellectual thread which connects all cultures across time, a wisdom lineage dating back over 5000 years. Even if we go back to 2677 B.C., we discover that the Chinese emperor Huang Ti believed that astrology was a vehicle by which humans could attain the natural order and harmony he dreamt could exist for the people in his empire. (Miller and Brown 1999)

Traditional astrology had five main branches: mundane, natal, horary, electional, and medical. **Mundane**, concerns society as a whole, and includes predictions about weather, harvests, politics, war, and epidemics. *Natal* astrology, the most common type of astrology, refers to one's nativity or birth moment and describes the character and destiny of an individual. **Horary** (meaning 'of the hour') is a form of astrology dealing with responding to a particular question. A chart is cast for "the hour" or moment when the question is asked and received by the astrologer. An answer to the question is then determined by this chart. **Electional** astrology is used to determine the most auspicious moments for an action or enterprise, especially useful for sacred rites such as weddings. **Medical** astrology has been practiced for thousands of years as well, and is one of the most underappreciated aspects of this cosmic language. From one's birthchart, chronic and potential health conditions can be determined. From the transits to one's birthchart, the onset of certain diseases can be predicted.

All of these traditional forms of astrology are still practiced today, and have been expanded upon. For instance, the most common use of electional astrology is to determine the most propitious moment for couples to be married. But elections can also be chosen for such widespread activity as beginning a business, leaving on a trip, sending a manuscript to a publisher, and much more.

In 2008, many people voraciously read astrology columns concerning the elections. Astrology associated with politics and world events is called *mundane* astrology, not because it's boring, but because it's named after the Latin word for world, *mundo*. All countries and even cities have their own birthcharts. In addition, due to the economic crises around the world, a specific type of astrologer is being consulted now more than ever: the financial astrologer.

An important and emerging synthesis of mundane astrology and natal astrology is a form of historical and biographical analysis of the collective psyche called **Archetypal Astrology**, which investigates cultural patterns across space and time, correlated to the cycles of the slower-moving outer planets.

Generational astrology flows directly out of Archetypal Astrology. It focuses on the roles members of a particular generation play in evolving collective consciousness.

Synastry and Composite Charts, extensions of Natal astrology, are profound tools used to elucidate the nature of partnerships. These relationships include connections between intimate beloveds, business partners, friends, and family members.

Relocation astrology synthesizes various traditions of astrology in order to guide the client to the best places for travel and relocation to support an individual's intentions.

Lastly, one of my favorite applications of the celestial language is **Experiential Astrology**, an emerging form of embodied astrology including astrodrama, astroyoga, and various ways of dancing the zodiac and the birthchart.

✳ ✳ ✳

I have always been cautious in the use of labels and definitions as they most often do not accommodate the reality of impermanence, change, or growth. But if I was to define myself in any way, it would be less as an astrologer, and more as a mystic: A Poetic Synchronistic Linguistic Mystic.

But mysticism has always transcended language, and so it naturally leans towards poetry—contemplative, artistic, illuminating, but defying structural bounds. Astrology is a symbolic language, and so, like great poetry, helps us to narrate our lives in a process of aesthetic and instructional reflection.

I chose to write this book because of the profound revelations this archetypal language has bestowed upon me. The mystic's experience is a completely subjective realm of epiphany, a recognition of interdependence at its core level. And synchronicity is the mystic's greatest perceptual instrument. I have been both humbled and empowered by the seemingly disparate elements that leap across space and time to bring meaning, wisdom, and spiritual understanding to each moment of my life.

With the assistance of the astrological language, one's experiences of synchronicity transform into an awakening in the soul we can call "astronicity," meaningful correspondences between the events of my life and the cycles of the heavens, whose patterns unfold with evolutionary purpose.

For instance, when you consider your life from the perspective of planetary rites of passage, you are first humbled by your recognition. Then you may feel yourself overflowing with inspiration and awe that indeed a map for the magical, but often treacherous journey of life, actually exists.

Even the word "consider" finds its roots in the heavens. To "con-sider" comes from the Latin, *considerare*, "to look at closely, observe," or literally, "to observe the stars," as *com*, means "with" and *sideris*, "constellation."

As you consider and apply this cosmic language, this astral revelation, a revolution occurs within you. In this sense, your birthchart is your soul's *rave-lation*. And the hermetic principle passed along from sage to scholar to magi to prophet that "As above, so below, as within, so without," becomes a visceral experience of gnostic epiphany.

It is this very mystery pulsing at the heart of astrology which actually makes it such an attractive art and science. It is a study of nature's process unfolding with my participation: a collection of observations and correlations, of pattern-recognitions, and wisdom-applications. My inner, personal experience mirrors the story in the heavens, and the reverse is true: the cosmos reflects my psyche and the shapeshift landscapes of my soul.

An Invitation to My Readers

Part 1 of *The StArchetypal Theater* answers the question, "Why bother with astrology?" Why should we learn this ancient, mystical language? What is its value and role in my life? How can it help me serve the world at my highest capacity? The second half of the first part explores the path of Divine Emanation as an astro-cosmology that unfolds to help us re-enchant our universe. This process leads us directly into the birth of the elements and modes, the primal vocabulary of astrology.

Part 2 introduces the vast language of what I call the StArchetypal Theater—planets, houses, signs, aspects. You are invited into the intricate dance of your multidimensional soul so that every aspect of your life may be illuminated as a pattern of energy—from your relationship intent to your spiritual vocation, from the food that you eat to the music you listen to. As you probe these patterns of energy, you are given the tools to interpret a birth chart, allowing astrology to guide your spiritual awakening.

Part 3 details the universal human experience of planetary cycles of initiation. Understanding these patterns awaken us to the mythical map of our sacred experience of incarnation. Many profound cycles that we all experience, such as the Saturn Return or the Uranus Opposition, are described with biographical portraits and counseling advice offered to assist you in finding the best way to harmonize with these cycles.

In this book, *The StArchetypal Theater* invites you in to the magical circus of your existence. Together we carve out the key to the Codex of your Soul. But you must unlock the door to the secret chamber of your heart. And you must step through the mirror, and ascend into You.

Part I

The Value of Astrology:
A Sacred Language for Delicate Times

*Astrology is a science in itself and contains an illuminating body of knowledge.
It taught me many things, and I am greatly indebted to it. Geophysical evidence
reveals the power of the stars and the planets in relation to the terrestrial. In
turn, astrology reinforces this power to some extent. This is why astrology is like
a life-giving elixir to mankind.*

—Albert Einstein

*Astrology is one of the most ancient Sciences, held in high esteem of old, by the
Wise and the Great. Formerly, no Prince would make War or Peace, nor any
General fight in Battle, in short, no important affair was undertaken without first
consulting an
Astrologer.*

—Benjamin Franklin

*The whole body of this world is as a man's body, for it is surrounded in its utmost
circle with the stars and risen powers of nature; and in that body the seven spirits
of nature govern and the heart of nature standeth in the midst or center.*

—Jacob Boehme

Chapter I
Surfing the Chaord

Every moment is pregnant with meaning, if you are listening. This game of life is not random chaos, nor a strict order. You find yourself in between, riding the "chaord." As you surf this chaordic existence, you inhale personal purpose and interpret spiritual significance for your life's events in proportion to your level of consciousness. At the most cosmic and inclusive level of understanding, every person is an angelic messenger, every moment a sacred reflection of a spiritual lesson you came to learn. Astrology is a language which elucidates this process.

The astrological camera lens is both macro and telephoto. First, it widens your horizons of understanding, interdependently linking what may seem distant and disparate elements. Simultaneously, it microscopically magnifies the totality of your internal and external environment to reveal the rich and complex hologram of life—the patterned systems of thoughts, emotions, and behaviors which synthesize to form your personal and collective Being. In utilizing an astrological framework for your earthly experiences, embodiment mutates into a magical education.

We are now urgently educating ourselves, teaching each other how best to imagine a new world, and how exactly to narrate the visionary dialogue of our shared evolution. In order to sing forth into being this emerging myth of human ascension and cosmic unity, you first need to understand the personal mythos breathing through you.

You feel a heroic calling, a spiritual warrior's invocation, pulsating from an internal depth of infinite potential. You wish to step out from behind any false masks, to unveil your true self behind any illusory outer identities. It is time to awaken to your mission. And so your personal alchemical opus beckons you.

To apply the astrological language in your life is an alchemical act: you learn how to transmute your base, shadow self, into a refined, golden work of art. This process was called the "Great Work" by the alchemists. This "Great Work" of your soul, and the healing of the Planetary Soul, begins with the contemplation of your sacred script. In the puzzle of life, where do your pieces fit and how do they shapeshift through time and space? How do you surf the chaordic edges of existence with clear intention? The word "surrender" means "to melt to the highest." So how then, do you melt the limited ego down in order to ascend and surrender to your soul's highest purpose?

When you first begin astrological exploration, you may feel intimidated by the journey into the birth-chart, afraid of what will be revealed there. This reaction to the astrological code, however, enslaves you to a disempowered and incomplete perspective of yourself. In this denial of your self-knowledge, you may find yourself drowning in avidya, the Sanskrit term for ignorance. You fail to accept the effervescent totality of your Being. And so you habitually play out the karmic patterns—the ego's desires for pleasure and aversions to pain. Meanwhile, you sacrifice the fruitful presence offered to you—the golden, effulgent revelation occurring in the perfection of the Now.

For you were born in response to a spiritual need in the universe. In every way, this was the most intentional of all possible acts in which the soul could participate. To bring the same intensity of intention to the realm of embodiment on earth, you are asked to remember this self-inscribed language of your soul. In the natal birthchart, you find a map which leads to the treasure of your essence. In the astrologer, you find a translator of the Codex of the Soul, a guide on the path to becoming the Astral Shaman.

Mindful Awareness and The Sacred Role of Astrology

Ye who seek, shall find.

—Jesus

The Buddha teaches that ignorance clouds all true understanding. "Individuals with mindful awareness," says the Buddha, "are free of harmful influence." In essence, the Buddha is stating that if you lack self-awareness, you cannot act wisely since you will be habitually and unconsciously responding to stimulus in your environment. Reactive behavior keeps you in the loop of seeking pleasure and avoiding pain, never understanding the fundamental nature of reality, and the importance of appreciating anicca or impermanence. This reactive ignorance is how you become a product of fate. However, as you become aware of your soul-contracts and incarnation agreements, you can learn to steer the ship of your destiny as a co-pilot, not just ride the roller coaster as a passive passenger.

And so this radical self-awareness is the alchemical mission of the modern avatar such as yourself. Your role as an Astral Shaman is to transmute your base, unrefined, reactive self, into a vessel of luminosity, an enlightened bodhisattva who seeks to serve all beings on their path of awakening.

In many ways, it is far more challenging today than in any other point in history to remain mindful. From multiple online chats while writing an email, to texting while driving, to talking on the phone while watching the news, multitasking is a standard, expected, and sometimes necessary behavior. Yet the need for intentional, mindful relationship to yourself, to others, to the body of the earth, and to the sacred dimension of the heavens is essential for all of our continued survival.

The astrological language provides parameters for this mindful attention, and its application in one's life actually increases free will as one applies and integrates the lessons of the birth chart. Past experiences are studied to gain wisdom and perspective to apply towards potential energetic expressions of one's future circumstances. Past and future meet in an enhanced and empowered present, as one compassionately strategizes one's life with evolutionary intention.

As the Buddha sat at the base of the Bodhi tree, he realized that every thought, action, idea, and feeling was interdependent with every other. No single part had substance in and of itself. No phenomena, sentient or inanimate, are separate from the causes and circumstances that create them, and so we are constantly relating to everything around us. We exist, relatively. The internet has increased our self-awareness as a global village, interconnected on every level. We both create and are created by all of life. As a guide of souls, the astrologer reveals these interconnected pathways, and in doing so, facilitates greater options for you to make more conscious choices in life..

The Astrologer as Scientist is a technician of a craft, familiar with a metaphysical and linguistic tradition dating back 5000 years and spanning every culture, a science which still applies to every aspect of life. The Astrologer as Artist is a counselor who translates the mirror of your consciousness, and coaches you on how to best to use your karmic toolset to actualize your dharma—your incarnate potential. With consciousness, you can transform your karma into your dharma.

And so the Art-strologer, the Astral Shaman is born—the synthesizer of the left-brain rational mind and the right-brain intuitive mind, the one who listens deeper in order to instruct more wisely. On the role of the astrologer, Robert Blaschke states,

> There is a spiritual responsibility in communicating the horoscope to the client. I think just like medicine where what is done by the physician can either heal or harm, astrologers are in a similar role. The astrological information can either be used in a negative and destructive way or in a positive and uplifting way.... People want to feel that connection to the divine, that connection to the cosmos. Yet I think that modern society has become so secular and so consumer-oriented, there's a lot of spiritual emptiness in present day society and astrologers are filing that gap the same way the priestly class used to do in ancient times. (Phipps, 2008)

Without the map of the birthchart, the psychologist, counselor, or coach, often views only a narrow field of vision into the individual soul. The delicate textures of the individual are lost to "standardized" complexes or overly generalized new age affirmations. Therefore, each of these counseling fields can benefit from the specific soul-cartography depicted in resplendent detail in the birthchart and its evolutionary transits.

Author and professor Richard Tarnas states that psychology textbooks of the future will look back on 20th century psychologists working without the aid of astrology like medieval astronomers working without the aid of a telescope. Likewise, history textbooks of the future will also look back at 20th century historians working without the aid of astrology in a similar way, increasingly as only perceiving events with a narrow lens. For astrology "opens up the deeper archetypal rhythms and patterning and cyclical evolutions of cultural phenomena." (Phipps 2008)

As Vedic astrologer Dennis Harness states, "The astrologer of the future will be more of psychomythologist." (Phipps 2008) Like the chorus of a Greek play, the astrologer can narrate and guide the client deeper into his or her journey into the emerging, evolving metapoem of the soul.

Transits, Participatory Synchronicity, and the Dialogue with the Divine

How do you become your own psychomythologist? How do you become an Astral Shaman?

Your birthchart unveils your very relation with the Source. It is your linguistic key into a conversation with the Divine. With a language to guide you in the dance of impermanence, you experience a richness of meaning at the orchestration of synchronicity in your life. Only a poetic, imaginative mind can grasp the magnitude of intelligence behind your life's magical design, as the Cosmos seems to sing both directly to you and to every other individual. You experience the supernatural textures of numinosity—the felt presence of the Beyond, the ineffable Mysterium Tremendum. And you ask, how can something so transcendent affect the phenomenal world in such a personal way? In awe and humility, you become empowered to live more authentically your verse of the interwoven Poem of Being.

Today we are gifted with so many techniques and tools to perceive the unfolding patterns in our lives. For example, knowing when a transit is going to occur in your life gives you the ability to actively seek omens in your life. In this way, astrology becomes interactive as you dance in the center of the holographic mandala. Here, everyone is your messenger, every event is meaningful. As you engage the unfolding design of your life, your consciousness brilliantly illuminates the patterns in the true meaning of the word psychedelia—"mind manifesting" before you.

When you meditate upon and engage with your transits—the current invitations and initiations of evolutionary forces—you experience your life in a cosmic context. You recognize that particular elements of your soul are seeking evolution and education. The transiting planet will trigger that point in your chart and will activate that realm within your soul. Your daily journal is transformed into a dialogue with a sacred dimension of synchronistic meaning. What was previously perceived as random chaos is transfigured into patterns of profound significance. You see the "signs" all around you, you hear the cosmos sing directly to you—and you wish to respond.

The language of astrology itself is neutral–it is a mapping of processes rooted in the archetypal dimension but occurring amidst the human sphere of experience. As you study and apply this language of the heavens, you understand that your life is not random, but pulsing with heavenly signs, overflowing with meaning, with an intelligent synchronicity orchestrating existence. For astrologer Robert Blaschke, astrology is the Holy Spirit, "a necessary language that connects heaven with earth." (Phipps 2008)

But synchronicity is participatory. And so this cosmic communication is not a fated monologue with the universe; rather, it is a dance of deeper listening which can affect a psychological regeneration and a spiritual liberation. Life becomes more of a magical play, an alchemical laboratory for learning, and immediate application of wisdom for personal and collective soul-evolution.

Let's say that you learn that Saturn is about to transit your Sun by conjunction. Knowing that the Sun symbolizes your life purpose and vitality, and that Saturn's evolutionary urge to mature and invite great responsibility to whatever point it touches, you can prepare yourself for a more serious time in your life, where you must discipline yourself and work hard. Since Saturn can limit or restrict what it touches, you may feel that you have less energy and you may even feel depressed or disappointed in yourself, especially in the house or realm of life experience where the Sun is located, and the area of life the Sun rules. Therefore, you will be invited to use your energy more wisely and with greater focus in these areas. You may feel increased pressure to bring something important to the world during this year to year-and-a-half transit, in these realms, so solitude and deep contemplation at this time would allow you to evaluate how you do or don't feel success in your life. By the end of this transit, you will discover a deeper level of wisdom within yourself and a more disciplined path to fulfilling a role in the larger community.

Thus, the transiting sky transmits meaning for the phases of personal growth and release. As Divine Inspiration astrologer Kelly Lee Phipps states, "Astrology empowers you to communicate with spirit and engage the conversation with love." (2003)

Quantum Astrology and The Paradox of Time

The archetypal language of the stars sings of the original forms, the divine fingerprints, the first images of being. But this language is fluid, malleable, and with a myriad of possible expressions. This leads us to an understanding of what Rick Levine calls "quantum astrology," whereby a planet is both a particle and a wave. (Levine 2005) We can describe the psychological force of a planet in a sign as the Moon in Libra as a specific kind of energy being transmitted. But these evolutionary urges of the planets are also *processes*, like wave forms, not located in a particular place. The Moon in Libra can express itself through time more neutrally, in a more shadow form, or in a more positive, luminous form, depending on the application of one's consciousness. This Moon in Libra process within an individual will undergo further transformations as other psychological forces trigger or catalyze it to new levels of understanding. If Pluto, for instance, conjoins that Moon, the emotions of that individual will go through a total regeneration, a process of death and rebirth, whereby the "particle" version of Moon in Libra will have changed dramatically.

This quantum phenomenon within astrology helps us to understand how we can both feel always "ourselves" and simultaneously the flow of perpetual change. Here we arrive at the language of Time and its unique qualities. Experiences and relationships are intrinsically paradoxical—both reflecting something familiar and shimmering with an effervescent uniqueness. Astrology provides a vocabulary to honor the subtle shades in the bardospace between the known and unknown. Celestial linguistics give us a poetic decryption of the delicately contoured code of sameness within difference, the repeating pattern pulsing within the body of the new moment.

Your birthchart can be expressed in an infinite number of ways; the archetypes are malleable and multivalent, filled with a myriad of possible expressions. Thus, a birthchart will be lived differently for those born at the same moment in space and time because of the level of intention, awareness, and conscious attunement capable in the individual soul. You choose how to archetypally describe your world through the language you inscribe to yourself. Becoming a student of your life requires this kind of intricate, breathing language for understanding how universal forces interpenetrate the experience of embodiment.

Chapter 2
A Cosmology of Resonance

I long to learn the things that are, and comprehend their nature, and know God. This is, I said, what I desire to hear.

He answered back to me: Hold in thy mind all thou wouldst know, and I will teach thee.

—Book I. Poimandres, the Shepherd of Men
The Corpus Hermeticum

As astrologer Caroline Casey points out, the religious idea that we are made in the image of God reminds us that we are actually dreamed in the mind of the Divine. And our own "capacity to imagine and dream is our honorable assignment as a spark of the Divine Source." (Phipps 2008)

Chaos is transfigured into an honorable order. We discover the pulse of consciousness as the primary reality, immanent in all things. A multiplicity of souls con-spire as One Spirit orchestrating events and encounters that invite your further growth and transformation in your return back to your Source.

With the astrological perspective, you become transparent to yourself and so can become clean in your relationships with others. In these processes of emptying into the fullness of oneself, you can at last meet your maker. "Astrology," as Phipps states, "is a way of paying fierce attention to this astonishing realm of mystery that forms the intersection of heaven and earth." (2003)

You are that sanctified intersection, that bridge between eternity and the world of space and time. You belong to a multiverse which works in tandem with humanity, and your birthchart reflects the unique expression of your involvement with and contribution to the creative challenge of life. The Cosmos is alive and breathes through you.

The Bardo of Becoming: Life Selection and the Descent of the Soul

For the Creator conceived that a being which was self-sufficient would be far more excellent than one which lacked anything.

—Plato, Timaeus

Your birthchart is the perfect script for awakening in a single experience of embodiment. As the soul matures, it begins to recognize its spiritual contracts and desires to both understand and honor these sacred agreements.

You might ask yourself why you chose the parents you did, and why they chose you? Why were you born in this particular time and place in history? Why do you have the gifts and challenges that you do? As you start to unearth the answers to these questions, you begin to perceive yourself more and more as a mythical metanarrative, in need of a language which will help you to fulfill your karmic agreements and realize your dharmic potential.

And in the course of your journey, you will naturally seek to understand the intermediary realm before you were born. To assist you in this process, I would like to offer three similar cosmologies that resonate with the application of astrological awareness in your life—the Platonic conception of incarnating souls, Carolyn Myss's three Angelic guides, and Dr. Michael Newton's *interlife* description of our sacred scripts and contracts with self, others, and places.

Plato's Myth of Er

The last chapter of Plato's *The Republic* recounts the Myth of Er, which elucidates the ascent and descent of the soul. This cosmology was circulated throughout the ancient world.

Er is hanging out at very edges of cosmos where souls wait to incarnate. There is a huge spindle there called the spindle of necessity, around which are the whirls and orbits of the different planets. On the planetary orbs, the Sirens sit, singing of the things that were and are and will be. The *Moira* are there as well, the three Fates—the apportioners of one's lot in life.

The souls engage in a process of life selection, whereby they choose a lifetime from all available based on their level of understanding, which is an accumulation of the wisdom and karma from other existences.

Once the soul makes its choice, *it is accompanied by a daimon*, an intermediary spirit, who brings the soul to the three Fates, who are sitting on the planetary orbits. They spin the orbits and ratify the decision the soul has made, making it irreversible. Then, the soul descends through the planetary spheres to earth and drinks of the water of the River of Forgetfulness, crosses the Plain of Oblivion, and proceeds to live out the life it has chosen, accompanied by the daimon, the guardian who makes sure the soul lives out its decrees.

In contrast, the process of ascent was achieved in the reverse motion, leading one through the seven levels of consciousness of the planetary spheres, arriving in the realm of what the gnostics called "the eighth"—the fixed stars. And finally, the most enlightened souls return to the "ninth"—the Divine Mystery, the Ultimate Source.

Plato's doctrine was popular in Greece before horoscopic astrology took hold of the Greek mind. It circulated through much of the ancient world and influenced even the great Arabic astrologer-astronomers and the astute thinkers, alchemists, and skygazers of the Renaissance. This cosmology was also the basis for much of Gnostic teaching, as found in such texts as *The Discourse in the 8th and 9th*, as well as the early mystery schools, such as Mithraism, an astral religion.

Mithraism was an initiatory astral religion, increasing in popularity in the Roman world around the time of Jesus' supposed birth in 7 B.C.E. Different grades of initiation were assigned to the different planets. The temples were underground caves with the depictions of the signs and the depictions of the planets. (George 2008) Mithra's birthday was celebrated on December 25th, three days after the winter solstice. On the winter solstice, the sun stops in the sky no longer descending at its horizon point. After an apparent entombment of three days, the Sun begins to rise again, beginning its march upward in the sky. (Joseph 2007)

Astral religions, hermetic doctrines, alchemical treatises, and gnostic teachings all emphasize the hermetic dictum of "as above, so below, as within, so without." Great mystics, sages, stargazers, and philosophers of all traditions have perceived knowledge as complete, intact, and perfectly reflected "on earth as it is in heaven."

Let us imagine that souls are the stars in the heavens. And when they are ready to incarnate, these star-souls descend through the planets, which ratify their choice of lifetimes. In this cosmology, the "choices" made by the soul are determined by the wisdom of the soul, which has much to do with the choices it has made before, what we might call *karma*. To paraphrase esteemed evolutionary astrologer Steven Forrest, nothing in this lifetime can cause you to have the birth chart that you have. It must be an accumulation of experiences from other places and times. (Forrest 2009) None of us in the vehicle of the body will know the vast extent of our souls' journeys. Likely, in death, we will still only grasp a fraction of Eternal Mystery's majesty. The karmic perspective brings compassion and understanding as we begin to appreciate the richly woven stories in the soul and how each life continues the great metanarrative, and eventually returns back to its original Source.

In this image from 1617 by alchemist Robert Fludd, the *anima mundi*, or world soul, is depicted, and represents a visual expression of Plato's cosmology. The philosopher's son is the ape of nature discovering his universal mother, this *anima mundi*. The woman with the crown of twelve stars for the twelve signs of the zodiac is the wisdom goddess of antiquity—known variously as Sophia, Sapientia, and Isis. She is chained to the Father and the mercurial monkey son (humanity) in a symbiotic unity. As the world soul, the universal mother, she mediates the corporeal, natural world with the metaphysical world of the Spirit.

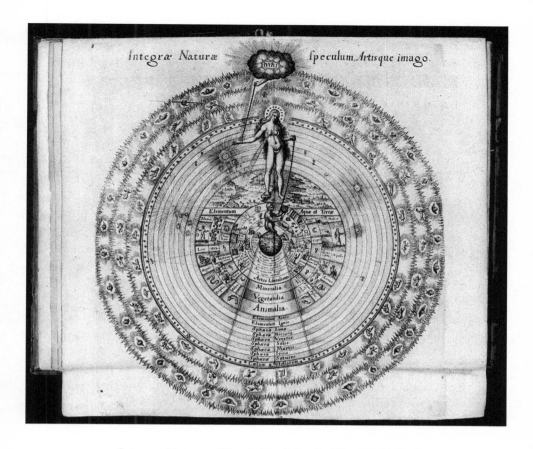

Integrae Naturae: The Anima Mundi, The World Soul
"The Mirror of Virginal Nature and the Image of the Art."

The soul's ascent to God-consciousness is depicted as a journey through the planetary spheres, ultimately embedding the soul in the realm of the heavenly children or unborn souls. The movement is towards paradise, the returning back to the central Source. The Source-Origin is encircled by angelic light situated beyond the sphere of the fixed stars, which are located just beyond the seven heavenly spheres of the planets. (Fabricius 1976)

Today, we might call these "planetary spheres" dimensions of awareness or planes of consciousness. These are the evolutionary urges within each soul. If we apply our modern astronomical discoveries, we realize there are more subtle levels within these spheres, since we are now aware of the outer planetary forces and the thousands of asteroids.

In her book, *Sacred Contracts*, medical intuitive and archetypal teacher, Carolyn Myss updates the concept of the Fates which Plato describes in the Myth of Er. She calls them the Angels of Necessity, Choice, and Compassion.

The Angel of Necessity is the organizing principle behind one's life, what we may typically call "fate." The Angel of Necessity dictates that there are places you have to be and appointments with people you cannot miss. Astrological language plays the role of the Angel of Necessity, elucidating these "cosmic appointments." Living life with this perspective can be very humbling, and can serve to keep us vigilant in our attention. Experiences that might frustrate you—missing the bus, losing your job, a breakup, having to sell your home—are now interpreted from a more vast perspective which includes the intricate web of innumerable other souls. When viewing events from this "bigger picture," you are more likely to remain patient, compassionate, and harmonic with yourself and others, avoiding the tendency to force situations. You remember that each situation you find yourself in is perfect because it is happening.

How you respond and integrate what is necessary is the domain of the Angel of Choice. This is where you can exercise the greatest amount of personal will. Astrology informs this realm of choice, intention, and will by demonstrating the possible paths of action given your circumstances—for example, deciding to move from shadow-fear to light-love or from ego-separation to unified wholeness. As astrologer Robert Blaschke says,

> The spiritual role the professional astrologer plays is to remind people of the blueprint we can see in their birthchart, the unfolding of the soul growing in to its fullest capacity through the progressed horoscope, and to help them to cope with the fated circumstances in their lives by explaining their transits. We also help clients heal their relationships with synastry and composite charts. (Phipps 2008)

The Angel of Compassion's role is to provide something in your life that reminds you of the better choice, of the larger plan and divine design. When you study your planetary transits and use other forecasting tools, you sense the changing of the tides. You are informed of the storm's approach and how to take shelter. You tune your antennae to intuitive signals that something is about to reshape your life. You are prepared, not with concrete prediction, for this is not astrology's domain. Rather, astrology is archetypally or energetically predictive. As a symbolic language, it paints an impressionistic image upon the canvas of events manifesting in your life.

The Platonic doctrine of the *daimon*, the intermediary spirit present at our births and accompanying us throughout our life, acts somewhat like a composite of Myss's three Angelic guides, helping the soul to continuously fulfill its duties and awaken to its lessons. The role of the astrologer is comparable to the role of the daimon in reminding individuals of their soul-contracts and how best to fulfill them.

Sacred Scripts: Contracts with Self, Other, and Place

I do not make sacrifice
I make the sacred face
I fashion revelation
in the moment's holy embrace
In the bliss
of Spirit-remembrance
I create contact
with my soul-contract

In *Journey of Souls* and *Destiny of Souls*, Dr. Michael Newton reveals his profound findings as an *interlife* hypnotherapist. His clients describe the entire journey of the soul and the sphere of the interlife—the life between lives. This journey includes the soul's meeting with other familiar souls and guides upon its death, the examination of its life lessons in the study of the records of the soul's existence, and perhaps most importantly, why and how the soul chooses the life and body it does.

Consistently, the patients of Newton and other interlife hypnotherapists describe our soul contracts with ourselves and others, including the memory triggers we give ourselves to remind us of our shared work together during incarnation. These memory triggers include keywords, phrases, gestures, glances that strike something much deeper in our souls. Astrology, as a language of the soul's ongoing odyssey, is a beautifully elegant instrument illuminating these soul-triggers as they occur through our contracts with the self, with others, and with places.

Contract with Self

It seems like a lot of people have an emptiness and a hungering for a deeper kind of life and yet all there is is consumerism, fetishism, and these false political struggles, but the government of the self would be about getting in to your own chart and understanding your archetypes and becoming in sense your own Hero of the Journey...

—Kelly Lee Phipps, Divine Inspiration Astrology

Evolutionary astrologer Steven Forrest imagines one on their deathbed, preparing to enter the next life, looking back with a feeling of triumph, accomplishment, peace, and wholeness. These are the sentiments of one who completely lived their birthchart, a blueprint written by you for the life you're supposed to live. Similarly, Robert Hand communicates that the birthchart symbolizes the individual potential which can be actualized in this lifetime. (Phipps 2008)

With the birthchart by your side as your map, you have a holistic manual for your multidimensional soul. With this manual of soul-information, you can gently negotiate with your life situations, you can compassionately compromise with your life circumstances, and you can liberate yourself more gracefully from environmental conditioning in order to live a more intentional and altruistic existence.

When you become conscious of the energies which create and sustain your life, you can now co-create. For you are not just the needs of your Moon, the drive of your Sun, or the mask of your Ascendant—you are a cosmic cocktail, a unique and dynamic blend of energies mingling in the InterdepenDance.

And you are both dancer and musician. As musician, you find yourself sometimes playing out of tune with your life. Astrology shows you how best to resonate with the other musicians, how to dance in step to each chord and beat, and also how to own and share your unique vibrational signature. Wholeness is achieved as you embrace all the instruments of your being. Then the symphony of your life can vibrate out through the entirety of the cosmos, into the body of eternity.

Contract with Other

We are a society of souls con-spiring with each other. Breaking the word con-spiracy down to its parts, we discover "spirits" (*spir*) working together (*con*). Hence, the great cosmic con-spiracy.

In our relationships, we are exponentially accelerating our interactions. Souls are flying in and out of our lives at lightning speed—we weave, we entangle, we imprint, we awaken, we change each other. In a sense, karma is ripening quicker now than ever. We are at the apex of a *concrescence*. The word means a "growing together," and signifies our roles as individual agents of the oversoul oneness-consciousness. Thus, now more than ever, we seek languages to elucidate the textures of our relationships and to illuminate our shared purpose.

Astrology presents an objectified mirror of yourself and another, helping you to build a solid foundation for understanding behavior and letting go of blame. In this willingness to make love not simply to the flesh, but to the soul, pathways of harmony open in all of our partnerships. We can discover what our souls intended to do together and without projection or expectation, we can embrace our mutual intentions.

"Synastry" means to join the stars and is an astrological technique by which you can compare the interaction and harmony of your planetary forces with another.

With Chart Transposition, you can see which archetypal fields of life in another you trigger with particular evolutionary forces, and which areas they activate most in you.

In the Composite chart, we combine the midpoints of every two planetary positions between people and discover the Middle Path between us: the single vibration of the energy pulsing between us, the soul of the third entity at the center of every two. With our composite chart, we learn how two people working together can positively affect the world as a unified force.

In addition, every event has a birthchart, including a wedding. With Electional Astrology, you can find the ideal date and time to marry and proclaim your contract between each other to the world. This important technique is one of the most ancient tools of astrology and should be considered by any couple wanting to insure a successful and enduring marriage.

Contract with Place

Every place on this beautiful Earth vibrates at a different resonant frequency for you. Anyone who has traveled can recognize how some places will hold an incredibly strong potency for us, while others barely inspire or change us. At different locations, we are influenced and invited by different evolutionary forces. Undoubtedly, we are called to locations that act as an evolutionary portal for us. Often, we cannot reference a logical reason from this lifetime why we should be drawn there. In addition to being magnetized towards places which activate some key urges within our souls, it is also likely that we resonate with places where we have incarnated before. In any case, we seem to have contracts with these places and the people we will meet there. Relocation Astrology, as an emerging branch of astrology, focuses on aligning you with your places of empowerment and transformation, helping you to find the best places to support your intentions for a home, for your travels, and for your continued evolution.

Illuminationist Philosophy: Emanations of Light

For the majority of mystical and esoteric traditions around the world, the Source is perceived as pure and absolute light.

In the mystical Jewish tradition, the Divine Consciousness impressed its intention and will upon Ain (Nothing) using words: "And God said: Let there be Light, and there was Light." This is known as Ain Soph Aur—"limitless light."

Tibetan Buddhism describes the bardo realm of Dharmata as the Ground Luminosity "of naked, unconditioned truth, the nature of reality, or the true nature of phenomenal existence....The arising of the Ground Luminosity is like the clarity in the empty sky just before dawn. Now gradually the sun of dharmata begins to rise in all its splendor, illuminating the contours of the land in all directions." In this place of minimal distraction, "the natural radiance of Rigpa manifests spontaneously and blazes out as energy and a light" (Sogyal Rinpoche 1993, 275).

In The Divine Pymander, a part of the *Corpus Hermeticum*, Hermes states, "Forthwith all things changed in aspect before me and were opened out in a moment. And I beheld a boundless view: all was changed into light, a mild and joyous light; and I marveled when I saw it." (Hauck 1999, 55)

The Iranian philosopher and Sufi mystic Al Suhrarwardi paints an illuminationist cosmology whereby all creation is a successive outpouring of the original Supreme Light of Lights (Nur al-Anwar). The absolute is pure immaterial light and creation unfolds as emanations of ever-diminishing intensities of light. The descending order of light includes something akin to the Platonic forms or archetypes which govern the entities of mundane reality. In his division of bodies, Al Suhrarwardi categorizes objects in terms of their reception or non-reception of light. (Bayrak 1998)

Thus, through these mystical cosmologies, we understand that our apparent separateness is simply different vibrational densities of the One Light. Our potential is to transcend them as we contemplate the luminous Source and live in accordance with the radiant principle of unification.

Additionally, we learn from both psychics and those who enter the interlife/afterlife, souls are perceived as auras—pulsations of light at certain frequencies. According to Michael Newton, the different color ranges of souls' auras refer to varying levels of development within the soul. (Newton 1994)

Christ Lucifer, the Feathered Serpent, and the Dual Urges of the Soul

For souls to continue to grow, they must take on their various and specific missions through the process of incarnation. Incarnating brings to a soul both feelings of excitement and of mild despair, for the soul will have to leave the spirit world where it shares intimately, in a unified dance of light, and is supported, appreciated, and known by clusters of other entities, in exchange for the experience of discovering itself embodied in apparent isolation from others, more anonymous, and at times competitive with others on Earth.

Given the luminous nature of souls, and their truth as Dharmata—the source ground luminosity of all things, we can begin to understand the importance of the Lucifer principle. The word Lucifer means, "light-bringer," and in the story, Lucifer separates from God to empower himself and make a kingdom upon earth. This is an allegory for souls' need to separate from the more perfected realms of the spirit-world in order to grow into their fullest capacities and potentials through experiences upon the Earth. The ultimate potential within each soul is its active willingness to return to the source, represented by Christ-consciousness. Christ's words are revealed within each one of us, that "The Kingdom of Heaven is within." The soul cannot grow or extend itself without the Lucifer-force, nor can it return without the unified awareness of the Christ-consciousness. The desires in the soul are but two-fold: the desire to separate and the desire to return.

The symbol of the caduceus and the archetype of the double-headed

Feathered Serpent represents this dual nature of the soul—the earth-bound serpent and the heaven-directed bird; the desire to separate and the desire to return interwoven together in every moment. The caduceus is known throughout the world as the symbol of medicine and healing. It is the role of the Astral Shaman to apply consciousness as medicine through archetypal linguistics, which, while enveloping your individual soul, simultaneously lead you back to the luminous source.

This is why the traditional shaman and the underworld guide of Hermes-Mercury carry a wooden staff representing the ascent and descent along the world axis of the cosmic tree. It is along this staff, like the witch's broom, where the initiate dances with the dual desires of the soul, and learns how to navigate the seeming paradox of separation-return. When the ego becomes over-inflated or exists in ignorance, the separating desires will overwhelm it and the shadows of planets in

Hermes-Mercury with the caduceus staff of the Feathered Serpent

signs, houses, and aspects will manifest more strongly.

To avoid the patterns of discontent and evolutionary stasis, the incarnate soul must become more aware of its spiritual nature and the textures of its various purposes while on earth. Astrology is the script by which you comprehend the reasons you established roots on this earth, and the pathways by which you can reach back through the boughs into the heavens. With the symbols of the planets and archetypal signs etched on your staff of life, you can consciously choose your ascension process, returning to the source by activating the most luminous potential of every planetary configuration.

The Being of Light and the Bodhisattvic Ideal

Your horoscope provides the map for the territory of your personal *paticcasamuppada*—the interdependent arising of qualities, conditions, circumstances, and relationships in your life. In addition, this map also points to the treasure chest of self-liberation, the tools which will help you to transcend the tethers of attachments as you walk on the path of the *bodhisattva*—one who works towards enlightenment for the benefit of all sentient beings.

Everyone's version of the enlightened/awakened (*bodhi*) being (*sattva*), appears differently, and shifts within the context of the soul-contract we fulfill with other entities. Living your buddha nature is simply the fulfillment of the supreme, luminous, and positive expression of the energies singing the chart through you.

The discovery of individual potential pregnant in your birth chart stems naturally from the intention of the bodhisattvic ideal. The coordinates of space and time for your birth were chosen by you and your guides to answer the question: How best can I work towards my own enlightenment in order to serve all sentient beings?

As an Astral Shaman, you remain in continuous apprenticeship. Everyone you share with, everything you do, every present moment is a reflection of what you should be learning about yourself and about your creative power. Every thought, word, and energy you generate has the power to either lift up or let down yourself or others. Your role as the Astral Shaman is to translate the map to this codex of the soul.

The effervescent sky at the moment of your birth radiates the language of your evolutionary potential. It is a call to prayer from the multiverse itself, a longing from the sacred heart of the Source, to know itself *through you*. Listen. Rise. Step up and Ascend. Answer that call to prayer from your ancestral AnceStar. Let the verse of your soul shine forth.

Become the most luminous You.

Chapter 3
Mystic Rhythms:
Sacred Geometry and the Archetypes of the Zodiac From Monad to Multiplicity

Astrology is the study of how the various forms contained within the Light of Consciousness or Monad affect the substance of Mind and cause the manifold experiences of life.

—Robert Zoller

Let the immortal depth of your Soul lead you, but earnestly raise your eyes upwards.

—The Chaldean Oracles

Archetypal Geometry

Only Oneness cannot be born. It simply is. "Am who am." Unconditioned BEING.

But with two, there is another and therefore the act of DOING. There is *desire*.

The word "desire" comes from the phrase *de sidere*—"from the stars." As we described earlier, the first seven spheres were known as the planetary spheres. The Gnostics called the field of the stars the "eighth" sphere. And the Source, the Unknowable, was referred to as the ninth sphere.

So what was this *original* desire which gave birth to the manifold universe of stars, planets, and earth? How were these archetypes born, these primal forms which imprint themselves upon matter?

Sacred geometry and astrology are means by which to answer this perplexing question, though the link between the two sacred sciences has not often been elucidated.

Plato considered geometry and number as the most reduced and essential, and therefore the ideal, philosophical language. Through the Neoplatonists, the Pythagoreans, and many mystery schools, the goal of geometric education was to enable the mind to become a channel through which the earth (the level of manifested form) could receive the abstract, and more primal truths of the cosmos. The practice of geometry and archetypal awareness was an approach to the way in which the universe is ordered and sustained. (Lawlor 1982)

The archetype is the underlying process and universal pattern, independent and prior to any form or structure. The reason why archetypes are sometimes hard to grasp is that we only recognize their myriad forms of expression. Thus Genghis Khan and Alexander the Great are the *types*, the forms, of the *archetypal* warrior and general, symbolically represented by the constellation of Aries.

Archetypes can be difficult to grasp because of their nature as core, fundamental building blocks of manifest reality. But just as science now dissects and describes the physical DNA, so does our metaphysical investigation of archetypes continue to evolve, especially as we synthesize astrology and geometry into a cosmology composed of an archetypal geometry

This kind of archetypal geometry re-enacts the unfolding of each form out of a preceding one. In this practice, we study how the essential creative mystery is rendered visible and tangible.

The following is a prayer, an inquiry, and a revelation, all intertwined—of the Divine Script which gave birth to the Twelve Holy Signatures—the luminous emanations of the starchetypal theater.

The Divine Divide—ShivaShakti and the Law of Polarity

What is your nature O Absolute One? How shall I know you through your multiplicity? Is there a language for this chaotic logic of division, a poem I may sing to the fragmented Unity? I allow the sacredness of your Number and the holiness of your myths to instruct me on my nature as a spark of your Eternal Flame.

How can we describe this First Principle? You seem veiled by your multiple forms, yet I feel You in your eternal immanence in the moments of my still mind, as the lineage of mystics and sages have taught me. Your Holy Word descends into the sanctum of my consciousness, the wakeful mind of this Listener. Studying Your equations, the mathematics of the Monad, I will always arrive at the One. $1 \square 1 = 1, 1 \div 1 = 1$.

One is one, nothing lacking, perfect. Unity never departs from unity, nor can it give rise to anything but unity. Change originates only in the Dyad, the flow of the yin and yang. For Spirit, Source, God, Allah, Eternal Light to know itself, You O Greatest One, must sever and so mutate into the manifest, into densities of light, and textures of darkness.

And so we pulse, as "Lila," your divine play, Purusha to Prakriti unfolding the magic of incarnation, Spirit and Matter in tantric union. In the passionplay of the Shiva lingam and the Shakti yoni, this multiverse of forms is created out of bliss, by bliss, for bliss….

Draw a line, say the masters, from point A to point B. Now take the exact midpoint. Draw a line directly above that midpoint. And behold the Holy Triangle, the reconciler of opposites, the re-establisher of Unity.

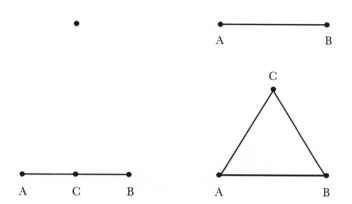

The Original point, the single dot is indivisible. But as soon as we draw a line, action begins, though unity is still the source of action. The reconciliation of the original Two causes activity, motion arising from the tension between the One, which is the Same, and the Two, which is the Other. A Circle of One surrounds the Tao of Yang and Yin, masculine and feminine.

And so our Divine pathos erupts in blissful suffering. In our longing to know the pleroma, the effulgence of Being, our existence is Your pained and perfect Breath-of-Becoming, Unity tearing asunder, Your hope of our will to return to You.

And Your hope is the Word, the Holy Spirit of the Third. In Egypt, the hieroglyph for "mouth" is the same sign used to write the word for the supreme being Re, known as Atum-Re the creator god. This hieroglyph for "mouth" and "Re" resembles the vesica piscis on its side.

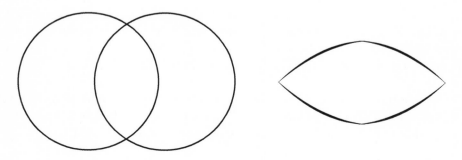

The vesica piscis is an ancient, mystical symbol further reflecting your Divine division. It is formed when we draw two circles with the same radius, with them intersecting in such a way that the center of each circle lies on the circumference of the other. Thus the Christ-Consciousness is born from the Yoni-shaped Vesica—the Divine Child of duality born as the Redeeming Third. And the Sacred Word emerges from the mouth of the One Source.

Thus the Third of the Holy Spirit, the Sacred Word, the Divine Child of duality, springs forth from the mouth of the One Source. And so naturally, three vesica piscis overlap to form the *triquetra*—an ancient pagan symbol adopted by Christians to represent all mystical trinities.

Christ emerging from the vesica piscis as the Solar Hero before the Sun on the Cross of Matter. He is flanked by the evangelical animal symbols of the four royal stars from the fixed constellations of Taurus, Leo, Aquarius, and Scorpio/La Aquila (The Eagle).
Evangelistar von Speyer, um 1220, Cod. Bruchsal 1, Bl. 1v

And so we dance the textures of division while the heart of heaven sings. And the Holy Child, the Third, is born, to heal the chasm between the Unity and the Division. This Holy Child is the Divine Breath of motion itself.

SPIRIT: "AUM" and The Three Modes of Divine Expression

In action, energy expresses itself in the threefold nature of motion: the Cardinal, Fixed, and Mutable modalities of energy.

Cardinal motion thrusts energy *outwardly* and so the crop rises. It expands energy out from the source, and so the tree blossoms. The Fixed mode sustains us. It moves *inwardly* and nourishes us with the fruit of the Tree of Life. And the Mutable mode allows the decay and withering of the old season, so the evolved form can *spiral* out in the synthesis of something entirely new.

We know that in India the sound *AUM* is said to be the original sound that contains all other sounds, words, language, and mantras. All of creation is encompassed in the sound of this Divine Breath, emanating from the mouth of the vesica piscis. It is the all-inclusive container of being and becoming and is the mystic name of the Trimurti, the union of the three gods, Brahma, Vishnu, and Shiva.

According to Hindu philosophy, "A" represents creation, when all existence sprouted from the golden nucleus of Brahma.

"A" resonates with the generative, activating, and initiating energy of the Cardinal/Outward mode of expression, the signs of the zodiac Aries (fire), Cancer (water), Libra (air) and Capricorn (earth).

"U" refers to Vishnu, the preserver of the worlds. This aspect of preservation is the role of the Fixed/Inward signs of the zodiac, which harness, cultivate, and utilize the energy of their element. These include Taurus (earth), Leo (fire), Scorpio (water), and Aquarius (air).

"M" is the final part of cyclic existence whereby Vishnu falls asleep and Shiva, the destroyer, breathes in the things of the world, reducing them to his essence, so the cycle can begin anew. This aspect of evolution is the role of the Mutable signs (and their Spiral motion), which adapt, shift, and demonstrate the energies of their elements. These include Gemini (air), Virgo (earth), Sagittarius (fire), and Pisces (water).

Mystical symbolism overflows in the art and architecture of the ancient

Celts as well. The three symbols of the triple spiral, the *triquetra* and the triskelion, are familiar images of the "holy trinity" of Cardinal, Fixed, and Mutable modes of motion. Translated as "three legged," the components of the *triskelion* are positioned in a way signifying constant motion. We can understand the image and the symbol for the "legs" as those which carry us, which move us through the world. Again, we feel the resonance of many holy trinities through this symbolism:

Creator, Destroyer, Sustainer;
Past, Present, Future
Spirit, Mind, Body
Father, Son, Holy Ghost
Mother, Father, Child
Maiden, Mother, Crone
Lower, Middle, Upperworlds
Cardinal, Fixed, Mutable

We can recognize in all of these trinities the intrinsic nature of movement, motion, progression, and cycle.

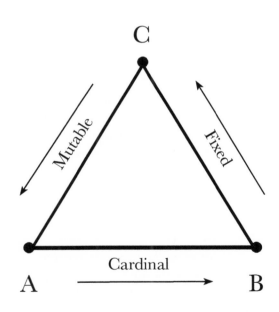

The Triplicities
Motion / Movement / Modes of Expression

Cardinal/Outward - *Take Action, Make it Happen!*

Seasons Begin

Activating
Initiating
Generating
Creating
Expressing
Catalyzing

"$\mathcal{A}$"

Aries (fire), Libra (air), Cancer (water), Capricorn (earth)

Fixed/Inward - *Harness the Energy!*

Seasonal Midpoint

Harnessing
Cultivating
Utilizing
Concentrating
Empowering
Sustaining

"u"

Taurus (earth), Leo (fire), Scorpio (water), Aquarius (air)

Mutable/Spiral - *Learn from It!*

Seasons Shift

Adapting
Evolving
Transmuting
Shifting
Demonstrating
Distributing

"ω"

Gemini (air) Virgo (earth), Sagittarius (fire), Pisces (water)

You will notice that two equilateral triangles are necessary to form the next fundamental geometry and basic shape of creation, the square, composed of four equal lines at 90 degree angles.

As energy moves, as the current of motion unfolds, it must do so upon matter, the even number four. Matter comes from the Latin word *mater*, which means mother. And the mother of all manifestation is the four elements. These elements are derived from observable "qualities." The ancient Greeks, like the Taoists, observed the conditions of the weather and environment outside and called these the qualities of matter. From these observations, the four elements naturally sprung forth.

The primary quality of the first principle (or light) is heat. This is apparent in our obvious source of life—the light-heat of the Sun. This Heat radiates upon the matter and forms its polarity, the Cold. Now, following the Law of the Three, the triangle which reconciles the two opposites, a mean arises called Moisture or Wetness. This offspring of Light-Heat and Matter finds its polar opposite in Dryness.

Now, one of these qualities cannot combine with its opposite, but it can bind with either one of the other two qualities, giving us the four primary symbols of life. The word "symbol" comes from the Greek *symbolos*, "to bind together." From the combinations of these natural qualities are born the living symbols, the binding forces of matter—the elements.

The quality of Hot combines with Wet to form *Air*, giving birth to Spring. Hot also combines with the quality of Dry to form the element *Fire* and this gives us Summer. Hot and Cold are in a dyad, a polarity relationship, so they cannot combine. Cold and Dry merge to form *Earth* and the season of Autumn.
Cold combines with Wet to form *Water* and the season of Winter.

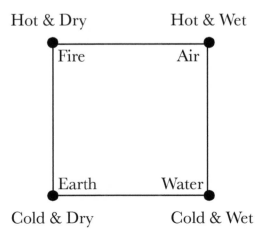

Hot & Dry   Hot & Wet

Fire   Air

Earth   Water

Cold & Dry   Cold & Wet

The Quadruplicities:
The Elements of Life

Masculine/Yang Elements

FIRE   - Hot & Dry

Spirit
Vitality
Consciousness
Essence
Identity

Aries (C), Leo (F), Sagitarrius (M),

AIR - Hot & Moist

Awareness
Ideas
Concepts
Thoughts
Knowledge

Gemini (M), Libra (C), Aquarius (F)

Feminine/Yin Elements

WATER - Cold & Moist

Emotion
Imagination
Sensitivity
Compassion
Feeling-Empathy

Cancer (C), Scorpio (F), Pisces (M)

EARTH - Cold & Dry

Substance-Form
Resources
Nature
Structures
Embodiment

Taurus (F), Virgo (M),Capricorn (C)

C = Cardinal/Outward; F = Fixed/Inward; M = Mutable/Spiral

The square contains the qualities of life, the elements. These are composed from the masculine and feminine triangles of motion. Thus, the square intrinsically holds every primal factor in the process of creation.

If we flip the square 45 degrees, we now behold the two triangles as the mystical symbol of the diamond.

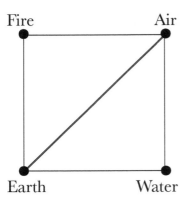

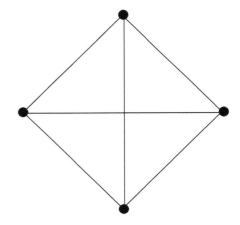

When we draw a line from each corner of the diamond, we find one of the oldest symbols of humanity, etched into petroglyphs and cave walls and fundamental to most religious and astrological symbology—the Cross of Matter, linking the four elements and four seasons. Often the Cross of Matter is perceived with a circle at the center, symbolizing the Sun rising, setting, and journeying through its stations of the four seasons. This symbol was adopted by Christianity as symbolic of Christ as the Solar hero, and is used widely in church iconography today.

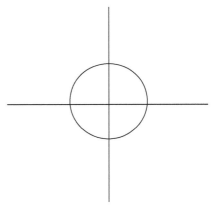

Because the Cross of Matter is naturally formed out of the diamond-square, we may find evidence here for the notion of the *diamond mind* in Buddhism. One who eradicates the defilements of illusory reality by ceasing to grasp at the objects of impermanence can liberate themselves, obtaining the mind of a diamond—the hardest natural substance, able to cut through all delusion.

The diamond-square is composed of the masculine and feminine triangles. The triangle is the strongest shape in nature. Thus an interpretation of the "diamond mind" may be that mind which perceives the immutable, sacred geometric truth of the triangle and the square, the sacred Three and Four, which we will see give birth to the Twelve primal patterns of energy—the archetypes of the zodiac.

Another symbol which merges the immutable creative truth of the Two, Three, and Four is the pyramid, with the vesica piscis for the eye, and the square base and four sides composed of triangles.

Thus, the symbol of the All-Seeing Eye on the pyramid, although used for occult purposes, is actually an incredibly holy symbol. It was also called "The eye of providence," and was depicted with rays of light and glory emanataing from each side of the triangle. The luminous Source radiates creation from its vesica piscis eye, motion triangulates, and the diamond-square of elemental matter forms.

♄umanity. the Five, and the Breath of Life

Five consists of two unequal parts, the two and three. Duality (two) and the reconciling return to Unity (three) combine in the Five, the merger of the rational three and the irrational two. Therefore, five is similar to humanity, a combination of rational and irrational forces, a synthesis of the threefold soul and dualistic matter. Five is at the midpoint or mean of the Source Monad and the fulfillment of manifestation int the Nine, the Ennead. Humanity, with its five limbs, (arms, legs, head) is at this crucial central pivot, where it must decide which way it will move, towards the Light or towards the Darkness.

Importantly, 5 is the numerical equivalent of the Hebrew letter *he*, which was said to be the divine breath, the spirit, and ether—what we may call the fifth element. In Arabic, 5 is *hamsah*, which in Sanskrit translates to "breath" and resolves down into the sacred mantra *Aham Sa*, "I am that." This signifies the point in the process of creation when the divinity becomes self-aware through its creation, hence the "breathing" in of life in Genesis 2:7—"And the Lord God formed man from the dust of the earth and breathed into his nostrils the breath of life; and man became a living soul".

The Latin word *anima* means "breath or soul" and the adjective *animalis* means "having breath or soul." The noun *animal* is derived from animalis and is used to indicate all living beings that breathe noticeably. The Greek word *zodiac* denotes a "circle of animals," and is truly signifying the circle of souls, and the emanations of the divine breath.

From the Divine In-spiration, we discover that the diamond-square also contains the 6-pointed star, which gives us the Seed of Life. If we allow the masculine and feminine triangles to interpenetrate each other with equal distances on each side, we form the 6-pointed star. This star contains the inner shape of the 6-sided hexagon as well as 6 equilateral triangles. When we draw the circle at each point of the triangle, we create the Seed of Life, the basic shape of all creation.

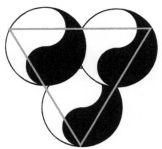

In the Seed of Life, we reach the totality of twelve archetypes since each point of the triangle contains the polarities of each element. We must remember that each circle is a yin/yang and must contain its opposite. So the masculine (Shiva) triangle, pointed upward, contains the Cardinal polarity of Aries-Libra, then moves to the Fixed Polarity of Leo-Aquarius, and reaches the point of reconciliation and return in the Mutable polarity of Gemini-Sagitarrius.

The Feminine (Shakti) triangle, pointed downward, contains the Cardinal polarity of Cancer-Capricorn, the Fixed polarity of Taurus-Scorpio, and the Mutable polarity of Virgo-Pisces. We now arrive at all twelve sacred signs of the zodiac.

The three Modes of Divine Expression emanate these four Elemental Substances, thereby giving rise to the twelve Arche-types,

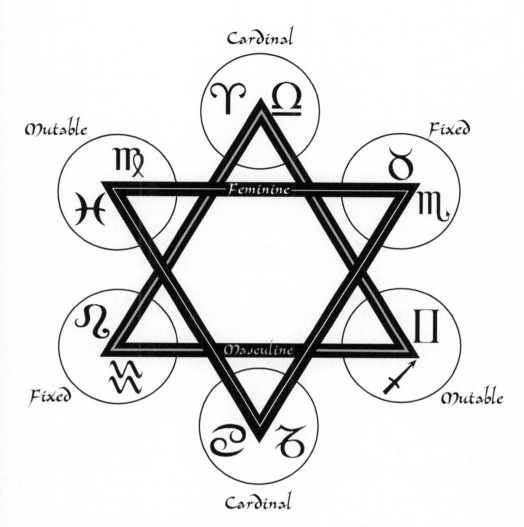

Cardinal

Mutable

Fixed

Feminine

Masculine

Fixed

Mutable

Cardinal

or "primal" "forms," the fingerprints of the divine pulsing all around us and circulating within us as the Seed of Life. We can give the following equation to describe this holy process:

$$E = M\,1 \times M\,2$$

E (Energy) = Motion (M1) x Matter (M2), with three possible motions and four possible elements of matter.

What we reveal in this powerful image of the twelve archetypes is in actuality the Star Tetrahedron, the most fundamental shape to be found in the three-dimensional universe of volume.

The 3-dimensional version of this shape is also the MerKaBa, the divine light vehicle allegedly used by ascended masters to travel between dimensions. The Egyptian term "*Mer*" means light, "*Ka*" means spirit, and "*Ba*" means body. So the Mer-Ka-Ba is the spirit-body surrounded by counter-rotating fields of masculine light and feminine light, the two triangles of motion containing the four elements. Human consciousness is the central, fifth element.

Since all twelve archetypes are contained within the Seed of Life and its 3-dimensional Star Tetrahedron, we can perceive how this shape functions as a vehicle for the soul to travel between dimensions and access all the possible forms or manifestations of the Source-Light.

Manifestation occurs by means of the seven energy centers of the chakras and the seven evolutionary forces of the visible planets. This sacred Seven can be seen by the total number of circles in the Seed of Life image. The chakras and planets are archetypally correlated and visualized in the ChakrAstrology Meditation in Chapter 6.

We may also add the three modes of expressive motion to the four elements, arriving at the sacred seven. We know that seven is often referred to as a holy number. In addition to the chakras and planets visible to the naked eye, there are seven whole musical notes, and the seven colors emanating from the white light prism, and the seven days of the week.

In the early verses of the Bible, the Seed of Life process is communicated as the seven days of creation, wherein God first creates the Vesica Piscis and each subsequent day adds another circle to creation, culminating with the shape of the Seed of Life on the sixth day. The seventh day is for rest. These seven days, as we describe in this book are named for deities associated with the seven planets visible to the naked eye.

In actuality, the seven circles contain the hidden eight, which is its circumference, the totality which includes the other circles. This eight gives us the perfected symbol of infinity and cyclic evolution. Nine follows as the number of regeneration. Upon this, manifestation is completed, from the Zero point of the Luminous Void, to the One Source, and through the archetypal unfolding of all Number. A universal language is born—precultural, primal, fundamental.

These sacred geometric archetypes are the seed-thoughts of the Source, the templates for all of energy's potential expression. You are a delicious meal born from this archetypal recipe. You are an exquisite painting spread across the canvas of life from the archetypal palette of colors. And you, as you are, are the perfect mixture of ingredients, the perfect shades and textures of paint, for every evolutionary process your soul requires. You are asked to respond to your script for your embodiment, and play your part in the StaArchetypal Theater. You have appointments to keep and lines to deliver.

The Vocabulary of the StArchetypal Theater

MODES - Motion:
-   -Movement of Energy

ELEMENTS - Themes:
-   -Primary Components of Matter

PLANETS - The Characters/Players:
-   -Evolutionary Urges
-   -Psychological Processes
-   -Forces of Consciousness
-   -Who?

SIGNS - Costumes/Masks:
-   -Styles of Expression
-   -Archetypal Images
-   -What?

HOUSES - Scenes/Stages/Setting:
-   -Realm of Life Experience
-   -Where?

ASPECTS - Dialogue:
-   -Relationships Between Characters, Evolutionary Urges, and Psychological Forces
-   -How?

TRANSITS/PROGRESSIONS/FORECASTING - Narrative Arc:
-   -When?`

Part 2

AstrLogos –
The StArchetypal Theater

With the planets
you shall align.....

*to decode
your divine
design....*

Chapter 4
The Verse of the heavens
Inscribed in the human heart

Do you believe that the sciences would ever have arisen and become great if there had not been before magicians, alchemists, astrologers and wizards who thirsted and hungered after hidden, forbidden powers?

— Friedrich Nietzsche, *The Joyful Science*

Science has this much in common with magic, that both rest on a faith in order as the underlying principle in all things.

—J.G. Frazer, *The Golden Bough*

Sages, Mages, and the Song of the Sky

Through focused attunement to the cycles and movements of the heavens, the magi, priests, and shamans of Babylon, Persia, Greece, China, and the Mayan and Incan worlds were able to correlate the literal movement of the planets with an event on earth, an archetypal force in the psyche, and an evolutionary impulse in the soul. In this way, these celestial movements were correlated to terrestrial events on earth. Thus, through observation and correlation, mythical significance was given to the manifested experiences of planetary positions in the signs of the zodiac, and to planets in sacred geometric relationships to each other, which we now call aspects.

The star shamans of old gave special attention to the *Zodiac*, a word which denotes the "circle of animals." This sacred circle is the wheel of constellations encompassing eight degrees above or below the "ecliptic." The ecliptic is the path of the Sun's apparent orbit through the sky, and the only circle in the heavens where the Sun and Moon can meet to form an eclipse.

Before the age of telescopes, the night sky was observed to consist of two very similar components: fixed stars, which remained motionless in relation to each other, and wandering stars, (*asteres planetai* in ancient Greek) which appeared to shift their positions relative to the fixed stars over the course of the year. To the Greeks and the other earliest astronomers, this group comprised the five planets visible to the naked eye and in the Middle Ages, the term "planets" began to include the Sun and the Moon, often called the luminaries or lights, making a total of seven planets.

Modern astronomers and astrologers have since discovered the outer planets, Uranus, Neptune, and Pluto, dwarf planets, and thousands of minor planets called asteroids, all of which can be used in interpreting birthcharts.

To ancient astrologers the planets represented the will of the gods and their direct influence upon human affairs. To modern astrologers the planets represent primary psychological forces, basic drives, and impulses in the human psyche. Overall, they are universal, evolutionary urges seeking expression.

The constellations where the planets would travel along the ecliptic were twelve relatively distinct, 30 degree segments of the sky, called signs. They act as qualitative adjectives or adverbs, describing the how by which a psychological force will manifest. Houses are like prepositions, denoting where, in what realm of life

ANCESTAR

experience, the planet will display its energy. They are the scenes where the story unfolds. The relationships between these psychoevolutionary forces are described by the aspects, the what which relates the dialogue between the planetary characters, the who within our psyche. The narrative develops between these characters over time. This is known as forecasting, which includes techniques such as transits and progressions. Forecasting describes when life events will occur. The why, however, is a mystical question only the individual soul can answer through the revelations of the various processes listed above.

So for instance, we can elucidate a certain quality of your psyche, for instance, your Sun, your urge to shine and radiate your life purpose, in the sign of Pisces, the mystical poet, dreamer, and artist. You radiate this Piscean life purpose in the area of the cosmic tribe and friendships, the 11th house. And if Uranus, the force of liberation, rebellion, and individuation, opposes your Sun, this will require you to constantly reinvent yourself, to free yourself from stuck patterns, and to radically change your current version of reality, a process both exciting and shocking.

* * *

One of the most profound revelations to the post-modern, tech-savvy, scientific mind is the connection between the astronomical data about the planets—such as size, geography, weather, orbit, etc—and the mythical significance of each planet. On almost every level, the planets move and act like the ancient gods with whom they were associated. Disenchanted at its rational distance, modern science, with its material astronomy corroborates the intuitive, felt, and magical experience received by our ancient ancestors. These were the first astronomers—naturalists, phenomenologists—who used only their eyes and their powers of meditation to correlate the planets to the deified psychical forces within each of us.

Because of industrialization and mass media, the majority of us have lost our connection to the sky. The vision beheld in our ancestors' heavenly gaze was the ancient version of the radio, television, theater, and internet—it was, and still is, the repository of information, the heart of every narrative. For thousands of years, sages, seers, magi, prophets, astrologers, and diviners studied the patterns of the heavenly movements, recorded their observations, and passed their wisdom down to preceding generations. Generals, popes, aristocrats, peasants, magicians, alchemists all consulted the stars. With the complexity and diversity of our modern world, today's astrology has only expanded its purposes and applications.

We can best recover the ancient's enchanted relationships with our sky by both exploring the heavens away from pollution and by simultaneously understanding these psychological forces and evolutionary drives within us in the full depth and breath of their archetypal significance, as observed and correlated over thousands of years. In this practice of communing with the heavenly language, you transcend space and time, you travel into the primordial realms of raw energy itself. You embrace the **ancestars** and remember the Codex of the Soul.

The mystical traditions from India such as elucidated in the Bhagavad Gita and Vedantic Hinduism, as well as Vajrayana Buddhism, emphasize the "emptiness" of the self, the unreality of the individual "ego." In *The Bliss of Inner Fire*, Tibetan Lama Thubten Yeshe states, "...in an absolute sense, the mind is empty, or non self-existent, while relatively it exists in dependence upon causes and conditions...." (Wisdom 1998)

This "dependence-arising" is an existential necessity, for as the Light of Absolute Truth, which we described in the opening chapter, descends and densifies into form, the subsequent multiplicity necessarily births the *relative* and *subjective* experience of the individual. We must in some way reconcile this apparent, but ultimately unreal, duality.

Thus, you can read these spiritual texts and be utterly transported to mystical heights of true self-awareness. And yet, you can finish reading the *Bhagavad-Gita* and realize that you're late for work. You quickly have to jump in *your car* and drive to *your job*. On your way to work, you check *your email* on *your phone*. You see a reminder from *your mom* about *your father's* upcoming birthday. You scroll down the list of contacts of all *your friends*. At that moment *your beloved* partner calls you to tell you how much he or she loves *you*. Your beloved reminds you that after work, you'll meet with *your friends* at a community potluck.

Your identity is constantly being reinforced, shifted, adapted, and evolved by every relationship you find yourself embedded within. The transcendent "no-self" of the mystics is no less "real" than the other aspects of one's earthly, embodied being. Try as you might to go beyond these relationships, you are multidimensionally identified. Your task is only to learn how to embody the most luminous expressions of these various energies within yourself and within your relationships.

The concept of the "holarchy" is important to understand here. The *holon* is a part that is whole unto itself, but is nested within greater or more inclusive wholes. In this model, the old value systems of hierarchy are replaced by the equanimous necessity of holarchy, where each slice of life's pie can be appreciated as both part and whole.

You attain an empowered humility as you learn how to identify yourself holographically, a holon *simultaneously* constituted by personal, social, and transpersonal psycho-evolutionary forces. The achievement of multidimensional self-awareness occurs as you integrate evolutionary lessons from every realm of life—family, resource-management, education, creativity, relationships, career, and spirituality—the totality of life experience described by the houses of the zodiac.

When the caterpillar in Alice in Wonderland asks, "Whooooo are youuuu?" To be honest, you must answer, "I am human, I am Gaia, I am galactic, I am cosmic, interdimensional, spiritual, one. I am that individual holon within the larger holon of family, of intimate relationship, of friendship, of spiritual lineage, of humanity, of earth, of star, of pure spirit."

In understanding the nature of the planets, and the evolutionary journey of the soul, from personal to transpersonal, through the signs and houses, the astrological language provides a framework for understanding the soul's fractal identity. A fractal is a self-similar pattern operating at different scales. The soul, on one scale, reflects on itself as personal and separately defined. On a larger, more holistic scale, the soul identifies as transpersonal, cosmic, and unified. Astrology maps this process of fractal identification and intrinsic soul-holarchy.

Psycho-evolutionary Forces

I use the term "pyscho-evolutionary force" to describe the evolutionary urge and psychological force present in the archetypal meaning of each planet in our birthchart. The psycho-evolutionary forces include first, the **Personalizing Forces** of the *Inner Planets*—Sun, Moon, Mercury, Venus, and Mars—which function to define our personality, our aesthetics, communications and perceptions, emotional needs, motivations, and life direction. Then, the **Socializing Forces** of Jupiter, Saturn and the asteroids embed us in a socio-cultural matrix where we educate ourselves and expand our self-definition, as we employ ourselves to the service of society as a whole. And finally, the **Transformational and Transpersonalizing Forces** of the *Outer Planets*—Uranus, Neptune, and Pluto—link us to certain generational motives and themes, in addition to our role in collective evolutionary processes. The planetoid Chiron, functions as the healing bridge between the socializing and transpersonalizing forces. Lastly, the Nodes signify the karmic dynamic and evolutionary intent of the Soul in its transformational journey of incarnation.

You are a synthesis of Personalizing, Socializing, and Transpersonalizing forces all frolicking in an archetypal contact dance. Returning to the above example for a moment, you may be undergoing a transit, an evolutionary trigger, of the *transpersonal* force Neptune to your Sun, so you immerse yourself in meditation and the absorption of mystical texts, like the Bhagavad-Gita. Meanwhile, the socializing force of Saturn is transiting your Moon so you are working long hours and feeling heavy pressures on your emotional body, questioning if your job can make you content. At the same time, the *socializing* force of Jupiter is blessing the realm of partnerships, so your new friendships and your romance with your beloved are blossoming and growing. And it seems for the last few weeks, while the *personalizing* forces of the Sun and Mercury have been in your fourth house of the family, the roots, and the lineage, your Mom keeps calling you, each time more distressed about someone's health in the family.

Without the language of astrology, it may seem that the many disparate forces described above are chaotically confronting each other. Yet, this example helps us to understand the interdependence and importance of each of these psychoevolutionary urges. They are each essential components in the individuation process, pathways towards integrating the full totality of your fractal Being.

You are at the center of the mandala, the sacred image of the whole. The multiverse orbits around your perception. The human family exists at the exact midpoint of our ability to both measure out macrocosmically and measure in microcosmically. Perhaps it is necessary for humanity to be at this midpoint between the quark deep within and the universe deep beyond.

But in fact, we are no different than the most infinitesimal and the most grand. We are a reflective jewel on the interconnected web of being. Perhaps the most astonishing revelation which the online revolution has provided for humanity is its metaphor of the "Web" and the "Net," signifying infinite, interlinking chains of consciousness, operating at various levels of self-awareness.

In the New Testament, when Jesus communicates, "I and my father are one," he is simply describing the fractal nature of the holarchy. Likewise, the hermetic maxim which guides astrology and many of the mystical traditions of "As above, so below" refers precisely to the same concept, that in truth, there is no outer or inner. Consciousness is a continuous spectrum of whole parts within greater wholes. Therefore, when he says, "The kingdom of heaven is within," Jesus is communicating holographic principles of archetypal identification.

Heaven, the skies, the planets, the stars are located within our own psyches, since the basic patterns of the universe repeat themselves everywhere, in fractal-like fashion, and "as above so below". Thus, the patterns that the planets make in the sky reflect the ebb and flow of basic human impulses. The planets are also associated, especially in the Chinese tradition, with the basic forces of nature.

The hermetic maxim of "As above, so below, as within, so without" was the fundamental root of all practices for Gnostics, alchemists, Pythagoreans, Neoplatonists, and mystics around the world. This foundational, archetypal truth is why these powerful forces of nature and the psyche were extrapolated out into deities and gods.

Archetypes are often difficult to grasp to the modern mind, because as Robert Lawlor notes, "European languages require that verbs or action words be associated with nouns. We therefore have no linguistic forms with which to image a process or activity that has no material carrier. Ancient cultures symbolized these pure, eternal processes as gods, that is, powers or lines of action through which Spirit is concretized into energy and matter. (Lawlor 1982, 8)

Whether in India, Greece, Rome, the Mayan world, or the birthplace of astrology in ancient Sumer and Babylon, gods have always been perceived as metaphorical extensions of the human psyche. But equally as important, just as humans made gods in their own image, so did the gods fashion humans in their own image:

> Then God said, "Let us make man in our image, in our likeness, and let them rule over the fish of the sea and the birds of the air, over the livestock, over all the earth, and over all the creatures that move along the ground." (Gen. 1:26-27)

In this important Biblical quote, God becomes plural. Notice the phrase, "Let us...." This seems to suggest the creative nature of the intermediary realm of the archetypes, the constituent components of the human psyche. Planetary configurations at the moment of one's birth reflect an internal, psychic configuration. The language of astrology then functions to illuminate the cosmic song of the incarnate soul. Carl Jung once remarked, "We are born at a given moment in a given place and like vintage years of wine we have the qualities of the year and of the season in which we are born. Astrology does not lay claim to anything else."

Whether the force is gravitational, electromagnetic, psychic, or mystical-spiritual—a planet's position compels you towards certain behavior. Indeed, it grasps hold of you. In India, the planets and eclipse points (Moon's nodes) are called Grahas, which means "graspings." But because the planet is extensive and reflective of energies within oneself, like all Hindu deities, planets can be propitiated. It has been a much more common practice in Vedic astrology to apply remedial measures for certain planetary conditions, either by birth or by transit. But there is no reason why this practice cannot be applied to the Western astrological tradition we describe in this book. This act of remediation is an attunement to the highest, most evolved expression of the psychological force operating through you. To return to the musical metaphor in Chapter 2, you are a musical instrument tuning up your vibratory potential to meet the frequency of each planetary force.

Archetypal Therapy

Besides India, in ancient Greece, the will of the gods could be understood by visiting the great oracular sites, places of tremendous natural power, such as was found in Delphi, Didyma, and Dodona in Greece. This was a consistent and widespread practice and as the historian Cicero wrote, the advice must have been good or people would not have kept coming back. (George 2008) This reminds us of the success and popularity of astrological guidance today.

The priest or priestess of the oracle would become literally inspired, breathing in the essence of the god and becoming filled with the god's spirit. Then they would give advice to all the pilgrims who had traveled there seeking counsel on business, love, family, finances, and health.

When a person was ill, there was a belief that when ordinary healing was not effective, the illness had been sent by one of the gods who had been offended. Imagine this "offended god" as an archetypal part of your psyche which has been neglected, suppressed, or distorted. Like those people today who consult astrologers, psychics, and all manner of energy workers and healers, the sick person of the ancient world would go to a diviner to understand which god was offended and why. The person was told to make a pilgrimage to that god's site and make offerings in order to become initiated into that particular god's rites. This type of healing was called *terapeia*, which is the basis of today's modern practice of therapy.

Planetary remediation is a type of terapeia, and we can see it in the following example. If you have Saturn opposite or square your Sun, it would be helpful to work with Saturn gemstones and to chant the mantra to Saturn while contemplating the Saturn planetary collage. In addition, you could set aside a sanctified time on Satur-day to fast or minimize food intake, to focus meditation on the root chakra, to study the Kaballah sephiroth Binah, and to reflect upon your relationship to time. All of these techniques would be especially powerful during a sky transit to either your Sun or Saturn. What you are doing in this process is recognizing a psychoevolutionary force within yourself reflected in the macrocosmic image of the planet Saturn. Through acute observation, the ancient stargazers and chroniclers of the sky correlated the placement of Saturn and every other planet in both nations' and individuals' birthchart to specific behaviors and experiences on the terrestrial plane. Those sages who observed the stars realized that there existed a primal urge to discipline oneself, perform a role in society, experience limitation and obstacle, and steadfastly take steps towards mastery. They noted the manifestation of these urges on the physical plane in relation to the heavenly movements of the planet Saturn. These urges, and all the evolutionary urges in the soul are intrinsic to the fundamental framework of life. The planets and stars reflect the basic organizing principles of the universe. They are original, divine imprints, and they play out their drama on the great stage of life as the Archetypal Theater.

Planetary Mandala

When I travelled for nine months in Asia in my mid 20's, I repeatedly noticed how each stranger reminded me of a friend or family member back home; they had the same energetic expression with a different mask. I was beginning then to decipher the codex of the soul—the archetypal resonance by which one recognizes the sameness in the difference.

The intention of the archetypal map presented in this book is to help you to invite in and integrate the wisdom of your soul in its multidimensional nature, while honoring the jeweled archetypal nature of those other souls you encounter on your journey.

Celestial events and terrestrial phenomena mirror each other. Hence, meditation upon, visualization of, and embodied invocation of planetary energies are simply experiences of deeper immersion within the totality of one's cosmic identity. As heavenly reflectors of our internal psychic processes, the planets function as meditative catalysts for spiritual awakening of core archetypal principles within ourselves.

In this sense, the planetary mandala acts as a mirror for absorption in the archetypal self. As an art-strologer, the planets compelled me to fashion meditative images of them for study and contemplation. These planetary images function as archetypal collages, and each one of us can make our own collage of archetypal energy for deeper integration of the psychoevolutionary forces within.

Therapist Carl Jung worked with mandalas in this same healing and instructive manner. The mandala is an ancient, cross-cultural tool used to focus and concentrate one's intention. It is a symbol of wholeness which assists the meditator in achieving a mystical relationship with the cosmic unity from which all manifold forms arise.

In India, a type of mandala, the "yantra," is a visual tool that serves as a centering device in meditation. It is also a symbolic representation of the energy patterns of a deity as seen by Tantric practitioners in their meditations. Yantra is a Sanskrit term meaning "to control" (*yam*) and "liberate" (*tra*). Yantra depicts both macrocosmic and microcosmic forces acting together—the simultaneous movement towards and away from the center.

In the Buddhist tradition, sacred *thangkas* serve a similar function as yantras. They often depict Buddhist deities—aspects of the transpersonalized self—to which one can offer prayers. At a more intensive degree of practice, the aspirant visualizes oneself as the *yidam*, or meditation deity. Thus an alchemical process occurs in the practitioner whereby the unrefined, personalized self is transmuted into the purified and exalted self.

Most often, thangkhas and yantras are engaged along with the practice of mantra. In these archetypal collages, I have also included the Sanskrit mantras for the planets, as received and transmitted by the yogis of India. *Mantra* literally translates as an "instrument of thought," and when repeated with devotion, is a profound, meta-linguistic tool of spiritual re-union.

When yantra and mantra are used in combination as a form of ritual prayer, *tantra* is created. The controlled and focused gaze coupled with the repetition of sacred sound produces a liberating truth that can bring about spiritual realization to the dedicated practitioner.

It is my hope that these planetary portraits will inspire a devotional practice extensive to the Buddhist and Hindu practices, with a potential to transform your relationship to the psycho-evolutionary forces which compose the totality of your being, weaving you through the complex holarchy of your spiritual identity.

how to Sing the hymn of your Soul with the StArchetypal Theater

Besides meditation with the planetary portraits, I have included a comprehensive list of archetypal correlations for each planet and sign to assist you in the integration of your archetypal structure as well as to open your perception to the archetypal energy pulsating all around you.

It is my hope that you will exercise your creative potential as you apply this language.

Perhaps you have three planets in Virgo. You can begin to work with the totem of the Owl. You can meditate upon The Hermit card in the Tarot deck. You can study the roles of the priest and priestess in different cultures throughout history and think of how you can update that persona now. You may cultivate a spiritual practice involving mantra and sacred, devotional music at the beginnings and endings of your day. You may seek to do a seasonal cleanse in order to assist you in maintaining your health.

Perhaps you would like to know why you always attract the same kind of man. In the list of correlations, you read that Mars can act as the projection of the sacred masculine, an energy which you must cultivate within. Your Mars is in Sagittarius. You decide to take yourself on an adventure—you begin outdoor activities, like rock climbing and kayaking. You decide to invoke the gypsy and travel on a spiritual pilgrimage to a foreign country. You feel the god in you flow as a global citizen as you listen to more world fusion music. Wearing more of the Sagittarius costume, you recognize yourself becoming more of the man you always attract, moving closer towards your version of masculine-feminine integration.

You're a Capricorn rising and your plate couldn't get any fuller. The pressures keep stacking up and everyone's turning to you to get the job done. You're burnt out, stuck, and weighted down from all the demands of work.

You read about Cancer, Capricorn's opposite sign, and you find that it relates to those you consider family and to nurturing yourself. So you call up your friend who does massage and you set up a weekly massage for the next month. You also realize that you're spending far too much time eating on the road. You determine to make yourself a nourishing meal with a beloved friend every Thursday night. And during that night, you watch nostalgic films that make you cry and you let your emotions fly. You allow yourself be vulnerable and break though that mask you must wear as the productive leader and the bastion of Capricornian strength, ambition, and hard work.

Maybe you're really irritated. You're feeling the dark, the doom, the gloom. This isn't something new. It's been creeping through over the last year with that Pluto transit opposite your Moon. You have to channel the intensity of the Lord of the Underworld somehow. So you find yourself drawn to listening to the goth and metal of your youth, and it feels absolutely cathartic. Film-noir and thrillers are the only movies that seem to be enticing you these days. Your friend just mentioned a past-life regression session she did and you're intrigued. You see an upcoming workshop on holotropic breathwork and you recognize how this could release all that lava boiling up from within.

You're trying to understand why your daughter hates doing math and history, but loves her art class. You read about her learning style, Mercury, and discover that the god of perception is in the sign of Pisces—the mystic, the poet, the dreamer, the artist. When you mention the possibilities of taking music or dance lessons, she gets very excited. You notice that she empathizes strongly with characters in film. You ask her to describe how they may be feeling internally, which they may not be speaking on the outside. You help attune her to her natural psychic gifts. Instead of amusement parks, you take her to the museum or aquarium. On vacation, you take her to the ocean and teach her how to meditate with the waves. At night, you put on the sound of the gentle shoreline for her to fall asleep to, and you invite her to write and paint her dreams.

These are just a few of the potential ways of combining the archetypal correlations in your chart so you can learn how to serve as instructor and guide into the luminous textures of your multidimensional soul. As a language, the possibilities are endless. As you read the following list of archetypal associations, please remember that what you read is a synthesis of information gathered from Western, Indian, and ancient astrologers for thousands of years. In attempts to update the archetypes for modern folk, I have included information from my own research and my own intuitive guidance. This is not an exhaustive list. You are invited to add your own correlations as you observe them over time. This dynamic nature of astrology and its archetypal foundations is what keeps it exciting and pertinent to our lives now. With the changing generations and with technological advancement, the archetypes wear new masks, but remain in their core the same primal energetic imprints governing all of life.

Author's Note:
*Unfortunately, I could not include color images of the planetary portrait, but all can be found and studied at my website, astralshaman.com
**The nodes are points in the sky created by the eclipse of the Sun and Moon, so there are no collages.
***I have not included collages for the asteroids, Chiron, and the dwarf planets Ceres and Pluto. They are composed primarily of rocky cores, and are irregularly shaped.
****Pluto has not been photographed by any spacecraft, so I have not included a collage for the Lord of the Underworld. Most likely, he would be ok with this, given that Pluto wears a helmet of invisibility while his powerful transits sneak up on all of us.

Planetary Symbols

Moon

Earth

Pallas

Jupiter

Uranus

Mercury

Sun

Vesta

Saturn

Neptune

Venus

North
Node

Ceres

Chiron

Pluto

Mars

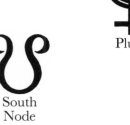

South
Node

Juno

Chapter 5
PLANETS
Wandering Stars:
The Evolutionary Urges of
The Planetary Cast of Characters

CIRCLE - Spirit
VERTICAL LINE - Mind
HORIZONTAL LINE - Body
CROSS - Matter
ARC - Consciousness/Soul

I have listed the planetary pantheon in the order of their speed and distance from the Sun. The order in which they appear in the solar system is a mirror of the extent of their forces in our lives—how they affect our inner, social, and collective levels of reality. This order correlates to their purposes as personalizing, socializing, and transpersonalizing forces within the human psyche.

Sun

I am the dance of Ra-diance.
But at dusk I meet my death
by the hand of my brother Set
Below the horizon west
I sail into the trials of the underworld
By the sacred dawn of each morning
I am the Second Coming,
I am the reborn and only
begotten Son of Heaven
I am the vital pulse of your heart
I am the Light of all vision
I am celebration's sparkle
in the playful child's eye
To my sky chariot
am I tied
And in service do I sacrifice
to bestow upon you
the promise of eternal life.

Evolutionary Urge, Keywords:	Vitality, life purpose, fuel, radiance, life force, confidence, appreciation, acknowledgment, creativity, self-esteem, accomplishment
Mantra/Affirmation:	Om hreem suraya namah
Planetary Dignity	
Rulership:	Leo
Exaltation:	Aries
Detriment:	Aquarius
Fall:	Libra
Directional Strength:	North, near the MC
Aspect Correlation:	N/A

Aum

Hreem

"I am the resurrection and i am the life,
and those who believe in me shall never die."
~ The Sun of God

Surya

Namah

Physical Characteristics: *My body is a mixture of hydrogen and helium, superheated into a plasma that burns at millions of degrees. I spew storms of deadly radiation millions of miles out of space. It is a yellow dwarf star, small compared to my stellar siblings, but I could fit one million earths within my boundaries. I have a surface temperature of 10,000 degrees Fahrenheit. In one second, I churn out more energy than has been used in all of human civilization. Photons, particles of light and heat, bring my life-giving rays to earth. My plasma rotates at different rates, creating a dynamic, tangled magnetic web with the possibilities of millions of poles, not just one north and south pole. When a sunspot unleashes its magnetic energy, what results are the most intense explosions in the solar system, solar flares, which can release the combined power of a million volcanic eruptions on Earth or millions of atomic bombs. I am 4.6 billion years old and will endure for another five billion years.*

Symbol:	The circle of spirit with the point of infinite awareness emanating from the center.
Quality:	Hot and Dry, Masculine, Yang; selecting
Duration in a Sign/House:	1 month

Where the Sun journeys through your chart, ask the following questions:

House: Where can I radiate my life purpose?

Sign: By expressing what archetypal energy do I feel most vitalized and alive?

Aspect: Which planetary forces constrict or increase my sense of vitality and creativity?

Historical Archetypes:	King, royalty, child
Deities/Gods:	Horus, Ra, Surya, Sol, Inti, Ahau, Lugh, Jesus, Helios, Apollo
Day of Week:	Sunday
Tarot:	Sun
Chakras:	Sahasrara, 7th
Sephiroth:	Tiphareth (Beauty)
Alchemical Stage:	Fermentatio
Angels and Spirits:	Michael
Animals:	Lion, hummingbird, falcon, lizard, all felines
Colors:	Gold, yellow
Music/Genres:	Jam music
Foods:	Orange
Metals:	Gold
Gems/Minerals:	Amber, topaz, citrine
Plants and Trees:	Sunflower, geranium, marigold; Birch
Essential Oils:	Naroli, patchouli, myrrh, frankincense, benzoin
Anatomy:	Heart, circulatory system, right eye (male), left eye (female), brain
Movement:	Excited, vibrant, spontaneous, childlike
Diseases:	Arrogance, narcissism, conceit, tyranny, fear of exposure, low self-esteem, anemia, heart and back problems
Medicines/Healings:	Sunbathing, Sun Salutation
Relations:	Royalty, presidents, father
Places/Natural Events:	The beach, the tropics

Moon

I am the Queen of the Night,
and the stars are my children,
In splendor and sparkle we reign,
Yet the home is my temple
For I am the soothing tea that you sip
And I am the bath of nourishment.
As my body waxes and wanes, so too do your emotions,
for as I magnetize the oceans of the earth, so do I tug on the tides of your heart.
I am the ache of instinct
the craving for contentment
I am the yearning to be heard in every need you acknowledge
Your soul seeks to be satiated by my sensitivity
For I am the mother of mercy,
And I am the vessel of memory
I am the cyclical pulse of time, the rhythms that repeat
I am the new seed planted, and the fruitful illumination in full abundance
For I am the moonth and the menses, and matron of maternal blessing
It is by my magic and mystery
the child you shall bear
the blossom of your belly.

Evolutionary Urge, Keywords:	Emotion, instinctive reaction, nurturance, nourish, feel safe, feel secure, receptive, absorptive, sensitive, memory, habit, birth conditioning, cycles, time-keeping
Mantra/Affirmation:	Om hreem chandraye namah, Om hreem somaye namah
Planetary Dignity	
Rulership:	Cancer
Exaltation:	Taurus
Detriment:	Capricorn
Fall:	Scorpio
Directional Strength:	South, near the IC
Symbol:	The arc of consciousness; Spirit listening to its own inward being

Aum

Hreem

Home

Moon

Mama

Emotion

Moon

Mary

Instinct

Chandra

Nurture

Namah

Physical Characteristics: *I am 234, 000 miles from earth, a travel time of three days from your home planet. My diameter is one-quarter of the Earth, making me the largest moon in proportion to my host planet, quite different than the other 150 moons in our solar system. I have no atmosphere, so there is nothing to carry sound waves. My temperatures mirror the emotional spectrum I signify in astrology: 270 degrees above zero at midday to 240 below zero at night. I pull the Earth's water towards my own body, creating the tides. Importantly, I play a fundamental role in stabilizing the Earth's climate. My gravitational effect keeps the degree of tilt and the Earth's rotational axis constant. This tilt is what maintains the repeatable cycle of seasons as the Earth orbits the Sun. Without me, the tilt of our north pole would vary widely and create much chaos on the planet. According to the Giant Impact Theory, the most accepted scenario of my formation, I was created 4.5 billion years ago, out of a collision between Earth and an object roughly the size of Mars. This collision started the Earth spinning, giving you your 24 hour day and launching material out around the Earth, including your satellite, me—Luna.*

Quality:	Moist and Cold, Feminine, Yin; absorbing
Duration in a Sign/House:	13 moons a year
	2.5 days

Where the Moon is located in your chart, ask the following questions:

House: In what area of life will I feel most comfortable?

What kinds of experiences give me the most emotional charge?

Sign: What is the energetic texture of my soul?

How do I naturally react to situations?

What style of being nourishes me and helps me to stay content?

Aspect: What planetary forces help me feel safe?

What other psychological urges give me insecurity?

Historical Archetypes:	Mother, nurse, chef, hostess, caregiver, hospitality
Deities/Gods:	Diana, Artemis, Selene, Isis, Luna, Mary, Ceridwen, Soma, Kwan Yin, Parvati
Day of Week:	Monday
Tarot:	High Priestess
Chakras:	Ajna, 6th
Sephiroth:	Yesod (Foundation)
Alchemical Stage:	Coagulatio
Angels and Spirits:	Gabriel
Animals:	Domestic pets—cat, dog, wolf, mouse, snail, duck, goose, amphibians
Colors:	White, Silver
Music/Genres:	Lullaby, crying
Foods:	Milk, rice, corn, watery fruits and vegetables, cabbage, lettuce, cucumber, celery, melon, comfort foods
Metals:	Silver
Gems/Minerals:	Increase sensitivity and intuition; Moonstone, Aquamarine
Plants and Trees:	Willow, lily, sappy those growing in water, grasses
Essential Oils:	Relaxing and comforting, work with female reproductive organs; dandelion, chamomile, juniper
Anatomy:	Stomach, breasts, digestive system
Movement:	Soft, gentle, internal
Diseases:	Co-dependency, food disorders, overemotional; Digestive problems, water retention
Medicines/Healings:	Holding, touch, massage, rocking, cradling, nourishing, and comfort food
Relations:	Mom, Babysitter
Places/Natural Events:	Home, motels, hotels, cribs, baby showers

Mercury

I am born of the Zeus and the nymph named Maia
Immediately after my birth, I stole one of Apollo's sheep
but I won his forgiveness by offering him the lyre
the instrument of my invention.
I choose no side but instead fashion the contest
Yet I must remain neutral,
For I am the messenger of the gods and the guide of souls
and the only one who can travel the domain of Hades
and return to the realm of the living.
Thus I am the shapeshift, I am the tragicomic
I am both the solemn and the god of commerce
When I am retrograde, I re-mind you
of the fragility of technology
and of the tongue's slippery body
to instead go within
and journal your memory into wisdom
By wing'd sandals I fly
and the sacred I inscribe
with my caduceus wand
I am Hermes Trismegistus
the alchemical magus,
in your ear I do whisper
the magic and the mischief
and the tall tales of the trixter.

Evolutionary Urge, Keywords:	Communication, thinking, perception, languages, education, intelligence, siblings, cunning, trickery, con-artist, clever, facile, adaptation, correspondences, internet, telephones, thieves, journeys, trade
Mantra/Affirmation:	Om hreem buddhaye namah
Planetary Dignity	
Rulership:	Gemini (M), Virgo (F)
Exaltation:	Virgo
Detriment:	Sagitarrius
Fall:	Pisces
Directional Strength:	East, near the ASC

Physical Characteristics: Closest to the Sun, I am without moon or atmosphere. I am the smallest planet, but I am full of paradoxes. They say I am lifeless, but I orbit the Sun faster than any other planet, in just 84 days. However, a year is shorter than a day for me. One of my days is equal to 180 earth days. For 6 months of the year, the side of me exposed to the Sun is 800 degrees Fahrenheit, while my other side is 300 degrees below zero. Without an atmosphere to protect me, I have been bombarded by asteroids and meteors, producing craters everywhere. I am full of what scientists have eloquently called "weird terrain," impossible to define shapes and sizes of rock. I surprise you by even having ice at my poles, which are likely due to meteor impacts. Since my poles never face towards the sun, this ice never melts.

Aspect Correlation:	Semi-sextile
Symbol:	Contains them all, potential for synthesis; Soul above mediates Spirit and Matter
Quality:	Neutral; mediating
Cycle around the Sun:	84 days. 3 Retrogrades per year.
Duration in a Sign/House:	About 3-4 weeks

Where Mercury is located in your chart, ask the following questions:

House: In what realm of life will I most often communicate?
Where will my thoughts naturally circulate?

Sign: Through what lenses do I perceive reality?
Look to the element to describe your learning style: watery and emotive/artistic, fiery and spiritual/creative, earthy and productive/sensual, airy and conceptual/ideas

Aspect: What planetary forces influence my thought processes?

Historical Archetypes:	Messenger, troubadour, performer, writer, scribe
Deities/Gods:	Hermes, Iris, Wodan, Odin, Castor and Pollux, Saraswati
Day of Week:	Wednesday, after Wodan (Norse)
Tarot:	Magician
Chakras:	Vishuddha, 5th
Sephiroth:	Hod (Splendour)
Alchemical Stage:	Distillatio
Angels and Spirits:	Raphael
Animals:	Birds, Crow, Fox, Monkey
Colors:	Blue
Music/Genres:	Eclectic fusion, uptempo, techno, breaks, 2 step, fingerpicking guitar, live improv, beat box
Foods:	Coffee, mint, most nuts
Metals:	Mercury
Gems/Minerals:	Strengthen mental clarity; Agate, tiger's eye
Plants and Trees:	Hazel
Essential Oils:	Stimulate respiratory and digestive systems; Peppermint, cardamom, fennel, lavender, rosemary, thyme
Anatomy:	Arms, hands, wrists, lungs
Movement:	Fast, chaotic, curious, distracted, excited, arms
Diseases:	Nervous, scattered energy, thievery, cunning; language/learning difficulties, asthma/lung problems
Medicines/Healings:	Cleverness, curiosity, humor, wit, adaptability, playfulness
Relations:	Siblings
Places/Natural Events:	Marketplaces, airports, post offices, playgrounds, libraries, bookstores

♀

Venus

Born of sea-foam
from the fury and semen
of the sky-god's castration
I am the source of all passion
the magnet of attraction.
Beauty beheld
the sensual seduction is my spell,
all affection is my realm.
I send the kiss you cannot resist
with amorous embrace
from my son Eros
lips so voluptuous
the curve
of Cupid's arrow
shall pierce you
with chocolate delight
and the song that shivers through your thigh,
the frequency of this flesh temptress,
of this courtship and caress,
your refusal is a futile attempt,
for by the finger and the linger
of love's scent
shall you enter
the rapture of the goddess.

Evolutionary Urge, Keywords:	Love, attraction, aesthetics, creativity, friendship, sacred feminine.
	*In women, the highest version of the goddess.
	**In men, the projection of the anima, or inner feminine essence.
Mantra/Affirmation:	Om hreem shukraye namah
Planetary Dignity	
Rulership:	Libra (M) Taurus (F)
Exaltation:	Pisces
Detriment:	Scorpio
Fall:	Virgo
Directional Strength:	South; IC

Aspect Correlation:	Sextile
Symbol:	The circle of spirit upon the cross of matter.
Quality:	Moist and Hot, Moist and Cold;
Cycle around the: Sun:	Feminine, Yin; attracting
	Roughly 1 year; 260 days as evening star, 260 days as morning star, 9 days conjoin the sun, orderly repeating
Duration in a Sign/House:	About 1 year

Where Venus is located in your chart, ask the following questions:

House: What area of life will I naturally feel myself magnetized towards?
Where can I apply my value system, aesthetics, and love?
Sign: What mask does my Sacred Feminine wear?
What energies attract me in friendship and partnership?
Aspect: What planets harmonize or challenge my love-nature?

Historical Archetypes:	Lover, artist
Deities/Gods:	Aphrodite, Freya, Radha-Krishna, Mary Magdalene, Cupid, Eros
Day of Week:	Friday, after Freya (Norse)
Tarot:	Empress
Chakras:	Anahata, 4th
Sephiroth:	Netzach (Victory)
Alchemical Stage:	Fermentatio
Angels and Spirits:	Hanael
Animals:	Dove, swan, sparrow, bumblebee
Colors:	Green
Music/Genres:	Dance—Trance, House, Club music
Foods:	Chocolate, sweets, desserts
Metals:	Copper
Gems/Minerals:	Open the heart chakra, help accessing the feminine principle; Malachite, aventurine, emerald, tourmaline
Plants and Trees:	Myrtle
Essential Oils:	Sweet smells, good for skin and aesthetics; Rose, jasmine, geranium
Anatomy:	Mouth, throat, neck, voice
Movement:	Graceful, seductive, sexy, beautiful
Diseases:	Vanity, co-dependence, hedonism, laziness
Medicines/Healings:	Unconditional Love, harmony, peace, sharing, mediation, co-operation, affection, sensuality
Relations:	Beloveds, intimate partners, friends

Aum

Hreem

VENUS

Love

am shree maha lakshmi namaha

affection

Aphrodite

attraction

creativity

Shukraye

Namah

Physical Characteristics: *I am the closest planet to earth, nearly identical in size. Like a mirror to beauty, I reflect 80% of the Sun's rays. I have a retrograde rotation, so that the Sun rises in the west and sets in the east. But my rotation is very slow—from one sunrise to the next takes eight Earth months! At 900 degrees Fahrenheit, I am the hottest planet in the solar system, due to my extreme global warming. Because of the plenitude of my volcanoes—some say I have near a million—I release carbon dioxide, 95% of my atmosphere. My atmospheric pressure is 90 times greater than on earth, preventing the vast number of lightning storms from ever hitting the surface. My clouds are composed of sulfuric acid, similar to toxic battery acid, which gives my skies an orangish tone. Because of my volcanoes, lava rock makes up 70% of my surface and I have been pummeled by meteors, which possibly changed my rotation. I am also full of canyons and mountain ranges.*

Places/
Natural Events: Weddings, the bedroom, art galleries, amusement parks, theaters, music clubs, shopping malls

Mars

I am the spark that enflames your will
I am the fearless general
And so I must lead with pride and power
As I catalyze the call to action
for I am the hero whom others shall follow
on the epic adventure
to conquer hesitation,
to destroy limitation
I am that which overcomes.
I am sexual desire,
the unquenchable thirst
the primal hunger.
For I am the spiritual warrior,
and I am the furious heart
of the eternal fire.

Evolutionary Urge, Keywords: Force of will, activates, motivates, drives, catalyzes, separation, territoriality, confrontation, conflict; Sacred Masculine, Yang
*In a man's chart, his version of the highest God-force.
**In women, the projection of the inner masculine essence, the animus.

Mantra/Affirmation: Om hreem mangala namah
I desire, I will, I can

Planetary Dignity
Rulership: Aries (M) Scorpio (F)
Exaltation: Capricorn
Detriment: Libra
Fall: Cancer
Directional Strength: North; MC

Aspect Correlation: Square
Symbol: Matter over spirit; The circle of spirit striking with the phallic, outward arrow

Physical Characteristics: *I am half the size of Earth. Dust storms darken my sky wile my nights' temperature descends to 100 degrees below. My atmosphere has no oxygen, composed of almost all carbon dioxide. My terrain is full of iron oxides, basically rust, which turns into dust particles. This combined with my red atmosphere, gives me the red glow in your night sky. My mountains, Olympus Mons, is the tallest mountain in the solar system—15 miles high. I am filled with canyons and dunes. Mariner Valley is a canyon the size of the United States and your Mojave Desert resembles many of my dune features. I was once far warmer and wetter than I am now, and today my polar caps are composed of ice.*

Quality: Masculine, Yang, Hot and Dry, separating

Cycle around the: Sun: Roughly 2 years

Duration in a Sign/House: About 2 months

Where the Mars journeys through your chart, ask the following questions:

House: What realm of life will excite and motivate me?

In what area will I likely find confrontation and battle?

Sign: What energy motivates me to act?

How best do I initiate myself out in the world?

Aspect: What compels the Sacred Masculine?

What compels the Sacred Masculine to act?

What other planets will either be more energized or suffer strife or confrontation within me?

Historical Archetypes:	Warrior, Hero, General, Samurai, Athlete
Deities/Gods:	Ares, Indra, Hercules, Achilles, Nergal
Day of Week:	Tuesday, after Tyr (Norse)
Tarot:	Tower
Chakras:	Manipura, 3rd
Sephiroth:	Geburah (Severity)
Alchemical Stage:	Separatio
Angels and Spirits:	Khamael, Samuel
Animals:	All predators, panther, jaguar
Colors:	Red, crimson
Music/Genres:	Metal, hard rock, industrial
Nature/Temperament	Hot and dry
Foods:	Spicy, cayenne, pepper, ginger
Metals:	Iron
Gems/Minerals:	Increase vitality, strengthen will and assertive energy; Red stones, bloodstone, carnelian, red jasper, garnet, flint
Plants and Trees:	Alder, thorny trees
Essential Oils:	Basil, pepper, ginger
Anatomy:	Adrenal glands, red blood cells, muscle tissue
Movement:	Aggresive, powerful, confruntaional; Martial Arts
Diseases:	Inflammation, anger, frustration
Medicines/Healings:	Physical exercise, competitive sports, caffeine
Relations:	Enemies
Places/Natural Events:	Battlefield, downtown city, freeway

SOCIALIZING FORCES:
The Asteroids, Jupiter, & Saturn

Asteroids are referred to as Minor Planets, and assist in the process of socialization. Thus, many of the more popular asteroids are named after myths that connect the individual to the culture at large. Below, I have described the most commonly used asteroids, often called the "asteroid goddesses."

Orbital cycles for the asteroid Goddesses:
Cycle around the: Sun: 4-5 years
Duration in a Sign/House: 4-5 months

Ceres

I am Demeter, the All-Mother
I am grain goddess,
and source of abundance.
But for half the year I weep
and the Earth remains barren
as my daughter Persephone,
is hurled down to Hades' underworld.
I was honored during the Rites of Eleusis
by the ergot plant.
I taught the initiate
to let go and surrender
I unveiled the traps of attachment,
the sorrow of separation,
and that only with loss can one transfigure
for then the return can occur.
And so in your willing transformation
I bestow the vision and the revelation
For I am mother to the orphan
and I nurture
the abandoned elder
within

Evolutionary Urge, Keywords:	Where do I seek abundance in life? How can I access wealth? What energies will nurture me? How can I nourish others and provide maternal energy? Where do I wish to share? Relationship with food; caring for children, elderly, those without caregivers, and animals; initiating the transformative process; grief and loss with certain attachments, antidote to loss—what feeds me and sustains me at my core?
Sign Affinity:	Taurus-Scorpio polarity, Virgo, Cancer

Juno

I am Hera, most ancient of goddesses,
My worship is older
than that of even my brother and husband Zeus
I was the ancient connection
to earth's mystic rhythms
before I morphed to become
social ritual and the Queen of custom.
I honor the sacred cycles of the feminine—
maiden, mother, crone.
I keep the sacred vow
of the marriage tradition
and so I cultivate the art of partnership
together we endure
locked in loyalty
and in karmic encounter
the process of negotiation,
relation, retribution
and yes, the struggle for power.
Delicate the dance I teach
to balance the scale's
in love's equality.

Evolutionary Urge, Keywords:	Urge to be in committed partnership; where is the source of power? Struggle, fears, and manipulations in relationships? Urge to find balance, fairness, and equality in relationship. Desire to share a sacred, cosmic connection with another.
Sign Affinity:	Libra, Scorpio

Vesta

The hearth I attend, the flame I sustain
with sacred devotion
chaste I remain
free of all distraction
Sexual repression or discerning selection?
For the detail of my intention
testifies to the body
as a vessel of divine reflection
I focus
I commit
I nurse the wounded
with the purified covenant.

Evolutionary Urge, Keywords:	Where am I devoted to a higher spiritual path? Where do I focus and commit my energy? Where will I sublimate sexual energy and practice purifying myself?
Sign Affinity:	Virgo, Scorpio

Pallas Athena

Born from Zeus' head, I am Athena,
the principle of wisdom incarnate
I am the strategy which rewards you victory
I am competition to achieve excellence
And I am all creative intelligence
fashioned into form
sculpted into utility
I am art in application
I am careful governance
I am the scientific aesthetic in politics
Neutral and androgynous
goddess of justice
I am psychic self-healing
and mental clarity.
I am visualization, affirmation, mediation

Evolutionary Urge, Keywords:	Where can my creative intelligence apply its wisdom? How can my strategic mind compete for excellence? Where can I apply my artistic talent?
Sign Affinity:	Libra, Aquarius

♃
Jupiter

I am Zeus, Thor, Jove—the king of the gods, and lord of the storm.
As an infant, my Mother Rhea, hid me in a cave,
secured from the horrible death of my father Kronos.
Then, as I grew, I at last forced Kronos to disgorge my siblings:
Hestia, Demeter, Hera, Hades, Poseidon
By the thunderbolt I decree justice, punishing the wicked, and protecting the weak.
I ride by eagle, and I anchor in Earth by root of the royal oak
My bounty is gifted upon those who prepare their table for the banquet of abundance.
I know no boundaries, I suffer no limits.
And so I share my fortune with mortals and goddesses alike
indulging in intoxicating ecstasy
my many moons are named after my many consorts
inspiring with wisdom and philosophy
I am your yoga path
by your prayer shall you receive my blessing
by proportion to the space you create
so shall you ascend in your faith.

Evolutionary Urge, Keywords:	To expand, to give opportunity, to bestow blessings, to teach, to inspire, fortune, faith, philosophy, humor, self-improvement, overindulgence, hedonism, extravagance, dogmatism
Mantra:	Om hreem brihaspatye namah, Om hreem guru namah
Affirmation:	I expand, grow, I believe
Planetary Dignity	
Rulership:	Sagitarrius
Exaltation:	Pisces
Detriment:	Virgo
Fall:	Gemini
Directional Strength:	East; ASC
Aspect Correlation:	The Trine
Symbol:	The arc of consciousness over the cross of matter; Soul elevated above matter

Aum **Hreem**

Intuition Growth

Expansion

Zeus

Guru

Opportunity

Jupiter

Brihaspataye **Namah**

Physical Characteristics: *I am composed of 84% hydrogen and 14% helium—the two lightest and most abundant substances in the universe. Thus I am the gaseous giant of the solar system, 77% the mass of all the planets, filled with many jet streams going in opposite directions. At 11 times the diameter of Earth, I could hold 1000 Earths in my body. Even My Great Red spot is larger than your planet. The Red Spot is a fierce storm 4000 miles larger than the Earth, traveling at 350 miles per hour. Composed of violent wind and lightning, it is ironically calm in the center. I have 62 Moons and my moon Europa appears to have water, but you must go through many sheets of ice to get there. My magnetic field is the largest object in the solar system, 450 million miles long, buzzing with electric particles. I conduct electricity all through and around myself, and auroras glow from my body, which are 1000 times more powerful than your northern and southern lights. Measuring 1200 miles across, they even emit noise.*

Quality:	Hot and Moist; joining, benefic
Cycle around the: Sun:	12 years
Duration in a Sign/House:	1 year

Where the Jupiter journeys through your chart, ask the following questions:

House: Where will my faith expand, where can I improve my confidence? Where can I take risks and feel the support of the gods?

Sign: What costume does the energy of expansion, faith, and idealism reign?

Aspect: Which planetary forces harmonize with or challenge my sense of faith, enthusiasm, and optimism?

Historical Archetypes:	Preacher, guru, teacher, traveler, gypsy, nomad, scholar, religious pilgrim
Deities/Gods:	Zeus, Thor, Jove, Indra
Day of Week:	Thursday, after Thor
Tarot:	Wheel of Fortune
Chakras:	Swadhisthana, 2nd
Sephiroth:	Chesed (Mercy)
Alchemical Stage:	Disolutio
Angels and Spirits:	Sachiel, Michael, Tzadkiel, Ganesh, Santa Claus
Animals:	Eagle, Elephant, Whale, Peacock, Horse, Bear, all large animals
Colors:	Turquoise, Purple
Music/Genres:	Upbeat, world music, fusion
Foods:	Fatty foods, butter, cream, naturally sweet, pumpkin, squash, berries, sugar cane, dates, honey, olive oil, mint, sweet wines, foreign cuisine
Metals:	Tin
Gems/Minerals:	Cleanse liver; Citrine, turquoise, chrysocolla
Plants and Trees:	Jasmine, Sage, Oak, trees bearing fruit
Essential Oils:	Cedarwood, Sandalwood
Anatomy:	Liver, Pancreas, Thighs
Movement:	Big, grand, extravagant, thighs, horselike
Diseases:	Overeating, obesity, cancer, cramps, gall-stones, liver troubles, sciatica, swelling
Medicines/Healings:	Prayer, philosophy
Relations:	Teachers, gurus, religious leaders, children
Places/Natural Events:	Churches, temples, synagogues, classrooms, college, foreign countries

Saturn

I castrated my father Ouranos
as he destroyed his young,
my siblings the Titans.
There was a prophecy that I too would be deposed
by my own son.
But I defy prophecy
in order to keep the status quo.
So I swallowed all my young as they were born.
However there is rumor there is still one almighty they call Zeus.
But I am Kronos—Timekeeper, Timeteacher, Father of Time.
Long-forgotten, I was originally god of agriculture, and so I bear the scythe
For with perseverance,
I am the harvest of your success.
Discipline conditions me to be serious
For only through concentration
can I achieve my ambitions
If you adhere to my limitations
and answer the challenge of my lesson
you shall be rewarded
with maturity, wisdom, and recognition.

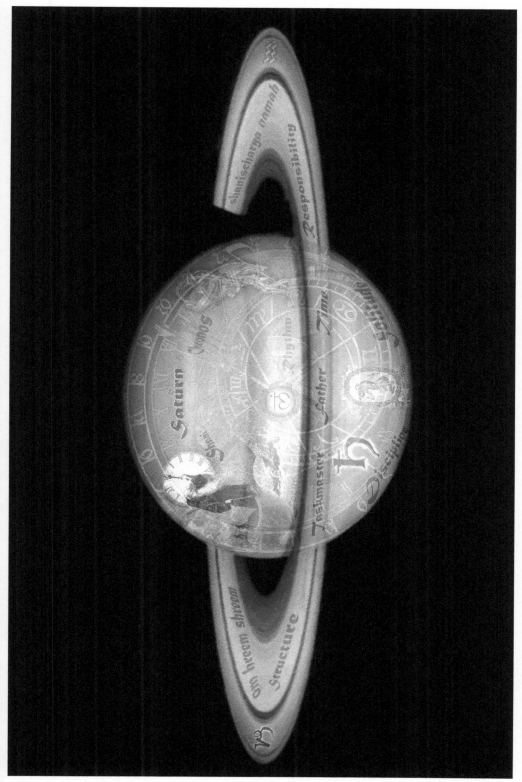

Physical Characteristics: *I may look peaceful and serene, but my lightning storms are a million times stronger than earth. Composed of hydrogen, with small proportions of helium and trace elements, my interior consists of a small core of rock and ice, surrounded by a thick layer of metallic hydrogen and a gaseous outer layer; some may even call me bloated. My weather may be more dynamic than even that of Jupiter's, with winds over 1000 miles per hour, though my storms shift slowly over time. I have the most eccentric poles in the solar system. My south pole is a hurricane 2/3 the size of Earth. Over the north pole, a perfect hexagon shape is found, a vortex of winds which can fit four Earths inside it. I am surrounded by majestic rings of ice and space debris, objects as big of houses down to as small as snow crystals. Although relatively paper thin, the rings are 173, 000 miles in diameter, wider than twenty-one Earths side by side. I have forty-eight named moons and my moon Titan is very special. The size of Mercury, it is the second largest moon in the solar system, and is the most earthlike body in our stellar family. It is the only body astronomers have found which has an extended atmosphere. Like earth, Titan's atmosphere is composed of oxygen and methane—natural gas. Its surface is a gooey substance of liquid methane. These rivers of natural gas feed into lake beds, and are surrounded by dunes.*

Evolutionary Urge, Keywords:	Responsibility, discipline, focus, mastery through hard work, concentration, solitude, hermit, misfortunes, routine exile, separation, losses, degradation, isolation, boundaries, obstruction, limitation, rigidity, inhibitions, sorrows, manifestation, failure, poverty, budgeting, debts, suffering, form, detioriation, decay, harsh, hard-hearted, cruel, conservative, practical, realistic, consistency, inhibited, resigned, melancholic
Mantra/Affirmation:	Om hreem shreem shanischarya namah I discipline, I concentrate

Planetary Dignity

Rulership:	Capricorn (F) Aquarius (M)
Exaltation:	Libra
Detriment:	Cancer
Fall:	Aries
Directional Strength:	West, DSC
Aspect Correlation:	Opposition
Symbol:	Cross of matter above shaping the form of consciousness; the sickle
Quality:	Cold and Dry, Malefic; challenging
Cycle around the: Sun:	29.5 years
Duration in a Sign/House:	2.5 years

Where the Saturn journeys through your chart, ask the following questions:

House: In what area of life will I have to discipline myself?
Where must I establish routines of hard work, focus, and responsibility?

Sign: Which energy will I initially fear and eventually seek to master?
How will I ultimately structure my consciousness?

Aspect: What planetary forces require commitment and stability? What forces may cause me to experience delay or obstacle in their expression in the world?

Historical Archetypes:	Father Time, Grim Reaper, wise elder, scrooge, boss, hermit
Deities/Gods:	Kronos, Shani, Pryderi
Day of Week:	Saturday
Tarot:	The World
Chakras:	Muladhara, 1st
Sephiroth:	Binah (Wisdom)
Alchemical Stage:	Calcinatio
Angels and Spirits:	Cassiel, Tzaphkiel, Aralim, Yama
Animals:	Tortoise, Black Horse
Colors:	Black, Orange
Music/Genres:	Minimalism, Silence
Foods:	Coarse, bitter food, salt, fermented foods
Metals:	Lead
Gems/Minerals:	Used to put ideas into form; Blue Sapphire, Onyx
Plants and Trees:	Elder, Pine, violet, sesame seeds, winter or dead trees, grey deep rooted, beet, potato, yam, carrot
Essential Oils:	Yin and cooling, camphor, pine, eucalyptus
Anatomy:	Skeletal system, tendon, ligament, joint, knee, skin, teeth
Movement:	Slow, weighed down, burdened, heavy-footed
Diseases:	Arthritis, rheumatism, emaciation, coldness, chronic complaints
Medicines/Healings:	Solitude, hard work, discipline, structure, rootedness
Relations:	Grandparents, elders, authorities, disciplinarians
Places/Natural Events:	Office buildings, corporate, governments, courts, jails, mountaintop, cemeteries

Chiron

In the body of the centaur
I merge instinct and intellect
as the bridge of consciousness.
Orphaned at birth,
Abandoned by my father Kronos,
and despised by my mother Philrya the horse,
I learned to survive on my own
until the great god Apollo became my foster father
He taught me the arts of healing and prophecy
music and poetry,
which I in turn taught others
For I am the wise mentor to the great heroes
I taught Achilles, Hercules, Jason, and Asclepius—father of healing
From astrology to herbology, I shared my counsel
the kind teacher, the coach to all
Wounded by my own student's arrow,
I offered my immortality up as a sacrifice
in order to free Prometheus—lover of humans.
For I am the dismembered shaman
And I am the wounded healer
within you.
I am the verse of service
inscribed upon your heart
and gifted to the world.

Evolutionary Urge, Keywords:	Shamanic consciousness, wounded healer, mentor, teacher, artistic craftsman, alchemy, sacrifice, service, wisdom, unfairness, chronic conditions
Mantra:	I heal
Durartion in a Sign/House:	Variable

Where the Chiron is in your chart, ask the following questions:

House: In what realm of life do I carry a wound?
Where can I learn to heal and eventually become a mentor to other?

Sign: What energy motivates my generation to explore deeper

Aspect: What planetary forces will have some primal, wounded aspect? What forces will be asked to make a sacrifice in order to more deeply heal?

♅

Uranus

I am Ouranous, oldest of the gods
Sky-father infinite,
and just when you think you can predict
the pattern of the weather
I shall surprise you
with the shock of mental storm
the electric charge
from which all ideas find their source
In my guise as Prometheus
I steal the fire from the gods
to liberate humanity
to innovate technology.
Through me,
your mind ignites in epiphany
the lightning strike increases
the quotient of synchronicity
you transcend dimension
in the sudden revelation,
now Rebel! now Revolt!
on your path of
Individuation

Evolutionary Urge, Keywords:	Originality, sudden change, impulse for freedom, radical energy, creative epiphany, divine mind, intuition, rebellion, breakthrough, individuation, innovation, eccentricity, inventiveness, youth, defiance of authority, intellectual brilliance
Mantra:	I rebel, I liberate, I individuate

Planetary Dignity

Sign Affinity:	Aquarius
Exaltation:	Scorpio
Detriment:	Virgo
Fall:	Taurus

Symbol:	Cross of Matter over circle of Spirit, bracketed by vertical lines of mind, or by two arcs of consciousness, uniting the past and future
Cycle around the: Sun:	84 years around the Sun
Duration in a Sign/House:	7 years
Previous Cycle:	Uranus in Pisces 2003-2010
Current Cycle:	Uranus in Aries 2011-2018
Next Cycle:	Uranus in Taurus 2018-2025

Where Uranus journeys through your chart, ask the following questions:

House: In what realm am I weird, eccentric, or different?
Where do I need to forge my own path and discover my uniqueness?
In what realm may I experience unexpected changes or sudden shocks?

Sign: How does my generation re-invent an archetype?
How do we shift the current paradigm of energy?

Aspect: What planets need freedom and radical means of expression?
What evolutionary forces in me may be traumatized by sudden changes?
In what planets will experience creative breakthroughs and innovative, youthful energy?

Historical Archetypes:	The inventor, The mad scientist
Deities/Gods:	Prometheus, Ouranus, Hephaestus, Hebe, Celi
Day of Week:	N/A
Tarot:	The Fool
Chakras:	N/A
Sephiroth:	Chokmah (Wisdom)
Alchemical Stage:	N/A
Angels and Spirits:	Uriel
Animals:	Bizarre and mythical—Unicorn, dragon, alien
Colors:	Blue
Music/Genres:	Jazz, circus, electronic, punk
Foods:	GMO's, almond, pecan, pistachio, caffeine
Metals:	Radioactive elements, uranium, radium
Gems/Minerals:	Mental stimulation, break up old, stuck ideas; can calm nervous system when too much Uranian vibrations; Lapiz lazuli, aquamarine, azurite
Plants and Trees:	Rowan, almond
Essential Oils:	Aromas are used to sedate the nervous system; Hyssop oil, marjoram
Anatomy:	Nervous system, blood circulation, lower legs, ankles, tibia, fibula
Movement:	Erratic, spastic, nervous, upside down, backwards, reverse

Physical Characteristics: *I am a pale blue marble in the sky, 32,000 miles in diameter, the size of four Earths. One of my days is seventeen hours long. I am composed of methane and I have no internal heating source. I am the planetary oddball as my poles point directly to or away from the Sun. Each pole gets around forty-two years of continuous sunlight, followed by forty-two years of darkness. I have twenty-seven moons and rings comprised of dust. Some of my moons orbit me in just a day and have collided forming some of the material in my two sets of rings.*

Diseases:	Nervous conditions, anxiety, trauma, stress
Medicines/Healings:	Third Eye stimulation, LSD, psychedelic man-made compounds
Relations:	Star family, alien beings
Places/Natural Events:	Alien planets, other dimensions, electricity, lightning storms, Abductions

Neptune

I am Poseidon, master of the seas
and all underwater entities,
As the waters that encircle the Earth
I can quake in fury,
I can be the tsunami of artistic imagination
that inspires you to both creative and destructive intoxication
Or I can be the calm waters
of receptive meditation
I can be your ascended master
your heart's reminder
that you must lose yourself, to find yourself
to dissolve the ego and instead imbibe
upon the eternal waters of spiritual re-union
to merge with the cosmic ocean
and receive the mystical vision
I invite you to escape
this mundane reality
for the lore of mythology,
And I have fashioned the horse
for your mystical journey
on the vast voyage of fantasy

Evolutionary Urge, Keywords:	To imagine, to unify, to return to Source, to dream, to universal love, to spirituality, to escape, to dissolve, compassion, mystical, transcendent, visionary, magical, musical, artistic, dance, cinema, fantasy, mythology, archetypes, role-play, anesthetics, hospitals, prisons, ego-dissolution, no boundaries
Mantra:	I envision, I imagine, I channel
Planetary Dignity	
Sign Affinity:	Pisces
Exaltation:	Leo
Detriment:	Aquarius
Fall:	Capricorn

Physical Characteristics: *My day is sixteen hours long and my diameter is 31,000 miles long, the same size as Uranus. I generate twice as much heat as I receive from the Sun, many think as a result of radioactive decay. I am striped with bright white, banded clouds, evidence of the highest winds in the solar system, over 1000 miles per hour. I have an anomalous Great Dark Spot— a highly unstable weather pattern, with erratic and unpredictable movements, for my storms appear and disappear. Thirteen of my moons have been discovered so far.*

Symbol:	Trident = Trinity; The cross of matter penetrating the upward reaching soul, longing for divine reunion
Cycle around the: Sun:	168 years around the Sun
Duration in a Sign/House:	14 years
Previous Cycle:	Neptune in Aquarius 1998-2011
Current Cycle:	Neptune in Pisces 2011-2024
Next Cycle:	Neptune in Aries 2025-2038

Where Neptune journeys through your chart, ask the following questions:

House: Where does my imagination most reflect itself?

In what area can I receive divine guidance and act as a channel?

Where am I likely to be confused or uncertain?

Where do my boundaries dissolve?

Sign: How does my generation reach its spiritual fulfillment?

How do we envision the most ideal expression of an energy?

Where can my generation be most clouded, confused, or deluded by an energy?

Aspect: What planets seek divine union and mystical awareness?

What planetary forces contain a strong spiritual vision as well as a tendency towards escape and fantasy?

Historical Archetypes:	Artist, martyr, savior, victim, mystic, prophet, psychic
Deities/Gods:	Neptune, Poseidon
Day of Week:	N/A
Tarot:	The Hanged Man
Chakras:	N/A
Sephiroth:	Kether—The Crown
Alchemical Stage:	N/A
Angels and Spirits:	All mythology, fairy spirits, sirens, nereids, nymphs, Quan Yin, Buddha, Christ
Animals:	Dolphin, whale, fish, algae, pegasus, all sea animals, fantastic—hydra, triton
Colors:	Indigo, blue-violets, underwater
Music/Genres:	B Major, Film scores, meditational, choral, chillout, ambient, spiritual; Reverberation
Foods:	Seafood, spirulina, blue-green algae
Metals:	N/A
Gems/Minerals:	Crystals to increase psychic sensitivity; amethyst, flourite, aquamarine, jade, coral, sugilite
Plants and Trees:	Ash, all psychedelics and opiates, seaweed, all plants growing in water
Essential Oils:	Euphoric, uplifting smells. Clary sage, Frankincense, Myrrh
Anatomy:	Pineal gland
Movement:	Liquid, seaweed, undulating, Chi Kung, Tai Chi, Savasana (corpse pose), meditation, stillness
Immune System:	Alcohol and drug addiction, depression, madness
Medicine/Healings:	Meditation, compassion, service, art, marijuana, mushrooms, LSD, Dream Yoga
Relations:	The web of multidimensional life, spirit beings, angels, guides, deceased
Places/Natural Events:	Cinema, outdoor festivals, the ocean, the womb; earthquakes, floods, tsunamis, hurricanes

Pluto

I am become death, the destroyer of worlds
-The Bhagavad-Gita

I am Hades, the Lord of the Underworld.
I wear my helmet of invisibility
for my transits sneak up on you and then cloak you for three years.
My name means "wealth," for as you surrender
into the depths of my infernal kingdom
the mysteries of your unconscious shall be revealed,
a treasure chest of your soul's riches
in your willingness to release the old
to reduce to essence,
to regenerate as the Phoenix—
but if you resist, in every attempt to possess,
and in every tendency to obsess,
you shall suffer
under the terror of volcanic crisis,
for I rule the abode of the shades
and I am the night's dense darkness.
But if you just let go
I shall unveil
the secrets of your soul.

Evolutionary Urge, Keywords:	Transformation, release, regenerate, rebirth, surrender, crisis, renewal, power, crime, violence, terrorism, secret societies, tantra, psychotherapy, past life regression
Mantra/Affirmation:	I surrender, I transform, I regenerate
Planetary Diginity: **Sign Affinity:**	Scorpio
Aspect Correlation:	N/A

Symbol:	The circle of spirit over the arc of consciousness, atop the cross of matter. Spirit overwhelms matter through the medium of soul.
Cycle around the: Sun:	Roughly 250 years
Duration in a Sign/House:	16-20 years
Current Cycle:	Pluto in Capricorn 2008-2024
Next Cycle:	Pluto in Aquarius 2024 - 2044

Where Pluto journeys through your chart, ask the following questions:

House: In what realm must I continually regenerate?

What area of life holds an overwhelming charge in my soul?

How can I consistently renew myself?

Sign: What role does my generation play in transforming and rebirthing a more evolved version of this energy?

Aspect: What planets have unconscious forces and motivations beneath them?

What planets must undergo a deeper investigation and constant rebirth?

Historical Archetypes:	Shaman, alchemist, psychotherapist, dictator, prostitute, criminal
Deities/Gods:	Kali, Shiva, Hades, Persephone, Ereshkigal, Orion, Yama
Day of Week:	N/A
Tarot:	Death
Chakras:	N/A
Sephiroth:	Malkuth (Kingdom)
Alchemical Stage:	The entire process of alchemy
Angels and Spirits:	Yama, Orion
Animals:	Bat, butterfly, serpent, scorpion, chameleon,
Colors:	Black
Music/Genres:	Goth, Death Metal, Gangsta Rap, Drum 'n Bass, cathartic, intense
Foods:	Onion, pepper
Metals:	N/A
Gems/Minerals:	Transform old energy, release heavy emotions; Obsidian, pearl
Plants and Trees:	Reed
Essential Oils:	Sandalwood, cedarwood, copal, palo santo
Anatomy:	Colon
Movement:	Intimidating, lurking, intense, powerful
Diseases:	Obsessiveness, control, power-hungry, manipulative, underhanded

Medicines/Healings:	Ayahuasca, DMT, Holotropic Breathwork, Rebirthing, Regression Therapy, Eyegazing, Evolutionary Astrology
Relations:	Therapists, doctors
Places/Natural Events:	Caves, underground, underworld, volcanoes, alleyways, basements, cellars cemeteries, ruins, Xibalba—The Road to Awe

Physical Characteristics: *They now call me a dwarf planet. My orbit is incredibly chaotic, and forms a huge ellipse. My moon is half my size and we are gravitationally locked whereby we revolve around each other every 6.5 days. I have only 1/14 the gravity as of Earth and one of my days is equivalent to six Earth days. At thirty to forty times farther from the Sun than the Earth is, my average temperature is 388 degrees Fahrenheit. Thus, I am composed of three types of ice, while my dominant surface features are from impact craters.*

The NODES:
Axes of the Soul-Myth

The North and South Node (Rahu and Ketu in India) are called the dragon's head and the dragon's tail. The dragon's tail refers to experiences that we have been "digesting" for many lifetimes or which are very constellated in our soul. These are habit patterns, behavioral norms, attitudes, and talents which are easily expressed, but often keep us in stasis. We are meant to fully digest the energy of our South Node and release these intrinsic gifts in order to fertilize other beings.

With the North Node, the dragons' head feeds on new experience. Although it may feel unfamiliar and sometimes daunting because of its opposite position to the inherent familiarity of the South Node, the soul will feel illuminated through the activities associated with its North Node quest. The North Node dares us to evolve rather than stay at home in our comfort zone.

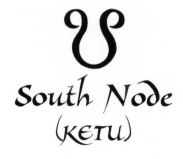

South Node
(KETU)

Mantra: Om hreem ketave namah

Duration in a Sign/House: 1.5 years

Where the South Node is in your chart, ask the following questions:

House: What kinds of activities was my soul primarily engaged in in other life-times? In what realm do I feel most familiar, but may I also discover trauma?

Sign: Where is my soul most strongly constellated in its identity?
What are my soul's habitual patterns and attachments?
What resources and gifts do I naturally possess and can give to the world?

Aspect: What forces or persons helped or hindered me on my soul's quest?

North Node
(Rahu)

Mantra: Om hreem rahave namah

Duration in a Sign/House: 1.5 years

Where the North Node is in your chart, ask the following questions:

House: What activities of life will help my soul best evolve?
Sign: With what energy will I find personal fulfillment?
Towards which archetype am I on a spiritual quest?
Aspect: What forces promote my soul's growth?

**Planets squaring the Nodes are like evolutionary gatekeepers, called skipped steps in the school of Evolutionary Astrology. They possess an energy that was a problematic obstacle in other lifetimes that holds a crucial key for one's evolutionary growth in this lifetime. They stand at the threshold of our spiritual quest, so that planet's sign, house, aspect, and realm of life it rules should be given special intention and attention in this life.

Retrogrades

Retrograde planets tend to express themselves more internally, with more consideration of the consequences of their outward expression. Karmically, retrogrades may indicate struggles with unachieved goals or unfinished life lessons. Their reflective and process-oriented natures allow you to develop your character. Although it may take longer to develop the confidence to express retrograde planets, when they are finally shared with the world, the tendency is for their expression to be more powerful and focused.

Essential Dignity and Rulership: The Conditions of Planets

In interpreting birthcharts, it is absolutely essential to learn about planetary rulership: what planets govern what signs. We utilize this information in order to learn more about the house, the archetypal realms of life. For instance, if we want to learn more about your relationship intent, we need to look beyond just the seventh house. We must look to the planetary rule of the seventh house. This planet, by its sign, house, and aspects will further describe the nature of your intimate partnerships.

Rulership is the most important aspect of *planetary dignity*. Ancient, Medieval, Vedic, and many modern astrologers will play close attention to the dignity of planets, which is essentially the condition in the birthchart. What do we mean by condition? Imagine you are hanging out in your home. You are the lord of the manor, the king or queen of the castle and you have free reign to use all your resources. This is similar to a planet in its sign of *rulership*. It has full strength to achieve its evolutionary force. But imagine you go to someone's house who you know is not very fond of you. You also don't care much for this person. In fact, you might even consider this person an enemy. This would be a very intimidating environment to find yourself in. Do you eat the food? Perhaps you'll be poisoned. Can you sleep at night or do you fear something may happen? This is similar to a planet in its *detriment*, the sign opposite its rulership. Here, it has no freedom to perform its evolutionary urge and so feels stifled and very uncomfortable.

You can think of Rulership and Detriment also like roles a movie actor may play. Let's say someone like Sylvester Stallone or Arnold Schwarzenegger back in their glory days went out for the part of a new world superhero, skilled in many forms of combat. Sounds like a role that fits very well. They would easily fit the part, like a planet in its rulership. But if our action heros went out for the part of Casanova or Don Juan, we might laugh at them. They would probably do a pretty horrible job, not fitting the part at all. Then their career would sink and box office sales would plummet. This is like a planet in its detriment. It can't do what it primarily wants to do.

Let's give an example. Let's say your Moon is in Cancer. It loves being there and can very easily fulfill its urges to nurture, create a safe and secure environment, and build a supportive and nourishing home. But if your Moon is in Capricorn, its sign of detriment, it only feels secure by continuing to work hard and achieve success out in the world. If your Moon is in Capricorn, you may experience quite a bit of burnout. You may neglect taking care of yourself, eating healthy and wholesome meals, or spending time with your family. Rest and comfort, the Moon's desires, would be very difficult for you to achieve.

The other important and often overlooked point to consider with planets in their rulership is a tendency for somewhat extreme behavior. Again, with the planet in its own home, its free to express itself at almost "arrogant" levels For example, we all know that the Sun is in Leo during most of August, and can be unbearingly hot and intense during this time, so it's almost too strong. Let us also consider the Moon in Cancer once again. The tendency here, although very nurturing, may be to experience the emotions with such sensitivity as to feel them flood with an overwhelming energy. Thus, special attention should be given to planets in their rulership so that they avoid extreme expression.

Now, if a planet is in its exaltation, it is like an honored guest at a friend's house. The friend busts out the fine red wine, they make a lush meal together. The two laugh all night. The guest gets to sleep in the plush bedroom. No, they're not at home, but they feel the excitement of being truly appreciated and admired, so they can truly shine here. A planet in its exaltation operates, then, at a higher level of being. It expresses itself with rich hues and juicy vigor. It may not be the actor's most famous role, but it's the one they win the Oscar for. Kate Winslet may always be remembered for Titanic, but she won the Oscar for her role in *The Reader.*

A planet in its *fall* is like a person in a foreign country they didn't really want to travel to in the first place. They don't speak the language, they don't understand the customs, and everyone's giving them a funny look. Essentially, they feel lost, unable to operate in that environment. Let's say your Sun is in Aries, its sign of exaltation. Well, everyone knows the feeling of the Sun after the Spring Equinox. He splashes his light and warmth on you, the days are growing longer, buds are beginning to come out, and everyone feels alive with new projects and reinvigorated life purpose. But if your Sun is in Libra, in its fall, it has to define itself through another, which is totally opposed to the Sun's nature. The Sun would much rather promote its own identity, not resolve to listening to another. The Sun wants to shine by itself in the sky: it doesn't want some other star outshining it!

In addition, you can examine planetary conditions by investigating how well planets like to be doing the activities of the house they're in. This is called *accidental dignity.* If Jupiter is in the ninth house, it can fully express its desire to study higher subjects, travel the world, philosophize, learn, and grow, because the ninth house resonates with the energy of Sagittarius, the sign Jupiter rules. If Venus in the sixth house, here, Venus, the goddess of love and affection, has to put her energies towards mundane tasks, her health, her diet, her fellow employees—Virgo territory—not the realm where Venus gets to express her fullest potential. She'd much rather be in the seventh house of partnership, akin to her sign of rulership, Libra.

Lastly, planets can better express themselves in directions of the horoscope. Mars, for instance, loves to be at the top of the chart, near the Midheaven, where his desires and ambitions have a focal purpose and can be seen by the world, but if Mars is near the IC, the home, this can create tension, confrontation, or a lot of movement in the home. You will find this referred to as directional strength below, an important technique from Vedic astrology.

It is helpful in analyzing one's chart or a client's chart to consider planetary dignity in order to understand how well these evolutionary forces can perform and exercise their essential nature.

A Planetary Prayer of hope

May the gods dance through you in every moment,
may you surf their song
may you pulse and throb
in divine harmony
With the planetary deities,
may you shake and shimmer
in cosmorgasmic ecstasy

When you return to your home sweet home
when you crawl into a bed of your own,
when family and friends
are the only ones who can comprehend,
when you wish to complain
and just let your instinct reign,
may the Moon goddess nourish you
as the tea kettel squeals
as you curl into your favorite meal,
when you laugh as you feel
the cat purr at your heel
may the Moon goddess nurture you

May you bask in the Sun's golden aura
the lion's roar of
living vitality
May you proudly radiate your purpose
to all you meet

May Mercury's mischief re-mind you
that language is perception

as you bounce between the satellites
across wireless transmission
give thanks and don't forget
this is mythmagic narration
through cellular translation
do you hear, do you know?
mystery's communication

May you taste Venus
in every glorious bite of chocolate,
in every amorous embrace,
may the goddess grace you
in every flirtatious glance
and every kiss of romance

May Mars ignite your palette
in every spicy curry
may the spiritual warrior
emerge fearless
as the hero of the journey

May Jupiter bestow
a season's greeting
beneath the mistletoe,
the yoga of laughter and hope
in the guru's holy revealing
in a philosophical teaching,
May optimism bless you
in an abundance of faith
in the joy of pastry
and the delight of cake

May you relish
in your mountaintop solitude,
and declare to the world,
I quarantine you!
I isolate by Saturn's rings!
I discipline myself
to become my own authority!"
And then may you descend
with serious integrity
to contribute your gifts unique
to building the foundations
of a sanctified society

As you pray for healing,
may the kind centaur Chiron coach you
through your duress
with celestial wisdom, with gentle caress,
may the mentor guide you
towards your path of success

May you let your freak flag fly
under Uranus' invitation
And feel the electrical pulse of intuition
to rebel against all limitation
May you open the channels of revelation
and embrace the fool within
as you discover your path of liberation
in the sudden lightning strike
epiphanous illumination
self-actualized
individuation

Heart of the Artist,
May you dream and remember the One,
when you receive the mystical vision
from divine imagination,
may Neptune awaken you
to the spiritual dimension

May the sweltering fires of the sweat lodge purify you
as Pluto transforms and rebirths you
May your old serpent-skin shed
may unconscious pain be lifted
With your willing surrender.
may the breath of catharsis regenerate you
May the phoenix rise from within
and renew

And may the gods dance through you in every moment,
may you surf their song
may you pulse and throb
in divine harmony
With the planetary deities,
may you shake and shimmer
in cosmorgasmic ecstasy

✳✳✳

I would like to give a really elegant example of how the evolutionary forces, psychological urges, and motivational impulses of the planets occur in one of everybody's favorite heroic myths, Star Wars.

It is easy to understand that Luke Skywalker is the Solar Hero, akin to all other heros we find especially prevalent in western mythology. Even his name—Luke, which means "light," and Skywalker, which is what the sun does (walk across the sky)—are related to the Sun. Early on, Luke meets Han Solo, the reckless mercenary. Han is the symbol of Mars, a renegade figure who does what he wants when he wants. The first time we see Han in the bar on Tattoin, he fires his weapon, a Martian symbol, at Greedo, who is trying to collect money from Han. Solo is the captain of the *Millennium Falcon*, which can travel at light-speed, and like Mars, Han is constantly on the move. Also, Mars is that part of us which fearlessly acts, and ultimately can help fulfill the life purpose of the Sun, like the knights of old. In Star Wars, Han assists Luke in his quest to defeat the Empire.

The Empire is a Saturnian force, with its concentration of rule, its strict hierarchies, and its cold detachment from the common people of the various planetary systems. The Empire is an all-encompassing system trying to control the galaxy, just as Saturn shows us how we must fit into society and fulfill a role, and if not, suffer the consequences of law and order. At the head of the Empire is the power hungry Darth Vader who lurks behind his black mask, steeped in his unconscious shadow. This is the underworld territory of Pluto, where repressed emotions can percolate to the surface in an intense desire to dominate, control, and wield negative influence over others.

The Uranian force of the Rebel Alliance battles against the Saturnian Empire and the Plutonian Darth Vader. The Alliance even carries the Uranian keyword, "rebellion" in its name. They desire the primal Uranian urges—freedom and liberation for all. It is through their inventive teamwork and innovative strategizing, Uranian concepts, that the Rebel Alliance eventually defeats the Empire.

Luke is trained by two Chiron figures, first Obi-Wan, then Yoda. Both Obi-Wan and Yoda act as mentors and guides toward Luke. They fulfill the same role as Chiron in our birthchart, revealing to Luke where his pain, wounds, and weaknesses are, especially regarding his family of origin, his lack of faith, and his physical training. In the myths, Chiron, the wise centaur, taught Achilles and Heracles, the great heroes. He also taught the healing power of herbs and astrology—the more subtle forces of the universe. This links Chiron's teachings to Yoda and Obi-Wan's instructions to Luke about the Force—the symbol of Neptune in the film. Neptune reminds us of our source. It is the seed of our divine imagination and our mystical union with all. In describing the Force, Yoda says, "It is the energy field created by all living things. It surrounds us, penetrates us. It binds the universe together...It cannot be fully described with words. You must feel the Force to understand it." It is often impossible to describe the spiritual dimension of our Neptunian experiences. Neptune can cloud or fog up our words in its attempt to dissolve our ego and allow us to merge with the universal field of energy. Where Neptune is in our charts is an area we have telepathic and psychic links, where we must feel things to understand them.

R2D2, C3PO, and Chewbacca combine the planetary forces of the Moon and Mercury in their archetypal energy. Throughout his adventures, Luke is accompanied by R2D2, his loyal friend. R2 often asks about the welfare of the others. In a sense, R2 and C3PO, as Luke's droids, function as his pets and recall the energy of the Moon as family and the source that cares for him and for which Luke cares deeply. In fact C3PO's original purpose was to help Luke's mother with farming. C3PO often worries, like a mother whose child hasn't called home. He is highly reactive, like the Moon part of us which is always concerned about feeling safe and secure. Chewbacca is also a Moon force in the films. Though he can be a warrior, Chewy is much more of a protective maternal figure, especially over his longtime friend Han Solo.

As machine intelligence, both R2D2 and C3PO function as Mercurial figures, consistently utilizing their enhanced mental, perceptual, and translating abilities, the realm of Mercury. On multiple occasions, R2's skills in deciphering codes save the lives of Luke, Han, and the others. Likewise, C3PO is versed in millions of languages, which allows him to infer that an intercepted signal was in fact an Imperial code, alerting the Rebels to the presence of a probe droid dangerously close to their base.

Lastly, the goddess Venus is of course Princess Leia. She is the exclusive feminine figure throughout the initial trilogy, and is portrayed in Venus' various costumes. In *Return of the Jedi*, she is a scantily clad object of beauty and adornment—Venus in Taurus and Libra. She is also a princess and in charge of making key decisions—Venus in Leo and Capricorn. She is an intrepid traveler and feisty warrior—Venus in fire signs. She is also Venus in her air signs, highly intelligent and a messenger, delivering a message to R2 to give to Obi-Wan. She shows sensitivity and a telepathic link with her brother Luke, displaying Venus in her empathic water element. Lastly, Leia is constantly pursued as "Her Highness" by Mars— Han Solo. In the Greek myths, Mars and Venus were lovers.

Supporting Actors in the StArchetypal Theater

Before proceeding to the angles, houses, signs, and aspects, I wanted to briefly mention some of the other heavenly bodies which can be used in an astrological analysis, often with the same degree of profound revelation attached to them. Often, the techniques listed below are used as an addendum to emphasize major factors shown in the study of the positions of the planets. But it is my feeling that as astrology continues to evolve, as we discover more heavenly bodies, as our world continues to complexify, we will seek this additional cosmic information to guide us.

The **Arabic Parts**, also known as "Lots," were a powerful and important technique used in the medieval and ancient world, which has been largely lost to modern astrology. The doctrine of parts is based on numerical or mathematical relationships between factors of the horoscope. These sensitive parts of the chart are determined by adding together two planets or points, and subtracting a third point. The most common in use today is the Part of Fortune, describing health, prosperity, and success for an individual. The Part of Fortune is calculated with a specific mathematical formula involving the degrees of the Sun, the Moon, and the Ascendant.

Parts are often used as a secondary tool in interpretations, to clarify or illustrate other key factors. **Midpoints** are also used secondarily. This technique takes the midpoints of two planetary positions, the center or meeting between two evolutionary forces. What arises is an alchemy of meaning between those two planets. When that midpoint is transited, an event in one's life can manifest pertaining to the meaning of that planetary pair.

The **Fixed Stars** can be used in a reading, just like the planets. In some ways, the majority of astrology focuses on only a small band of the sky, the ecliptic, the path of the Sun. Yet, the sky is vast and so as ancient astronomer-astrologers like Ptolemy discovered, that the fixed stars can be used to denote character or the fate of a nation, and they can be used in prediction as well.

The appeal of working with the fixed stars is the sharing of the rich mythical lore of the constellations—stories that transcend time and span every known culture. However, the disadvantage is the difficulty in interpreting the various stories and translating them for a client. We also have much less information about the delineation of particular stars and their meanings. Our sources for understanding a star's relationship to parts of the chart are minimal.

However, Bernadette Brady, on her website, skyscript.co.uk, compels astrologers to utilize the full sky in their astrology, noting that:

> This ecliptocentric astrology only permits a celestial object a voice in humanity's dialogue with the heavens if through mathematics it is made to walk the single line of the sun. Or another way of seeing this is to realize that we have adjusted our sacred and personal relationship between earth and sky to encompass only the sun's point of view.

The last technique I would like to mention, which I have studied and used in my own chart interpretations, is the use of **Minor Planets**, also called **Asteroids**. No area of astrology confounds me quite so much as asteroids.

The majority of asteroids are located between Mars and Jupiter in the asteroid belt. Their astronomical position is significant as a large majority of the asteroids recognizable to us are named after mythical characters. These stories link the individual person to the social matrix, and the narrative serves a function in instructing the culture. It is quite appropriate then that the asteroids, with their hundreds of mythical associations should be found located at the bridge between the personalizing and socializing planetary forces—between Mars and Jupiter.

When considering the metaphysical significance of asteroids, we should remember our earlier discussion of the *daimon*, that spiritual entity of Plato's cosmology assigned to us just prior to our incarnation. In her talk on asteroids at the 2007 Blast Astrology Conference, Demetra George briefly mentioned the possibility that the notion of the daimons may be connected with our modern understandings of the asteroids. The daimons were semi-divine spirits, part mortal and part divine, invisible messengers as numerous as the incarnating souls, carrying information between the gods and the humans.

Asteroids, as well, are nearly imperceptible in a solar system and only 4% of the mass of the Moon, nothing compared to the grand, deified forces of the planets. Just like the daimons, their number is almost unfathomable—millions have been found. And there are over 13,000 asteroids that have been discovered, named, and numbered, all of which can be placed into one's birthchart. (George 2008)

One of the foremost experts on asteroids, Demetra George states,

In my 35 years of research, I have seen over and over again, that when a planetary body, whether it's a planet, a star, or an asteroid, is prominent in the skies at a moment of a person's birth, then the mythic biography of that celestial body is a shaping motif in the person's life. And one possible reason for this is that the myths of the gods and goddesses are nothing other than the symbolic externalizations of the eternal structures of the human psyche. (George 2008).

When she refers to "prominence" in a person's birthchart, George is referring to an asteroid which is placed within just a few degrees of the Sun, the Moon, the angles, and the planet which rules the Ascendant, since these points are the heart of the life force in an individual's chart. However, in the examples that follow, you will see that asteroids connected with any point of the birth chart can reveal layers and layers of symbolic meaning.

In his excellent article, "The Significance of Asteroids," Jacob Schwartz proposes that asteroid use in astrology is a monumental advancement which harmonizes with the needs of the onrushing Aquarian Age, an epoch of information. Our challenge today, he asserts, is to sort through, prioritize, and integrate vast quantities of information without completely overwhelming ourselves. (Schwartz 1995) In addressing asteroids, an astrologer utilizes a highly specific language to elucidate the depths of the human psyche. As John Challen proposes in his article "The Expansive Mirror of the Asteroids," the compact, but highly specific utility of information found in the asteroids is mirrored in advances across other fields, such as the personalized data compression of modern technology in iPhones or the individual codes of DNA found in forensics and medicine. (Challen 2007)

In addition, Schwartz argues that the asteroids represent an evolutionary breakthrough for humanity because of the basic premise that the naming of new planetary bodies correlates with the blossoming of new centers of consciousness within us. We witnessed this effect in a pronounced manner with the discovery of Uranus in 1781, synchronous with events representing the Uranian significations in a birthchart: revolutionary impulses for freedom in the Americas and in France, the increasing demand for individual rights, as well as the onset of a more technologized society with the beginnings of the Industrial Age.

"If," as Schwartz suggests, "we are on the precipice of a quantum leap in consciousness where a greater proportion of the brain will be utilized, then the awareness of asteroid relevance can stimulate those newly utilized brain cells." (Schwartz 1995) In light of this proposal, we should realize that by 1950, only 10,000 asteroids were known. By 1982, the number had increased to 100,000; the number today is in the millions. Also, in 1995, the number of named asteroids only totaled 5,000. As we all know, the mid-90's saw the peak explosion of the global brain, as the internet began to circulate worldwide. By 2007, the number of named asteroids has increased to 13,000.

It is important to consider how asteroids are named. They are named by the astronomers who discover them. One could even say the astronomers "channel" the names at times. There is no logical process to their naming, nor do astronomers consult with astrologers. The process is similar to how many parents name their children—they receive the name through some act of prayer or simply because they like the sound of it. The fact that astronomers can receive the names of these heavenly bodies, and that these names can instruct, inform, and guide my life in a meaningful way testifies to the unified field of consciousness to which we are all interwoven—the vast and mysterious archetypal theater.

Asteroids are not only named after mythical characters. Places, plants, animals, fictional characters, famous figures in the arts and sciences, and a seemingly infinite number of first and last names also comprise the names of asteroids. In short, the sum total of the collective human psyche is reflected in the asteroid lexicon, resulting in a situation whereby the majority of people with whom you consider yourself kindred—family, friends, and cultural icons—all can be found as heavenly bodies floating in the asteroid belt and dancing through a section of your birthchart. Again, a name is a vibration, and the people, icons, places, etc. who hold this vibration all help to create your identity, just like other parts of your birthchart.

Why are you drawn to a particular artist's work? How come this geographical location keeps calling you? Why do you consider that scientist the most inventive genius of all time? Why do significant people with a certain name keep popping up in your life? As John Challen writes, study of the asteroids demonstrates how each of us is connected to humanity's collective mental and cultural realm. Let's examine some highly revealing asteroid signatures to understand their important role in astrology.

According to Demetra George's research, former president Bill Clinton has the asteroids Paula, for Paula Jones, Monica, for Monica Lewinsky, and Asmodeus, the Persian demon god of lust, all in Scorpio, the sign of intrigue, suspicions, and lies, and opposite his place of security and comfort—his Moon in Taurus. Meanwhile, the asteroid Hillary is conjunct the IC, the angle signifying the place of roots and family. Even through the affairs and turmoil, Hillary stood by her husband as an anchor.

Like planets, asteroids can also be used in transits and to signify cultural events such as in the following examples. Jacob Schwartz notes that Peter, Paul and Mary first performed as a singing group in the summer of 1961. The asteroids Peter, Paul, and Mary were also together then too, in the theatrical sign of Leo.

At the moment of his wedding to Princess Diana, the asteroid Diana was traveling over Prince Charles' Ascendant, the point of outer identification to the world. At the couple's divorce, the asteroid Diana was opposite Charles' Pluto–the planet signifying power struggles, control issues, joint resources, manipulation, jealousy, and intense emotions. In another fascinating example about Princess Diana, at the moment of her death in Paris, the transiting asteroid Karma conjoined the former princess' asteroids Diana and Paris.

The first personal breakthrough for me regarding asteroids involved a synastry reading between two beloved friends, a couple who had met six months prior and was planning to get married nine months after my visit. I was curious to find the asteroids in their charts, noting their instantaneous falling-in-love, their desire to have children together, and the strength of their bond.

I decided to search where the proper name of the beloved was placed in the other's chart. What house, what sign, was it touching another planet? Perhaps this would unveil more about their cosmic connection. Although the male partner's real name was Nicholas, he went by Nicky, so I looked up the name Nicky in the asteroids list and to my surprise, found an asteroid named Nicky. I also found an asteroid named Ashley, the female partner's name.

In Nicky's chart, the asteroid Ashley was very near the IC, the roots of the chart, the place of home, family, and often past life connection. The asteroid Nicky was conjunct his Jupiter and opposite his Sun.

In Ashley's chart, the asteroid Nicky was conjunct the asteroid Juno, the point of sacred union, signifying the marriage partner in the chart. Nicky was also located in the eighth house, the realm where we share resources and intimately blend our souls with another. The asteroid Ashley was also widely conjunct her Sun.

Not only were both asteroids positioned in significantly personal places in each other's birthchart, but each of my friend's personal names were also connected to the source of identity and vitality, the Sun in their own chart. This seems to suggest the metaphysical importance of a names' vibration. This fact is well known in various esoteric traditions, such as Gematria and other schools of numerology. It also invites us to consider the value we place on how we choose to identify ourselves to the world through the frequency of our name. For those seeking to re-name themselves in a sacred context, a study of prominent asteroids and their subsequent myths can be a helpful tool of self-discovery.

I decided to look up the asteroids for James Cameron, Sigourney Weaver, and Sam Worthington, the director and stars of the best selling box office film of all time, *Avatar*. I found asteroids named Pandora, Cameron, Sigenori, and Weaver, and inserted them into the charts of the actors and director with amazing results. We should also keep in mind that as I write this, a trilogy of films is scheduled to be released, according to James Cameron. So this team will be working together for each of them.

In the director's chart, his name Cameron appears within just a few degrees of the asteroid Pandora, linking his identity forever to the name of the magical planet in the film Avatar. If one studies Cameron's career, one can quickly notice that films like Avatar, Aliens, and the first two Terminator films both heavily relate the myth of Pandora—the first woman who carries the box that when opened, unleashes terrible things upon mankind, such as illness, turmoil, and all evils. Interestingly, hope was all that remained in the box after she closed it. We see these evils in the form of planetary colonization and the rape of nature in a monstrous alien species and in the apocalyptic, destructive potential of artificial intelligence. We can also easily notice a female protagonist like Pandora in the films mentioned.

In Sigourney Weaver's chart, the asteroids of her name show up prominently. The asteroid Weaver is in her first house of personal identity, and it is opposite to the asteroid Sigenori. Sigenori is in the transformational sign of Scorpio conjunct her version of the goddess Venus. Sigourney Weaver will likely be remembered for her identification with her roles as a tough, resilient, fearless, and powerful Scorpionic woman, such as her characters in *Aliens, Gorillas in the Mist, and Avatar.*

It is hard to imagine that Sam Worthington will top any film after *Avatar*, and will likely be known for his journeys to the mystical planet of Pandora for the rest of life. Interestingly the asteroid Pandora can be found within a few degrees of his ascendant—the mask, the persona, the vehicle which carries our soul through this life.

Meanwhile, the asteroid Cameron is directly conjunct Worthington's Saturn, within 2 degrees of his Sun, and within 3 degrees of his Midheaven point of career. The asteroid Cameron, in the mask of director James Cameron, is promoting the identity, life purpose, work ethic, discipline, ambitions of Worthington and all in his house of career in the sign of Leo—the actor and performer!

We can see how contacts with Saturn play a fundamental role in collaborative work efforts in two other famous charts as well.

Johnny Depp has worked with Tim Burton on over seven films, achieving one of the most enduring and successful working relationships in all of film. The asteroid Burton opposes Depp's Saturn. It falls in Johnny Depp's first house, Leo, and certainly Tim Burton has helped Depp develop his Leo talents as creative artist and performer.

In George Lucas' chart, the asteroid Ford is located within 2 degrees of Lucas' Saturn in Gemini, the sign of the storyteller and messenger. Harrison Ford was not only a key star of the *Star Wars* trilogy, but he was also the lead actor in the Indiana Jones films, all written by and executively produced by Lucas. In this sense, we can see that Harrison Ford was helping to structure, focus, and manifest (Saturn) Lucas' role as storyteller.

Interestingly, the asteroid Ford is within 1 degree of Steven Spielberg's Midheaven, the point of career in Pisces, the sign of the imaginative artist and visionary filmmaker. Spielberg directed all four of the *Indiana Jones* films, grossing nearly one billion dollars at the box office. Indeed, Harrison Ford helped to advance and amplify Spielberg's career as an influential filmmaker.

Actor Liam Neeson was nominated for an Academy Award for what will likely be his most famous performance of all time, his role as Oskar Schindler in *Schindler's List*. The asteroid Schindler is within 2 degrees of Neeson's Jupiter, planet of expansion, inspiration, growth, and faith. It is also in a flowing, graceful, friendly trine to Neeson's Ascendant—his outer mask and persona in the world.

With just the few examples above, it is hard to deny the metaphysical magnitude of the asteroids. There seems to be an act of heavenly providence in the spiritual function of these cosmic bodies as intermediary messengers, connecting clusters of souls across the dimensions.

I would like to share a personal story which elucidates both the work with invoking the planetary archetypes and the significance of the asteroids in my own life, including the creation of this book. As I was finishing the writing process on this book, I invoked the evolutionary force of Jupiter quite regularly. During one morning's meditation, as I did a visualization practice with the Jupiter mandala, envisioning the vast size of the great planet, I let its magnitude reflect the infinite potential which unconditional faith can grant us. As I chanted the Jupiter mantra, I asked for assistance in finding an editor and for help in the process of publishing, as Jupiter rules publishing and the social connections which help us spread our message to the world.

Following my meditation, I entered the sphere of email where I found a message from a friend suggesting I contact one of her friends regarding editing my book. She thought the connection between us would be ideal. Within moments, I was online chatting and then on the phone with the woman who would edit my book, Tara.

Immediately, our link found spiritual and etymological roots. The Buddhist deity Green Tara is the goddess I have been working with longest as a deity of maternal guidance and protection. In many cultures, the name Tara refers to "star"—quite appropriate for an astrological connection. When I researched the asteroid Tara's position in my birthchart, I discovered that she was within just a few degrees of my Venus. Venus, as you know, is the goddess of love, friendship, and important social contacts, and my Venus and Tara are both in the sign of

Gemini—the messenger, storyteller, and writer.

These kinds of spiritual synchronicities are how Jupiter answers our prayers. When we are open, we can receive. For me, the asteroids represent one of the most exquisite, humbling, and empowering examples of "astronicity." It is this kind of "revelation," this kind of archetypal weaving of the vast web of inter-dependence, which I hope this book will inspire for you on your own journey of awakening.

Chapter 6
ANGLES and HOUSES
The Map and Mirror:
Your Cross of Incarnation,
Your Realms of Life Experience

Angles And the Angels of Destiny

From the akashic soup,
a spiritual conspiracy of your guides,
your karma, your fate,
the tapestry woven,
the space-time and family chosen,
gestation,
preparation,
then the cosmic womb bursts open.

This is your sky, different than any other.
Determined at the exact moment of first breath
with the sacred, mystical soul's intent,
The incarnate birth trauma
and the miraculous gift,
This life, this precious human rebirth.
In that first breath, you inhale the celestial poetry.
In your infant baby fat and hungry tears,
you imprint the macrocosmic dance of soul's necessity.
That second of birth, you implant yourself upon the sacred cross of matter,
the four cardinal points of being and becoming.
The constellation that rises: the mask of your Ascendant, the moment of your birth,
this is where Father Sun lights the horizon each morning in the magic of his rebirth;
the constellation at the zenith: the golden purpose of the Midheaven,
where your glorious star, your life-giver, shines his brightest
signifies where you too can reach your spiritual apex,
the height of your soul's incarnate vocation.

The constellation that sets: the dance with the intimate other of the Descendant,
this is where Father Sun meets the night of his rest, the embrace of the darkness.
The constellation at the base of the earth: the hidden roots of the Nadir,
where Father Sun sinks into the heart of the underworld,
the realm where you dig in to your home,
and the Sun within reminds you
of the primal myth of your soular self,
preparing to be reborn
once again
at the Sacred Ascendant

This is the skeletal frame of your earthly reality
So welcome to your relationship with Earth
Embrace your e-lationship with embodiment.

Find the archetypal image, the primal energy that dances
as the angels of destiny
on your sacred angles
of incarnate mystery.

As your personal cross of incarnation, the exact degrees of the angles are very
sensitive points. The houses that follow—the first, fourth, seventh, and tenth houses—
indicate much of the dominating energies of life we have discussed above including
outer persona, home, relationships, and career. *(See fig. 6.1 for Angles and Houses)*

When planets transit these points, significant life events occur, including
new and destined contacts, changes of residence and job, issues with our family,
and ways we outwardly identify. When we meet people whose planets trigger one
or multiple angles, they can have an important role to play in our life's direction.
When we move to locations with specific planets on the angles, we will breathe in
the nature of the planet very strongly in that location. Its energy, as expressed in
our birth chart, will be emphasized there.

Nadir (IC):   Who am I to me? Portal to my personal mythos. Soul Vision.
A collection of karmas, sanskaras, and constituents parts.
The awareness of the soul as privileged to embody itself
and grow. Inner sphere, the Roots of my Tree of Life, the
heart of Eternal Being, Spiritual Ancestry.

*What journey will I sail on in this life?

Planetary Ruler: By house, sign, and aspect, will further
describe the sphere of my inner life, the textures of my
personal mythos?

Ascendant (ASC):   How do I arrive at my purpose? Elucidates in depth:
how I will achieve my life calling.
Giving form to the ideal, the soul-vision of the nadir.

Toolbelt to realize the vision and activate the Midheaven path of mastery.

Point of obvious self-identity, outward persona, character. An "ego" mask which compares itself to its external conditions and other people.

The Horizon point: the Inbreath—that which opens all around me.

*What ship do I sail to arrive at my destination?
What vehicle will I ride upon in this life?

Planetary Ruler: Steersman/Captain of the ship; the "ruler of the chart" who guides me on my journey. By house, sign, and aspect, describe much of my daily life energy and focus.

Midheaven (MC): How best can I serve the whole? What is my path of mastery? How will I profess myself to the world?

What is my dharma as a planetary agent of transformation? Point of no-self, the wholly transpersonalized self, connected to everything around me, illuminating the whole of reality with my energy.

My highest goal and purpose.

The golden unfolding of my being, where I translate myelf into the celestial sphere, where I ascend to my heights. Vocational Life Calling: that which calls me.

*What is my ship's destination?

Planetary Ruler: By house, sign, and aspect, further describes the mission, the achievement of your path of mastery.

Decendant (DSC): Who's helping me on my mission? The others which reflect my mission back to me.

What experiences do I encounter to evolve me?
My approach to relationships and intimacy.

*Who are the other passengers on my ship?

Planetary Ruler: By house, sign, and aspect, will further describe my soul-mate passengers. Elucidates the kinds of important connections I need to fulfill my soul-vision.

Transits to the planetary rulers can often be as potent as transits to the angles themselves and will likely manifest through outward events in your life. Transits to the ruler of the Nadir will cause some shift in your home or family. Transits to your Ascendent will affect your life trajectory and outer persona. Transits to the ruler of the midheaven will affect your career, while transits to the ruler of the Descendent will impact your relationships.

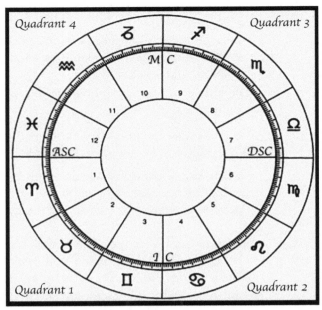

6.1 - Angles, Houses, Quadrants

houses
Experiential Realms of Life:
The Stage and Scene

Houses are the twelve fields of life experience, the archetypal stages and scenic realms where the characters (planets) play out their roles (signs).

Planetary forces wish to evolve components of the psyche through particular areas of life experience. A certain style of behavior, one of the twelve Signs, will be at the "cusp" or beginning of a house, indicating that this style best express itself through that specific house, that archetypal realm of life experience.

In addition to a Sign being at the cusp of a house, planets will occupy certain houses. In this case, ask yourself, "What evolutionary force (planet) wishes to express itself in this area of my life?"

Even if you do not have planets in a particular sign, the archetypal energy of that sign still rules that area of your life. In this way, you can begin to interpret a chart just by knowing what signs are on the cusps of what houses. For instance, you may have no planets in Cancer, but Cancer is the sign on the cusp of your second house. Your resources and money will somehow be connected with Cancerian activities; perhaps you will take care of children, work with families, make food for people, or do healing work to earn some amount of money. You will also highly value the home and nurturing activities. So ask yourself: "What costume (sign) is best for me to wear to integrate the evolutionary lessons of that house, that realm of life?

Planets in houses function like the adjectives in those realms, further elucidating the flavor of that archetypal realm. For instance, if I have Jupiter in the second house of resources, then the symbol of Jupiter will affect how I earn money. Perhaps I will earn money as a teacher. Also, a lot of money can be earned because Jupiter expands whatever realm it occupies. However, Jupiter could simultaneously mean that I will spend a large amount of money. Whereas, for instance, if Neptune is in the second house, I will likely place a great value on art and spirituality, and may even earn a living from these activities. But because Neptune, by its nature dissolves things, money may seem to slip into and out of our lives very quickly.

Lastly, you will see listed below "accidental dignity." Accidental dignity occurs when a planet is posited in a house of its natural rulership. So, for instance, if the Moon is in the fourth house, it has accidental dignity, because naturally the fourth house is associated with Cancer, the sign which the Moon rules. The effect is to give the planet more strength because it is in a house it likes to be in, similar to the notion of planets in the Signs they rule.

houses/Experiential Fields of Life

1.   Outward persona and mask, the vehicle carrying your soul, appearance, behavior, complexion, body, impulse, fame, health, longevity, livelihood, present moment, projection of self-image out into the world
        Sign Affinity: Aries
        Accidental Planetary Dignity: Mars
        Directional Strength for: Mercury, Jupiter

2.   Value system, money, resources, possessions, earning ability, self-esteem, relationship with self
        Sign Affinity: Taurus
        Accidental Planetary Dignity: Venus or Ceres

3.   Languaging and perception of the world, learning, early education, siblings, short journeys, communications, networking
        Sign Affinity: Gemini
        Accidental Planetary Dignity: Mercury

Whatever sign and planets vibrate in this field describe the images and energies which will help you learn the best. They are the path of intellectual synthesis.

4.   Home, roots, lineage, family of origin, experiences of upbringing, past lives, primal personal mythos, inner identity
        Sign Affinity: Cancer
        Accidental Planetary Dignity: Moon

Directional Strength: Moon, Venus

5.   Creativity, self-expression, children, play, pleasure, romance, gambling
           Sign Affinity: Leo
           Accidental Planetary Dignity: Sun

6.   Health, diet, daily practices and duties, skills, employment activities,
        apprenticeships, fellow employees, karma yoga (path of service)
           Sign Affinity: Virgo
           Accidental Planetary Dignity: Mercury or Chiron

7.   Relationships, reflective other, balancing partnerships, open enemies, marriage
           Sign Affinity: Libra
           Accidental Planetary Dignity: Venus
           Directional Strength: Saturn

8.   Psychological regeneration, joint resources, inheritances, deep intimacy,
        sexuality, soul-blending, death and rebirth
           Sign Affinity: Scorpio
           Accidental Planetary Dignity: Mars, Pluto

9.   Foreign travel, journeys abroad, philosophy, religion, cosmology, faith,
        higher education, broadcasting, publishing, law, sport
           Sign Affinity: Sagittarius
           Accidental Planetary Dignity: Jupiter

10.   Career, vocation, path of ambition, mastery through time and effort,
        place of greatest recognition, status, reputation
           Sign Affinity: Capricorn
           Accidental Planetary Dignity: Capricorn
           Directional Strength: Sun, Mars

11.   Friendships, cosmic tribe, ideals, group association, goal-setting, hopes,
        wish-fulfillment
           Sign Affinity: Aquarius
           Accidental Planetary Dignity: Saturn, Uranus

12.   Spiritual union, ego-dissolution, archetypes, myths, imagination, dreams,
        retreat, sanctuary, meditation, contemplation, escapism, confinement,
        hospitals, mystical
           Sign Affinity: Pisces
           Accidental Planetary Dignity: Jupiter, Neptune

One helpful way to initially understand the energetic concentration in the birthchart is to study where the majority of planetary characters are located by quadrant. This will indicate a general emphasis for your life, including the overall motifs that will tend to dominate. See Fig. 6.1 for quadrant layout.

Quadrant 1   Personal Development

With many planets in the first quadrant, you concentrate the majority of your energy on self-development. You seek to discover your value system and enhance your communication skills in order to evolve your personal identity. You may need more time alone in order to evaluate how you feel and think about what others say and do.

Quadrant 2   Expanding through your Immediate Environment

The primary focus in this life is about developing personal relationships, including a strong foundation and home base. You will need to learn about the conditioning of your early environment in order to understand how to creatively fulfill your vital essence. Healthy routines and daily practices help you refine your gifts and offer them back to the world. Your family, children, and co-workers will reflect back to you the appropriate paths of service.

Quadrant 3   The Art of Partnership

If many planets occupy this quadrant, there is a strong desire to share life experiences with partners. You must learn to listen and accommodate others' value systems. You must allow yourself to be changed by others so that you can help in their transformation process. You are learning to balance, cooperate, and listen with the depths of your soul to discover the Middle Way. As you grow, you will begin to refine your communication with others, and develop a broader perspective of reality, applying foreign philosophies, ethics, and religious ideals to your engagement with the world.

Quadrant 4   Integrating with Society

If a majority of planets occupy this quadrant, your focus extends outside of yourself to society as a whole. You are concerned with how best to integrate your skills for the evolution of the whole. Your work, friendships, and spiritual path reflect your deepest commitments. You have much to achieve and the setting and realization of goals will be accomplished through powerful alliances and important causes.

Chapter 7
The SIGNS:
Archetypal Images/Styles/Costumes/Masks

As we discussed earlier, every Sign of the zodiac is an archetypal image, a combination of Mode (motion) and Element (matter). Planetary characters (evolutionary forces) will express themselves through the masks or costumes of these Signs. Archetypal expression is multivalent, which means an archetype can express itself through a range of possibilities. Energy can move from unconscious to superconscious, from wounded to healed, from distorted shadow to naturally luminous. By becoming conscious of the range of expressions of these twelve primal archetypal images, your free will increases. When you learn to recognize the essence of the different primal energies, you can choose the expression which will guide you towards greater wholeness and return you at last to the luminous, unified Source.

Evolutionary Journey Initiation through the Zodiacal Mystery School

The sign and house which follow any given archetype will be a place of resolution and evolution when a sign can no longer move forward or learn more in its own nature. So for instance, when Taurus gets too stubborn, self-reliant, and insular, Gemini, the following sign, says, "Hey, come out and play! Let's connect with these people and this fascinating piece of information. Let's take a trip and go learn something. Get curious and excited about something—Don't stay stuck in the mud!"

But, on an evolutionary level, you must honor and master the lessons of each sign before you transition to the succeeding archetype. In this sense, each archetypal energy is also an initiatory journey, whereby you must answer the call of one sign completely before entering the mystery school of the next sign. It was most likely this kind of initiatory rite of passage which the aforementioned Mithra cults and other astral religions were focused upon.

Continuing the above example, if you do not learn to find peace and stability within, that solid, inner value system of Taurus overflowing with an appreciation for the abundant sensual sustenance of the present moment, then the

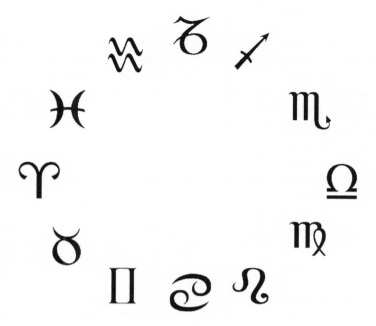

tendency for the Gemini shadow will overwhelm the nervous system as you try to step out in the world—you will be scattered and fragmented in a million directions chasing every last bit of information, every friends' online profile updates, every news story—you will essentially be lost in the hurricane of the mind. So you must honor each sign for its step on the initiatory journey, an evolutionary odyssey from one sign to the next. Even once you arrive at the transpersonal, cosmic realms of spirit in Pisces, the journey does not end there. If you stay in the womb, and never emerge, then of course you will never incarnate and learn your evolutionary lessons. And so we give praise to Aries, which generates the vital essence, declaring "God helps those who help themselves—Here I am! I seize the day!"

It can be of great assistance to also understand that the sign *opposite* one of the twelve archetypes will be the agent of balance, the polarity which gives instruction on the path of awareness and integration, especially helpful if you are strongly expressing the shadow of a sign. In a sense, you must *adopt* the polarity to *adapt* into a more conscious state of wholeness. So, for example, if Capricorn stays too focused on its ambitions, constantly attempting to achieve some huge measure of success out there in the world, it will neglect its personal needs for a fulfilling and nurturing Cancerian home. Cancer reminds Capricorn to take its shoes off and relax. "Take a healing bath," Cancer reminds Capricorn, "receive some massage, eat nourishing food, and spend loving moments with the family."

Aries ♈

Symbol:	Ram's horns, Fountain of flame bursting forth
Motion of Expression:	_Outward/Cardinal-_ activating, initiating, generating
Element:	_Fire-_ vitality, identity, consciousness, spirit
Geometric Apect:	_Conjuntion-_ new energy, beginning the journey
Planetary Ruler:	Mars
House Association:	First House
Key Phrases:	I am
Affirmation:	I seize the moment
Archetypes:	Adventurer, Hero, Warrior, Leader, General, Pioneer
Tarot:	Emperor
Anatomy:	Head
Herbs:	Have stimulating effects, usually with thorns, spines, prickles; Nettles, burdock, cayenne, red clover, sassafrass
Yoga:	Face stretches, eye and neck rotations, headstands, warrior poses
Movement:	Explosive, aggressive, martial arts
Film:	Martial Arts films, War films; Bruce Lee films, Hero, Fight Club, 300, Braveheart, Gladiator
Music:	Aggressive, confrontational; punk, hardcore, grunge, metal; Rage Against the Machine
Sexuality/Turn-Ons:	Impulsive, assertive, the quickie, freedom to discover, one-night stands. Instinctual, primal, opportunistic, passionate spontaneity

Archetypal Image, Expression, Symbolism:

Natural/Neutral:	Vital, energetic, athletic, bold
Shadow/Wounded:	Anger, rage, violent, intolerant, thrillseeker, abusive, selfish, narcissistic, pushy, rash, insensitive, childish, competitive, reckless and constant "doing"
Healed/Luminous:	Athletic, outgoing, enterprising, courageous, fearless, pioneering, independent, initiating, focused, superhuman energy
Past Life Imprints:	Early death, anxiety and urgency Hunter-prey, fear, Fight or flight warrior, samurai Repressed or thwarted will Rushing, risky action Separate, different, pain of aloneness, ostracized

Taurus

Symbol:	The bull's horns
Motion of Expression:	*Fixed/Stable/Inward-* harnessing, cultivating, empowering
Element:	*Earth-* substance, form, structure
Geometric Apect:	*Waxing Crescent-* nourishing seeds or refusing the call
Planetary Ruler:	Venus, Ceres
House Association:	Second House
Key Phrases:	I have, I value
Affirmation:	I appreciate the abundance of the present moment.
Archetypes:	Dancer, Musician, Chef, Gardener, Druid, Builder, Tree Hugger, Earth-Mother
Tarot:	Hierophant
Anatomy:	Throat and shoulders
Herbs:	Soothing to throat; licorice, fenugreek, slippery elm
Yoga:	Shoulder stands
Movement:	Slow, plodding, all fours, crawling, stable, contact dance
Film:	Movies related to food, gardening, nature: Chocolate, Like Water for Chocolate, Scent of Green Papayas
Music:	Downtempo, chillout, trip-hop, lounge; Massive Attack
Sexuality/Turn-Ons:	Raw sensation, massage, touch is essential, contact dance, "nuts & bolts sex"
	Neck caresses, ears, massage, pressing, squeezing, chocolate, sensual oils, comfortable environments, plush pillows, sensual music

Archetypal Image, Expression, Symbolism:

Natural/Neutral:	Practical, tranquil, fertile
Shadow/Wounded:	Stubborn, slow, resistant to change, materialism, attachment to pleasure and the body, cautious, poverty or hoarding, stagnant, rigid, emotional suppression, cautious, poverty or hoarding, stagnant, rigid, emotional
Healed/Luminous:	Self-sufficient, perseverant, zen, hard-working, practical, loyal, abundant, patient, enduring, serene, grounded, composed, affectionate, reliable
Past Life Imprints:	Impoverished, sustenance level, survivor mentality Farmer, shepherd Greed, miser, hoarding, material obsession Prolonged death; problems with fertility Self-reliance, "I can do it alone," "I won't give in," "I am what I own"

Gemini ♊

Symbol:	The Twins
Motion of Expression:	*Spiral/Mutable-* evolving, adapting, distributing, demonstrating
Element:	*Air-* ideas, concepts, knowledge
Geometric Apect:	*Waxing Sextile-* empowering synthesis, creative opportunity
Planetary Ruler:	Mercury
House Association:	Third House
Key Phrases:	I think
Affirmation:	I channel versatility and mental agility to synthesize information. I shapeshift to share the story.
Archetypes:	Messenger, Storyteller, Writer, DJ, Comedian, Performer, Teacher, Marketer, Merchant
Tarot:	The Lovers
Anatomy:	Arms, hands, wrists, lungs
Herbs:	Strengthen the lungs and respiratory system, some relax nervous system; Hyssop, lemon balm, mullein,
Yoga:	Wrist and arm stretches
Movement:	Fast, curious, chaotic, scattered, excited
Film:	Comedy; Ferris Bueller's Day Off, Austin Powers, Rushmore, Pi
Music:	Eclectic, fusion, drum n bass, glitch, breaks
Sexuality/Turn-Ons:	Highly curious, naturally polyamorous and bisexual, flirtatious. Accents, foreign languages, talking whispers in the ear, voyeurism

Archetypal Image, Expression, Symbolism:

Natural/Neutral: Communication, thinking, writing, information, shapeshifter, travel twin, sibling

Shadow/Wounded: Superficial, scattered, con-artist, trickster, liar, unfocused, immature, overwhelmed with information, cynical, over-talkative, distracted, unemotional, foolish

Healed/Luminous: Intelligent, light-hearted, curious, clever, versatile, mobile, spontaneous, humorous

Past Life Imprints: Thief; living double life
Messenger who could not deliver or was killed for message
Scribe
Merchant, trader
Troubadour, minstrel
Negative consequences from curiosity

Cancer

Symbol:	Mother holding child, yin-yang
Motion of Expression:	*Cardinal/Outward*- activating, initiating, generating
Element:	*Water*- emotion, imagination, compassion
Geometric Apect:	*Waxing Square*- foundation laying, crisis calling for decision
Planetary Ruler:	Moon
House Association:	Fourth House
Key Phrases:	I nurture
Affirmation:	I embrace and nourish with the tender heart of Mother
Archetypes:	Mother, Nurturer, Protector, Healer
Tarot:	The Chariot
Anatomy:	Stomach, breasts
Herbs:	Soothing to the stomach and digestion; peppermint, spearmint, papaya leaf
Yoga:	Half-moon pose, Goddess pose
Movement:	Slow, undulating, holding, fetal, nested
Film:	Family Films, nostalgic films from youth, cartoons
Music:	Nostalgic, theme songs, lullabies
Sexuality/Turn-Ons:	Nurturing, holding, emotional Eyegazing, caressing, holding, massage, long hours in bed, breasts

Archetypal Image, Expression, Symbolism:

Natural/Neutral:	Caring, domestic, tribal, familial, sentimental
Shadow/Wounded:	Moody, attached, emotional, worried, clinging, insecure, cranky, nagging, shy, oversensitive
Healed/Luminous:	Compassionate, maternal, healing, empathic, intuitive, caring
Past Life Imprints:	Death in Childbirth Wounded Child Abandoned Orphan Cocooned internally, afraid of the world

Leo ♌

Symbol:	Circle of spirit spun in creative flair from the lion's mane
Motion of Expression:	*Fixed/Stable/Inward*- harnessing, empowering, sustaining
Element:	*Fire*- vitality, identity, consciousness, spirit
Geometric Apect:	*Waxing Trine*- flowing, inspired, creative, harmonious
Planetary Ruler:	Sun
House Association:	Fifth House
Key Phrases:	I create, I play, I perform
Affirmation:	I manifest the divine spark
Archetypes:	The King/Queen, Performer, Actor, Child
Tarot:	Strength
Anatomy:	Chest, heart, spine
Herbs:	Strengthen heart and regulate blood pressure; Borage, hawthorn, motherwort
Yoga:	Surya Namaskar (Sun Salutation), spinal stretches
Movement:	Prideful, thrusting chest out, arrogant, loud, superstar, stride
Film:	Evita, Amadeus, the Lion King, Elizabeth, Moulin Rouge, Frida, Chicago
Music:	Pop; African
Sexuality/Turn-Ons:	Romantic, passionate, courtship, knows what it wants, desire to play and have fun, dramatic, warm, affectionate, generosity increases with more attention Role play, dress up, being worshipped, strong, full body

Archetypal Image, Expression, Symbolism:

Natural/Neutral:	Vitality, fun-loving, theatrical, expressive
Shadow/Wounded:	Egotistical, conceited, childish, always seeking approval, dramatic, power-hungry, narcissistic, arrogant, extravagant, temperamental, stubborn, dominating
Healed/Luminous:	Generous, confident, joyful, creative, gifted, romantic, charismatic, courageous, self-aware, noble
Past Life Imprints:	Royalty—misuse of power or power taken away Famous, need for applause Child prodigy or wounded, ignored solar child Starving artist; overwhelmed by talent, can't channel gifts Tragic, dramatic

Virgo ♍

Symbol:	Female winged angel holding an ear of corn in her hand.
Motion of Expression:	*Spiral/Mutable-* evolving, adapting, distributing, demonstrating
Element:	*Earth-* structures, resources, form, nature
Geometric Apect:	*Waxing quincunx-* adjustment, refinement
Planetary Ruler:	Mercury, Chiron (affinity)
House Association:	Sixth House
Key Phrases:	I serve
Affirmation:	I devote myself to a path of spirit; I discriminate the subtle textures of interdependence
Archetypes:	Disciple, Mentor, Sacred Servant, Healer, Craftsmen, Technician, Monk, Priest(ess), Druid, Yogi
Tarot:	Hermit
Anatomy:	Intestines, digestion
Herbs:	Aid in digestion, high in potassium; Blackberry, flax, dill, fennel, plantain
Yoga:	Side stretches, side bends
Movement:	Detailed, careful, precise, subtle, Chi Kung, Yoga
Film:	Nature and Animal films, Films about health, the sacred and mentorship; Planet Earth, Fast Food Nation, Sicko, The English Patient, Karate Kid
Music:	Healing, devotional, sacred, mantra; Deva Premal, Dave Stringer, Krishna Das, massage music, native
Sexuality/Turn-Ons:	Sacred, devotional, efficient, technical, masterly, taoist, pure/chaste. Ritual, in nature, S&M

Archetypal Image, Expression, Symbolism:

Natural/Neutral:	Healthy, realistic, pragmatic, ecological, neat
Shadow/Wounded:	Critical, uptight, inferiority complex, timid, perfectionist, narrow-minded, stuck in routine, discriminating-judging
Healed/Luminous:	Patient, humble, realistic, logical, discerning, orderly, efficient awareness of interdependence, intelligent
Past Life Imprints:	Nun, virgin, martyr
	Servant, slave, peasant
	The victim, masochism, self-sacrificed
	Lack of self-worth, guilt, fear of mistakes
	Apprentice not yet ready, lack of confidence in skills
	Priest, priestess, sacred prostitute, witch—persecuted for practices

♎ Libra ♎

Symbol:	The Scales of Balance
Motion of Expression:	*Cardinal/Outward-* activating, initiating, generating
Element:	*Air-* ideas, concepts, knowledge
Geometric Apect:	*Opposition-* tension for reconciliation, illuminating fulfillment through unifying the duality
Planetary Ruler:	Venus
House Association:	Seventh House
Key Phrases:	I balance
Affirmation:	I harmonize my heart with the rhythm of another
Archetypes:	Lover, Peacemaker, Harmonizer, Counselor, Judge, Don Juan
Tarot:	Justice
Anatomy:	Hips
Herbs:	Balance the kidneys and bladders, are diuretics; Corn silk, juniper, parsley, uva ursi
Yoga:	Balance poses
Movement:	Graceful, harmonic, poise, partner yoga
Film:	Romantic comedy; Sleepless in Seattle
Music:	Trance, house, club, pop, radio
Sexuality/Turn-Ons:	Romantic, giving, attuned to partner's needs Parties, dance, eyegazing, romance

Archetypal Image, Expression, Symbolism:

Natural/Neutral:	Just, diplomatic, cooperative
Shadow/Wounded:	Indecision, co-dependency, projection, fantasy, gossip denial, facade, inauthentic pleasantries, surface, comparison, need to be needed, excessive flirtation
Healed/Luminous:	Diplomacy, peacemaker, social grace, valuing multiple perspectives, righteous judgment, deep listening, harmonizing, inclusiveness, idea-spreaders
Past Life Imprints:	Damaged trust, betrayal Sophisticated bourgeoisie roles, Identity only as partner; loss of lover

Scorpio ♏

Symbol:	Direct penetration to the heart of the mystery
Motion of Expression:	*Fixed/Stable/Inward-* activating, initiating, generating
Element:	*Water-* emotion, imagination, compassion
Geometric Apect:	*Waning Quincunx-* adjustment, compromise, surrender
Planetary Ruler:	Mars, Pluto (affinity)
House Association:	Eighth House
Key Phrases:	I transform
Affirmation:	I probe the mystery
Archetypes:	Shaman, Investigator, Researcher, Psychologist, Banker, Alchemist
Tarot:	Death
Anatomy:	Genitals, colon
Herbs:	Balance the hormones, soothe the colon, aiding elimination; black cohosh, aloe vera, dong quai Root, ginseng, pennyroyal, senna
Yoga:	Scorpion pose, eagle pose
Movement:	Sensual, bellydance, mysterious, cathartic
Film:	War and Horror films, Film Noir; David Lynch films, Apocalypse Now, Fatal Attraction, The Godfather, Basic Instinct, Batman, Silence of the Lambs, Terminator, Seven, The Shining
Music:	Intense, cathartic; Metal; Tool, Dark Side of the Moon
Sexuality/Turn-Ons:	Intense, passionate, death and rebirth experiences Anything taboo, S&M, tantric

Archetypal Image, Expression, Symbolism:

Natural/Neutral: Passionate, deep, esoteric, hypnotic

Shadow/Wounded: Possessive, suspicious, controlling, extreme, compulsive, confrontational, dark, intense, secretive

Healed/Luminous: Powerful, probing, magnetic, magical, psychic, resilient, intimate

Past Life Imprints: Betrayal, abandonment
Sexual abuse and trauma, prostitution
Psychological torture
Paranoia, spy, suspicion, vengeance
Powerlessness or misuse of power; sorcery
Violent death
The centaurian archer's arrow poised to seek the truth

Sagittarius ⚐

Symbol:	*Spiral/Mutable-* evolving, adapting, distributing, demonstrating
Motion of Expression:	*Fire-* vitality, identity, consciousness, spirit
Element:	*Waning Trine-* ripening vision, harvesting creativity
Geometric Apect:	Jupiter
Planetary Ruler:	Ninth House
House Association:	I explore
Key Phrases:	Follow your bliss
Affirmation:	Explorer, Philosopher, Sage, Teacher, Gypsy, Pilgrim,
Archetypes:	Scholar, Seeker, Guru
	Temperance/Art
Tarot:	Thighs
Anatomy:	Large and nutritious, good for liver and pancreas, in-
Herbs:	crease bile flow; Horsetail, dandelion, wild yam, oregon grape root
	Triangle pose, squats
Yoga:	Extravagant, big legs, horse-like, leaping, jumping, high
Movement:	energy
	International, ethnic, spiritual; Baraka, Gandhi, Sound
Film:	of Music, Forrest Gump
Music:	World music, fusion
Sexuality/Turn-Ons:	Powerful sex drive, sexual teacher
	Foreign lovers, humor, adventurous, outdoors

Archetypal Image, Expression, Symbolism:

Natural/Neutral: Outdoorsy, freedom-loving, athletic, religious-philosophical, traveler

Shadow/Wounded: Dogmatic, obnoxious, opinionated, restless, blunt, wanderlust, overidealistic, restless

Healed/Luminous: Enthusiastic, faithful, ethical, optimistic, scholarly, expansive, humorous, judicious, wise

Past Life Imprints: Homeless nomad, displacement
Overabstraction
Manipulating truth
Missionary, convert
Fundamentalist, preacher
Persecuted for beliefs

Capricorn ♑

Symbol:

        A mountain goat with a dolphin's or mermaid's tail, sig-

Motion of Expression: nifying extremes of height and depth.

Element: *Cardinal/Outward-* activating, initiating, generating

Geometric Apect: *Earth-* structures, resources, form, nature

Planetary Ruler: *Waning Square-* reorientation, crisis in consciousness

House Association: Saturn

Key Phrases: Tenth House

Affirmation: I utilize

Archetypes: I activate ambition and self-discipline

Tarot: Executive, Soldier, Politician, Leader, Wise Elder

Anatomy: The Devil

Herbs: Skeletal system, joints, teeth, skin

        High in calcium, help in arthritis, rheumatism, and bro-

        ken bones or teeth; Comfrey, sarsaparilla, white oak,

Yoga: wintergreen, rue

Movement: Knee rotations, pigeon

Film: Slow, heavy laborious, pressured, weighty

        Political, imperial. A Few Good Men, The Firm, JFK,

Music: Schindler's List, Metropolis, Wall Street, Devil's Advocate

        Minimalism, classical, melancholic; Arvo Part, Henryk

Sexuality/Turn-Ons: Gorecki

        Need for trust, slow and building, strong stamina

Archetypal Image, Expression, Symbolism:

Natural/Neutral:

Shadow/Wounded:

        Traditional, achievement-oriented, conservative

Healed/Luminous: Nationalistic, authoritarian, disciplinarian, sober, fearful, bound by law and tradition, patriarchal

Past Life Imprints: Successful, determined, patient, organized, mature, responsible, linked to ancestors, integrity

        Conformity, conditioning, slave to social position
        Oppression by or misuse of authority
        Overburdened
        Guilty, "it's all my fault"
        Soldier
        Trapped in futile situations of hierarchy

Aquarius

Symbol:	Waves of electrical energy, prana, chi
Motion of Expression:	*Fixed/Stable/Inward-* harnessing, cultivating, empowering
Element:	*Air-* ideas, concepts, knowledge
Geometric Apect:	*Waning Sextile-* exciting renewal, paradigm shift
Planetary Ruler:	Saturn, Uranus (affinity)
House Association:	Eleventh House
Key Phrases:	I reform. Give me freedom or give me death!
Affirmation:	I envision a humanitarian future of universal freedom and tolerance.
Archetypes:	Scientist, Reformer, Genius, Inventor, Revolutionary, Rebel
Tarot:	The Star
Anatomy:	Shins, the circulatory system
Herbs:	Helpful for circulation and relax nervous system; Chamomile, passionflower, prickly ash, scullcap, catnip, valerian, hops
Yoga:	Pranayama
Movement:	Free, erratic, freakish, like being electrically shocked, spinning, jumping, highly individualized
Film:	Sci-Fi and Postmodern; Star Trek, Alien(s), Blade Runner, 2001; A.I., Minority Report, K-Pax, Close Encounters; Matrix, Zeitgeist, Powers of Ten, Being John Malkovich, Truman Show, Ed Wood, Cirque du Soleil
Music:	All electronic, esp. techno, psychedelic; Shpongle
Sexuality/Turn-Ons:	Anything goes, eccentric, inventive, weirder the better, naturally polyamorous and bisexual, multiple partners who are friends. Voyeurism, toys, online, video, pornography

Archetypal Image, Expression, Symbolism:

Natural/Neutral: Non-conformist, unique, radical, communal, detached, intuitive fighting for cause and for freedom

Shadow/Wounded: Anarchist, alienated, fragmented, impractical, cold, unemotional, overly intellectual, robotic, over rational, zealous, insensitive, aloof

Healed/Luminous: Liberator, innovative, humanitarian, altruistic, philanthropic, globally/cosmically minded, tolerant, futuristic, genius

Past Life Imprints: Ostracized, cast out for difference, wounds to individuation
Group hysteria and mass trauma
Anti-social, anarchist; Secret and fringe societies, aristocracy
Futurist ahead of one's time, mad scientist
Atlantis, extraterrestrial

Pisces ♓

Symbol:	The two fishes swimming in opposite directions, unified by the bridge of transcendent consciousness
Motion of Expression:	*Spiral/Mutable-* evolving, adapting, distributing, demonstrating
Element:	*Water-* emotion, imagination, compassion
Geometric Apect:	*Waning Crescent-* release and dissolve, spiritual revitalization
Planetary Ruler:	Jupiter, Neptune (affinity)
House Association:	Twelfth House
Key Phrases:	I imagine
Affirmation:	I dissolve my ego to channel the divine artist
Archetypes:	Dreamer, Mystic, Artist, Musician, Nurse, Savior
Tarot:	The Moon
Anatomy:	Feet
Herbs:	Strengthen immune system, antibacterial, heighten states of awareness; Goldenseal, echinacea, myrrh, chapparal, mugwort, kava kava
Yoga:	Fish pose, Corpse pose, Tai Chi
Movement:	Slippery, liquid, undulating, seaweed, sleepy, drunk
Film:	Mystical, mythical, fantastic, animation, Films about dreams and madness; Waking Life, The Fountain, Avatar, One Flew Over the Cuckoo's Nest, Ashes and Snow, Alice in Wonderland, Harry Potter, Lord of the Rings
Music:	Movie scores, classical, chillout, ambient, lush, transcendent
Sexuality/Turn-Ons:	Desire to merge, very sensual, imaginative, ego-dissolution, tantric, naturally polyamorous, group sex Fantasy, role-play, hot tubs, ocean, intoxication

Archetypal Image, Expression, Symbolism:

Natural/Neutral:	Sensitive, psychic, dreamy, idealist
Shadow/Wounded:	Escapist, spacey, vulnerable, impractical, indiscriminate, foggy, confused, evasive, weak boundaries, depressed
Healed/Luminous:	Artistic, psychic, compassionate, romantic, spiritual, poetic, contemplative, an open channel, mystical, empathic
Past Life Imprints:	Dreamer, visionary, prophet, seer Escapist—alcoholic, drug addict, lost in fantasy; going insane Poet, musician, artists Pirate, lives in or around the sea Naiveté, in denial; Being projected upon Victim, martyr; depressed; Disassociation

The Archetypal Odyssey of Awakening

Burst out from the Piscean womb, you encounter the self—Aries, I AM who am and I AM here! Without fear and without forethought, you have only the impulse to action. You navigate this life on the ship of your Ascendant—you wear that mask for all to behold. In your first house, you find the vehicle to carry your soul through life. You are the pioneer. And you must overcome in order to bear the light, so you dare to bravely embrace this life. How do you defend, as would Mars, your right to wear your persona with pride? For this Rising Sign is your carrier wave on the path of Ascension through time.

As you boldly pounce into the Taurean stage, into the second house, what costume will you wear, what art direction and set design will you decorate yourself in? Now, you cannot just do, you must also possess, as you pronounce I HAVE. You glorify your values and define your relationship with yourself. To appreciate embodiment, you celebrate your sensual essence, you play in nature's succulence, you cloak your body in the bark of a tree, and you soak in Gaia's honey. So how will you manage your precious resources? How will you design your dance to receive the earth mama abundance?

But do not get stuck in the mud of the material world, for there is much to learn in the Gemini mind of the third house, I THINK. The cat is curious as you wear Mercury's thinking cap and learn to perceive the world. First, you meet your siblings here, then your system of education, as you distribute and evolve concepts, ideas, and knowledge.

"But do not scatter yourself in a world of endless information," says Cancer. "Remember your family, your roots, your home, and who you are in your deepest personal mythos." Heal and nurture yourself by means of the Moon and the fourth house. Here you react and utter I FEEL in your state of ultimate vulnerability and maternal sensitivity.

"If you leave your protective shell, you just may learn how to play and laugh like me!" shouts Leo. For here in the fifth house, you are the Solar Child, and you celebrate spontaneity. You are the creator of your universe, you are the king and queen of make-believe as you re-create reality. I CREATE

Now, in Virgo, you must craft your art, you must refine your skill, you most hone your gifts. In the sixth house, I SERVE. You recognize that there is much work to do to heal the planet, and you must begin with your own health, your diet, your daily practice. You must make your to-do list an act of sacred service on the path of devotion.

You are ready now, to ascend to the realm of relationship, for you recognize that you cannot perfect the world on your own. You need partner and beloved and so you must meet the other in Libra and the seventh house. You are imbalanced on your own and you must learn to honor the desires of another and so you affirm I LISTEN. You weigh the scales of justice and find yourself magnetized towards Venus' attractive scent.

And then you dive in—to the throbbing heart of Scorpio's mystery. Re-sistances, control, and obsession all crawl out of the monster mirror. And so your psyche must purify and regenerate as you confront every eighth house inner shadow. In the thralls of passion and the delicate dance of compromise, you share resources and blend souls with another. Pluto demands you shed skin and rise from the ashes in the breath of rebirth as you battle the dragons of the unconscious—Serpent Shaman and Alchemical Phoenix—I TRANSFORM

But the archer's optimistic arrow will point you out of the dark, dungeon depths of Scorpio. The Sagittarian centaur invites you to the upper world odyssey. Inspired by faith, a pilgrim without limits, the hero exclaims I EXPLORE as you sail though the ninth house—the exotic dreams of foreign cultures entice you with the expansive aroma of majestic cosmologies. You are uplifted by Jupiter's gracious theologies, the guru's wise philosophy, and the heart's intuitive synchronicities.

And now you must serve the world on your path of mystery. At the Mid-heaven, your vocation calls you, for it is here that you may radiate your light to the ends of the earth. The wise elder emerges in Capricorn after years of generating structures with dedication and discipline. In the tenth house, you take the weight of the world on your shoulders as Saturn whips you into shape, demanding that you walk the path of integrity and be held accountable for you response-ability. With steadfast determination, you declare I UTILIZE, and so invoke the leader within.

Yet you are not alone in your quest. The Aquarian visionaries surround you. In the eleventh house, your cosmic tribe conspires to grant you every wish in the sacred act of friendship. Individuals, gathered together, you harness all knowledge and allow the lightning flash of Uranian intuition to liberate you from the rigid and the old. You text edit the revolution which will end the status quo. You are the tech savvy mad scientist evolving the new paradigm of Being. You are the future freedom, the radical idealist emancipating humanity. With a rebel yell, you cry "Give me freedom or give me death, for I REFORM!"

And then you must let go, and let god in. You must dissolve your ego, as but a drop of the Piscean ocean. In the twelfth house, you must submerge to return to One. Now you remember that all is fantasy and so you whisper as you retire into sleep, as you retreat into dream, you are the artist enwombed in divine imagination. In the holy sanctuary of meditation, you are the open channel and the angelic musician. And your spirit guides sing poetic vibration as you Neptune the inner ear towards psychic revelation.

I IMAGINE I IMAGINE
I AM MADE IN THE IMAGE OF HEAVEN
I IMAGINE I IMAGINE
I AM THE CELESTIAL REFLECTION
I IMAGINE AND UNVEIL
THE DIVINE and MYSTIC VISION
I IMAGINE
IN THE IMAGE I AM
WHO AM IN THE IMAGE I AM
WHO AM

Chapter 8
ASPECTS:
Dialogue and Narration

Aspects are the dynamic dialogue between the planetary characters within you. They are the heart of the unfolding narrative between the various psychological components of your being.

Dynamic aspects, sometimes called hard aspects, include 90 degree squares, 180 degree oppositions, and some conjunctions depending on the planets involved. These dynamic aspects invite you into the dance of life by describing where internal and external conflicts and challenges may lie. You will repeatedly need to reconcile and integrate dynamic aspects such as the opposition and square. You may be able to more easily integrate flowing or graceful aspects such as the trine or sextile, but you may also may be lazier in practically applying their intrinsic gifts to your life. However, if you bring consciousness to these flowing aspects, you can learn to enhance your natural gifts and better serve the world to your fullest capacity.

Often times, a friendly aspect to one planet can assist a harder aspect to the same aspect. So if Saturn is square your Venus, but Venus is trine Jupiter, look to the benefits of Jupiter trine to Venus, such as inspiring and optimistic friendships or travel opportunities, to help remediate the tense pressure of Saturn on the goddess of love.

Think of the square as two forces running down the street that bump into each other. They must pay attention and work out their differences. Often one planet wins out in the battle of the squares. But a square can be exponentially rewarding when integrated because the two planets, although in different genders and elements, will be in the same mode of expression, such as masculine, mutable fire Sagittarius and feminine, mutable earth Virgo.

The major spiritual goal of oppositions is to move towards wholeness by uniting the polarities. These two planets will once again be in the same mode of expression, but this time in the same gender and in elements that need each other, such as the masculine, cardinal fire and air Aries and Libra, and the feminine, fixed earth and water Taurus and Scorpio.

Also, give attention to the 150 degree quincunxes, as these planets are neither in the same element nor mode of expression, essentially speaking a different

ASPECT NAME	SYMBOL	MEANING—*Evolutionary Purpose*	DEGREES	RESONANT SIGN
*Conjunction	☌	new energy, beginning the journey	0	Aries
Semisextile/Waxing Crescent		nourishing seeds or refusing the call	30	Taurus
Semisquare		disruption, frustration, agitation	45	N/A
*Waxing Sextile		empowering synthesis, creative opportunity (nature of Venus)	60	Gemini
Quintile		divinely inspired creative genius	72	N/A
*Waxing Square	□	foundation laying, crisis calling for decision (nature of Mars)	90	Cancer
*Waxing Trine	△	flowing, inspired, creative, harmonious (nature of Jupiter)	120	Leo
Waxing Quincunx		adjustment, refinement	150	Virgo
*Opposition	☍	tension for reconciliation, illuminating fulfillment through unifying the duality (nature of Saturn)	180	Libra
Waning Quincunx		adjustment, compromise, surrender	210	Scorpio
*Waning Trine	△	ripening vision, harvesting creativity (nature of Jupiter)	240	Sagitarrius
*Waning Square	□	reorientation, crisis in consciousness	270	Capricorn
*Waning Sextile		exciting renewal, paradigm shift (nature of Venus)	300	Aquarius
Waning Crescent		release and dissolve, spiritual revitalization	330	Pisces

language altogether. They will need constant intention and refinement in your life.

Synastry charts between two couples are heavily associated with understanding the aspects between two people's evolutionary forces. You can apply the meanings below to inter-aspects between your chart and a friend, lover, business partner, or family member.

In the chart below, you will also notice that each aspect relates naturally to a sign of the zodiac. Beginning at Aries, for instance, if you move 90 degrees you arrive at the sign of Cancer. Cancer is naturally resonant with the themes of the waxing square—building secure foundations, making key decisions towards establishing security, etc.

Understanding this helps us to answer a common question about orbs. People tend to ask how large of an orb should we apply? Is it quincunx if it's 3 degrees but not 5 degrees? In terms of aspects, I find the classical techniques most helpful. In Hellenistic (Greek) and Vedic (Indian) astrology, whole sign aspects are used, which means that if you have a planet in Gemini and another planet in Pisces, they are square because the signs are naturally square to each other. This is very useful. With this technique, you simply assume that the closer the aspect is to exact, the more intense and obvious will the nature of that aspect be experienced in your life.

Aspects are categorized as either waxing or waning, also called "applying" and "separating." An applying aspect occurs when a faster moving planet is moving towards a slower moving planet in the natural order of the zodiac, which is a counterclockwise direction. These applying, or waxing aspects, serve to build and create structures and are filled with anticipation and learning. Whereas an aspect which moves away from exact is called separating and, because the exact aspect has already happened, seeks to be more gracefully integrated into one's life experience. These waning aspects re-orientate, reflect, and consider the meaning behind the activities.

Another way to think of the aspects is to understand their planetary nature, which we describe in the next section on the Thema Mundi. For instance, the graceful, beneficial, friendly energy of the trine is akin to the nature of Jupiter, while the challenging hard work of the opposition is similar to the force of Saturn.

By applying planetary and sign associations with the aspects, you can truly integrate the archetypal nature of the zodiac. Planets, signs, houses, aspects—are all the same language of primal, divine energy, manifesting for different functions.

The asterisk marks the most commonly used aspects, called Ptolemaic, as they were elucidated by the great Greek astrologer Ptolemy.

Chapter 9
The Thema Mundi:
Sacred Geometry and
The Astro-Logic of the Ancients

This section owes an incredible debt to Hellenistic astrologers Robert Schmidt, Demetra George and Chris Brennan, who have been working tirelessly to translate and distribute astrological wisdom from the ancient world, including Greece and Egypt.

The Thema Mundi refers to a chart cast for the world itself. References appear in Hellenistic, Persian, Medieval and Renaissance literature and artistic representations. The first mention of the Thema Mundi comes from Thrasyllus, who died around 36 ce. He was the head librarian at the Library of Alexandria, a philosopher and commentator on Plato, and became court astrologer to Roman emperors Augustus and Tiberius. Of the Thema Mundi, the philosopher Macrobious says that the demiurge—the creator of the manifest world—assigned the planets to these positions at the creation of the world.

The Thema Mundi was used as a teaching tool to understand the logic behind rulerships, aspects, and other fundamentals of astrology, which is why I include it here.

The Thema Mundi was timed according to the Egyptian New Year— when Sirius rose heliacally, in the summer. "Heliacal rising" means to rise before the Sun, and this sacred and important time announced the flooding of the Nile River and so the beginning of the Egyptian new year festivities. If one was looking at that time, for a heliacal rising of Sirius, then Cancer needed to be the sign on the Ascendant. The Sun would then be in the following sign, Leo, so the Sun was given rulership of Leo.

The Moon was then given position in and rulership of Cancer, with the likely logic that the Sun and Moon are the two Luminaries and, in the signs of Leo and Cancer at that latitude, are the signs with the greatest number of daylight hours.

As you continue, you will see that the formulation of planetary rulerships was a matter of geometry, rather than a matter of affinities. For example, you can see in Fig. 9.1 each of the inner planets and Jupiter and Saturn fan out equilaterally in both directions from the Sun and Moon, and each planet but the Sun and Moon

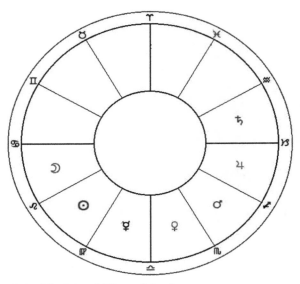

9.1 - *Traditional Thema Mundi*

rule two signs, one masculine and one feminine, one on the solar side and one on the lunar side. The Sun and the Moon, because of their strength in our own perceptual nature, as huge and important bodies to our life sustenance and to our emotions, rule only one sign each.

From the Moon ruling Cancer and the Sun ruling Leo, you then move outward in the order of the speed of the planets and the distance from the Sun, in an alternating masculine and feminine assignment. Mercury, the fastest planet, closest to the Sun, is given rulership of the sign following masculine Leo, feminine Virgo, the Virgin. Venus follows in speed and distance, so she becomes ruler of masculine Libra. Mars is the next fastest and next outer planet, and so takes the sign following Virgo, feminine Scorpio. Jupiter is the next planet out and takes masculine Sagittarius. And lastly, Capricorn, a feminine sign, is given over to Saturn, the slowest and most distant of the planets, the known edge of the solar system to the ancients.

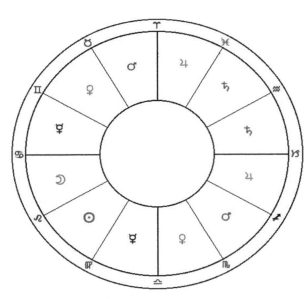

9.2 - *Thema Mundi with mirror image containing all planetary rulerships.*

If you fold over the chart (Fig. 9.2) between the Sun/Moon axis then you arrive at a mirror image for the doctrine of rulerships, which is astronomically accurate, since for instance, Mercury can never be more than one sign away from the Sun. Traveling in reverse order from Leo then, moving back one sign, you arrive at feminine Cancer, which you know is ruled by the Moon. The next sign in reverse order is Gemini and so Mercury is given rulership of this masculine sign. Venus, similarly, can never be more than two signs away from the Sun, so she is given rulership over feminine Taurus, two signs before Leo. Continuing with the mirror image, Mars is then given rulership of masculine Aries, Jupiter of feminine Pisces, and Saturn of masculine Aquarius.

In modern astrology, assignment of the outer planets Neptune to Pisces, Uranus to Aquarius, and Pluto to Scorpio neglects the elegant symmetry and geometric order of the original system as well as thousands of years of its multicultural application. It is better to say that these outer planets have affinity with the above signs.

It is important to acknowledge here the shamanic, phenomenological, and astronomically accurate associations of these planets to these rulerships. Observation led itself to archetypal correlation. Let's explore further.

To ancient and modern stargazers alike, the Moon and Sun are the lights of the cosmos, while Saturn is the dark boundary, the last wandering star visible to the naked eye. If you fan out either side from the Sun and Moon, you will uncover the meaning of the sacred geometric aspects. If you move 60 degrees from the Sun in Leo to the sign of Libra, and you move 60 degrees in reverse from the Moon in its home in Cancer you arrive at Taurus. Both Libra and Taurus are ruled by Venus, so the 60 degree angle takes on the nature of Venus, synthesizing, harmonizing, creative.

Starting at the Sun in its home in Leo again, if you fan out 90 degrees, you arrive at Scorpio ruled by Mars. Moving back from the Moon in Cancer 90 degrees, you arrive at Aries, also ruled by Mars, so the 90 degree angle, the square, resonates with the conflictual agitation of Mars.

From the Sun, if you move 120 degrees, you arrive at Sagittarius, ruled by Jupiter. Likewise, if you move 120 degrees back from the Moon, you arrive at Pisces, also ruled by Jupiter in his feminine mask. And so the trine is of the nature of Jupiter, and was traditionally called the greater beneficial aspect of friendly, flowing ease.

Lastly, if you move from the Sun in Leo out 180 degrees to the sign of Aquarius, you find Saturn's home. Moving back from the Moon in Cancer out 180 degrees, you find Saturn's rulership in Capricorn. And so the opposition is of the adversarial and challenging nature of Saturn. This makes logical sense since the Sun is in its weakest energy output and lowest point in the sky during its journey through the signs of Capricorn and Aquarius.

Although this was not described in the classical texts, it may logically be argued that the 30 degree angle from the Sun in Leo to Mercury in Virgo may resonate with the rational, contesting, and analytical nature of Mercury. The semisextile and semisquare aspects both require this refinement of perception akin to Mercury's energy.

Now this last point wouldn't be true in the southern hemisphere, but this map was made by Egyptians and circulated through the Greek and Roman world—all locations in the Northern Hemisphere.

It is my hope that this presentation of the Thema Mundi helps to elucidate some of those questions you might have regarding sign rulership and the metaphysical meaning of the aspects.

Chapter 10
Introduction to Chart Interpretation

Since we have now concluded reviewing the basic language of the archetypal theater, I'd like to introduce you to a few ways of integrating this information into chart interpretation through some famous charts. Chart interpretation is a craft, a practice, a science, and an art. Your own chart is your greatest teacher in the craft. When you begin to interpret a horoscope, you should allow your consciousness to meditate for a few moments on the energy you behold in front of you. Allow your right brain to soak in the picture of the sky at the moment of the individual's birth. After a few moments, you will begin to notice major life themes emerge as you give attention to the elements and modes. You may see clusters of planets in certain quadrants of the chart, highlighting realms of focus for the soul. You may notice outstanding configurations such as grand trines or t-squares—planets involved in these configurations will require special attention in interpretation.

Then you can begin to dissect the chart, planet by planet, angle by angle, noting the sign, house, and aspect with each planet. Begin with the Sun, Moon, and Ascendant, and work your way from the personal planets, to the agents of socialization, and finally to the transformational forces of the outer planets. As you practice, the major motifs will stand out in prominence and you may forego a structured interpretation, replacing it instead with the needs of the client in that moment.

A narrative sculpture unfolds before you. You see the outline of the life and begin to storytell the primary themes which dominate the life. Allow the individual's mythos to sing through your observations. Before you lies a mystic poem and you are a bard, a celestial translator for the Codex of the Soul.

Examples of Interpretative Statements

Ex. 1: You have the (Planet/Evolutionary urge) wearing the mask/costume of the (Sign) playing out its scene in the realm of life experience (describe the House) and dialoguing with (Planetary Force) in this type of relationship (describe nature of Aspect between two planets).

Ex.1: You have the soul of (Moon) radiating the life purpose of (Sun) wearing the mask of (Ascendant).

Ex. 2: You are emotionally nurtured by (Moon sign, house, aspect). You walk the path of (Sun sign, house, aspect). The lifestyle vehicle which carries you is (Rising sign and Ruling planet by sign, house, aspect).

Brief Astro-Biographical Interpretations

The descriptions below are partial interpretative statements to help you begin to narrate the chart as an unfolding, individual mythology.

Revolutionary Civil Rights Leader MARTIN LUTHER KING, JR:

You have the soul of the mystic, dreamer, poet, and visionary in the realm of spiritual friendships and idealistic revolutionaries (eleventh house). You walk the path of the leader, organizer, and wise elder of integrity, wearing the mask of the grounded realist, the peaceful pragmatist, and the lover of beauty (Taurus).

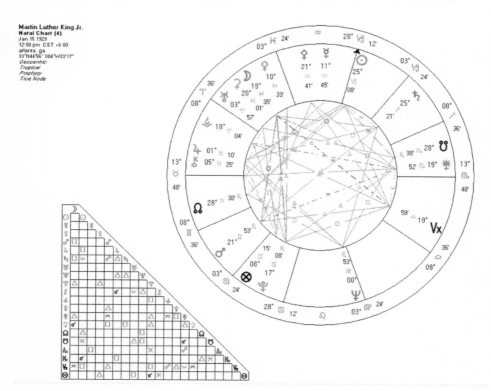

Martin Luther King Jr.
Natal Chart (4)
Jan 15 1929
12:00 pm CST +6:00
atlanta, ga
33°N44'56" 084°W23'17"
Geocentric
Tropical
Porphyry
True Node

Popular Talk Show Host OPRAH WINFREY:

You are instinctually nurtured (Moon) by an ability to broadcast, publicize, and expand people's horizons (Sagittarius) about very personal stories, family, lineage, and the interior depths of the soul (fourth house). Your life purpose is to radiate the popular visionary genius (Sun conjunct Venus in Aquarius) in the realm of your personal creativity and self-expression (fifth house).

Your vehicle in this life is the sacred servant and mentor (Virgo rising), who must use technology, networking, and friendships (ruling planet Mercury in Aquarius) to fulfill a path of daily devotion to spirit (sixth house).

Deep, probing questions, investigation, and research into the psychological motivations (Scorpio in the third house) behind people's actions will motivate and activate you (Mars), although you may create or suffer heated arguments or passionate speech (Mars square Mercury).

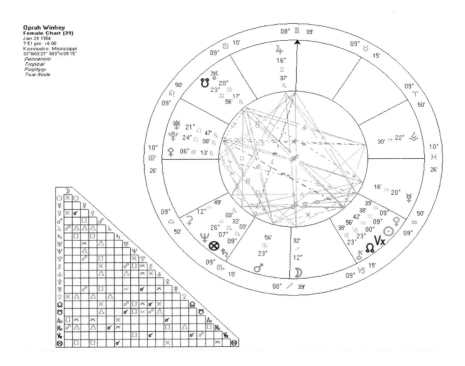

U.S. President BARACK OBAMA

You wear the mask of the visionary idealist and you radiate the life purpose of the performer, leader, and creator in the realm of service and hard work. (Sun in Leo in sixth house). You will have to integrate dreams and visions (Neptune) into your life path, but you may be deluded, foggy, or confused as to how to vitally express yourself, as your identity dissolves in lofty beliefs (Neptune in the ninth square the Sun in the sixth).

You have the soul of the powerful and influential orator, writer, and shape-shifter (Pluto square the Moon in Gemini). Your relationships and associations will be with wealthy or elite individuals who will have a transformational, threatening, (Pluto), damaging or mentoring (Chiron) effect on your sense of security and your family (Pluto opposite Chiron, both square the (Moon in the fourth house).

You will seek power and influence in your career (Scorpio MC). Your career will depend on your ability to transform and regenerate yourself through psychological death and rebirth and the assistance of other peoples' resources (Ruler of MC in eighth house).

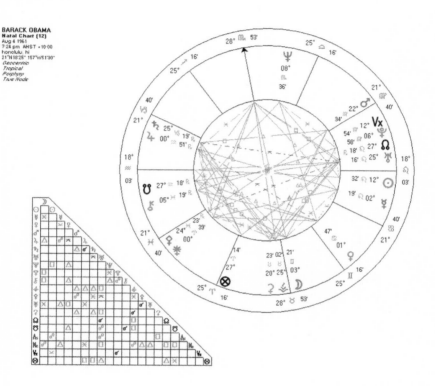

BARACK OBAMA
Natal Chart (12)
Aug 4 1961
7:24 pm AHST +10:00
honolulu, hi
21°N18'25" 157°W51'30"
Geocentric
Tropical
Porphyry
True Node

Actor BRAD PITT:

You seek to be a craftsman and technician in your career (Virgo Midheaven). The realms of career and relationships are linked, both ruled by Mercury, so that you will likely work with your partner, in the same field as your partner, or meet your partner while working. You may enjoy multiple relationships with intelligent and multitalented individuals (Gemini Descendant), who are respected and successful in their careers (Ruler of Descendant Mercury in Capricorn). You will likely want to have children with your partner and build a sustainable relationship where your money, resources, and popularity will be highlighted (Ruler Mercury conjunct Moon and Venus in the second house).

You have a strong tendency in your soul towards workaholism, constant striving, and pressure and burden of hierarchical systems of approval and outward success. You may even feel that you will never do enough in this life (Capricorn South Node in the first house conjunct Mercury and Mars). But you must learn to nurture yourself and build a secure home and supportive family. Caring for others and allowing your heart and your soul to be nourished will bring spiritual fulfillment and enduring peace (Cancer North Node in the seventh house; Jupiter squaring the Nodes).

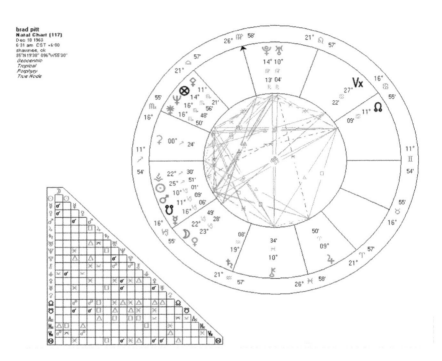

Actor JOHHNY DEPP:

You are emotionally nourished by a dedication to success, and daily seek recognition in your career (Capricorn sixth). You sail on the ship of the performance artist (Leo rising) whose life purpose involves wearing many masks, cultivating talents in storytelling, shapeshifting, and play amidst many friends with a similar vision (Sun in Gemini eleventh house). You have a natural ability to gracefully utilize enduring relationships towards achieving your life purpose (Saturn in Aquarius seventh house trine Sun in Gemini eleventh house). You seek a unique and eccentric partnership that defies convention (Aquarius) but also involves commitment and stability (Saturn in seventh house). Your desire for a structured and disciplined relationship may take extra time and effort to manifest (Saturn retrograde), and is challenged by your love of sensual pleasure and beauty and your magnetism towards work (Saturn in seventh square Venus/Mercury in Taurus in tenth house).

You assert yourself as a craftsman in your trade who must forge his own unique path of detailed effort (Mars conjunct Uranus in Virgo). Your masculine essence must have complete autonomy in order to continue to reinvent and regenerate itself fearlessly as you empower yourself (Mars conjunct Uranus and Pluto).

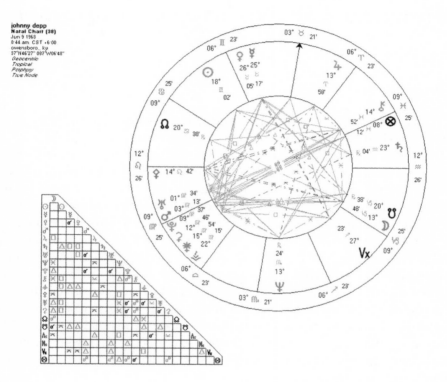

Chapter II
Experiential Astrology:
Practices for Archetypal Integration

The Horoscopic Soul-Collage

One of the most interactive and engaging exercises you can do to understand your archetypal map is to make a soul collage of your horoscope.

Gather art supplies including poster board, colored pens, pencils, magazines, construction paper, glue stick, and photos of yourself, friends, and family. If you have Photoshop skills, you can also make a horoscope mandala with that amazing tool. In either case, this collage can not only be a fun interaction with your sacred script, but a powerful, meditative exercise of archetypal self-reflection.

You can do this exercise a few different ways. First, you can make an image board of the planets just by themselves, to begin understanding the energy, similar to what I did for the archetypal collages of the planets. In some way, make or obtain images of planet, either one from online, one from my website, or you can draw one if you like. Now place the image of the planet in the center of some poster board. Begin to encircle this planet with photos, images, and other drawings of the archetypal mask this planet wears, the zodiac sign it occupies in your birthchart. So if you have the Sun in Gemini, take images of a cell phone, computer, a written letter, a book, a student or any other images that resonate with Gemini for you.

A simpler technique involves making twelve image boards for each sign and then placing them around the wheel of your personal horoscope. You can sit in the center of the wheel as you do this, facing towards the Midheaven top of the chart. By meditating upon the positions of the signs by what houses they occupy, you can see how each realm of life is influenced by a certain style of behavior and energetic theme.

If you want to take this exercise to the next level of archetypal synthesis, you can include music as part of the process. First, you can play music for each planet, moody, internal music for the Moon, the raw and intense hard rock for Mars. See the suggested music in the sections above. Play this music as you create your planetary image boards. This can be a very revealing exercise especially, if you have say, Mars in Cancer. You'll notice the friction and disconnect between the natural Martian music—passionate, loud, aggressive—and the images of family, babies, a cup of tea or coffee, a bed, a bath, a massage, all associated with Cancer. This process is helpful because it demonstrates Mars in his fallen position in Cancer, and which may reflect certain hesitancies in your life towards self-assertion outside of the home.

Another way to employ music is to play the wheel of the zodiac in its natural order from Aries to Pisces. In this exercise, you create your mandala house by house. So let's say you're at the fifth house, Leo's home. Here you can put on playful, fun, celebratory, solar music—maybe African music or children singing. Then put in the images of the sign you have on the cusp of the fifth house which reflect how you play. Maybe you have the sign Taurus on the cusp of the fifth house, so you can collage in trees, flowers, tasty foods, massage, etc., to show how you prefer to play and express yourself. When moving into the sixth house, natural Virgo territory, listen to sacred or devotional music while you create an image for the sign you have on the cusp of the sixth house.

What if you have a planet in this house? Allow that planetary energy to also speak through images or keywords. If you have Uranus in the sixth house, you can place symbols and images such as technology, someone who looks independent, bolts of lightning, a mad scientist, a zodiac wheel, or the words "freedom" and "individual" to signify how your path of devotion, service, and daily practice can include these inventive, higher mind Uranian themes.

In the seventh house, the domain of Venus and Libra, throw on some romantic music, some Spanish serenades, cheesy love songs you may secretly like— and collage the images of the sign on the cusp. Let's say Saturn is in the seventh house. You may put someone older than you here, who looks successful and serious. This may seem like a dry image in the house of love, but will ring true as a fundamental relationship need for a disciplined, stable, and enduring relationship. You could add images such as pyramids and ancient trees, which weather the storms of time and still maintain their integrity.

Solar Return Mandala and Transits

A variation on this soul collage is to create a birthday mandala utilizing your Solar Return chart. This chart is described in detail in Part 3, the Rites of Passage section, but is essentially a chart cast each year for the moment the Sun arrives back to the exact degree and minute of your birth. This chart is usually cast for the place you will live for the upcoming year. This amazing tool was used in much of the ancient world, by the Greeks, Arabs, and Persians, and is one of the most popular forecasting tools used by astrologers today. It is profoundly revealing.

So you can do the same exercises we listed above for creating an archetypal mandala, only this time using your solar return chart to demonstrate the major life themes in development. Notice how the styles of engaging each house now change for the year. Notice what realms have the most planetary emphasis. Pay special attention to the house of the Sun. This mandala will reflect back to you the areas of emphasis for your life in the coming year, areas which will require cultivation and concentration for your evolution.

Once you have made or printed out planetary images, you can also apply them to transits, which are the positions of the planets in the sky currently. If Saturn is going through your fourth house, take the image of Saturn and move it through the fourth house very slowly. Listen to Saturn's voice demanding you concentrate and discipline yourself for two-and-a-half years in this realm of home, family, and roots. If Uranus is opposite your Sun, allow a conversation to unfold between the two planets. Study the images of Uranus's house position by transit and the images of the Sun's natal position. What dialogue is occurring there? How does Uranus seek to reinvent and liberate the Sun? Let the images teach you.

With experiential astrology, the possibilities are endless, for the archetypes can be expressed through so many different media in a multitude of styles. The point is to play, to engage your sacred script with an active imagination and an open heart. Allow the heavens to sing through you!

Astro Drama

Drama therapy can be traced back historically to Greek theater. In his Poetics, Aristotle states that the function of tragedy is to induce catharsis—a release of deep feelings–to purge the senses and the souls of the spectators leading to harmony and healing in the entire community. Drama and embodied therapies continued to be updated and evolved by psychologists of the 20th century, especially Wilhelm Reich, Jacob Levy Moreno, who created psychodrama, and various Gestalt psychologists, post-Jungian psychotherapists, and movement therapists.

With astro-drama, an individual, couple, or collective can story-tell and role play the various components of the birthchart. Astro-drama facilitates two important therapeutic processes described by Phil Jones, author of *Drama as Therapy, Theater as Living*. One of these, "projective identification" occurs as a person identifies with a character in a story. In the case of astrology, you can identify with a planetary archetype. "Dramatic distancing" assists in the understanding and engagement with emotional or psychological issues and circumstances. By watching two other people perform a part of one's chart, or playacting a part oneself, the dramatic metaphor helps you to witness the situation from a more objective standpoint and can make each element of your chart more tangible and tolerable. On the other hand, your visceral embodiment of your chart can have a regenerative and cathartic effect, transforming your perceptions of core elements of your personal narrative.

Begin by creating a few playlists for each of your planets from your own music selection. If you have three planets in Gemini, then include three songs with the archetypal texture of Gemini—fast, dynamic, eclectic. Refer to the section on the movements and music of the planets and the signs, and then mix and match to fit your chart. Now take one planet at a time and dance it in its sign. If you can do this practice with a friend, notice the differences in your charts. How does your Moon in Virgo move differently than your friend's Moon in Sagittarius? This exercise leads naturally to aspect integration.

Aspect Integration

You can do this next exercise by yourself, or you can play one planet while one friend plays another, or you can gather together some friends and role-play each other's charts. Let's say you wish to know more about your Pluto opposition to Venus. One friend can take on the role of Pluto and you (or another friend) can take on the role of Venus.

It would be great, for instance, if Pluto could wear a long black coat. He would sneak into the room, looking dark and foreboding. You could see him undergoing an internal, psychological crisis. Venus would look over and initially be frightened, then somewhat enthralled and magnetized by this powerful presence. She may ask him what's wrong, and he would day nothing, but just turn away. She would ask again, and this time, as she approached, he would howl and hiss at her. She would run off frightened, but come back again, almost obsessively hypnotized by this dark force, with a conviction that she could help him. This time, he would not wait for her. He would thrust himself into her face with an intimidating dominance. He would seem to threaten her with every move and give her no room to breathe, and finally cloak her in his black cape. Venus could try to escape, but with every resistance he would grip her tighter, so she would eventually learn to surrender. Then the two, at last, would embrace in full body union, merged, staring into each other's souls.

What is interesting about this exercise is that it maintains archetypal coherence across planet, sign, house, and aspect. For example, this highly tense and dramatic scene would not only resonate for someone with Pluto opposite Venus, but could also apply to Venus in Scorpio, or Venus in the eighth house. The potential which emerges in role-playing your chart is to viscerally feel the archetypes vibrate and pulse through you. The goal here is to recognize the overlay of archetypal affinity between planets, signs, houses, and aspects. In this practice, you will realize that you can channel the whole wheel of archetypes because they are the primal energetic patterns of all existence.

How would the above example change if Uranus was square or in opposition to Venus? Can you envision how Uranus would throw open the door and rush right up to Venus, tickler her, do crazy tricks for her, toss her into a dance of wild abandon, and then suddenly skate away, never to return? How would Neptune or Mars change the scene?

In film, theater, and other media this archetypal dance is always unfolding—we just don't use the planetary references. For the Pluto-Venus example, one only has to consider the archetype of the femme fatale, such as in *Basic Instinct*, or the attraction to money and power, such as in *Wall Street* and *The Devil's Advocate*, or the seductive, black eye makeup galore of Robert Smith of the Cure, or the hypnotic pull of total oblivion in the death metal mosh pit.

As you engage this practice, notice the importance nuances of different aspects—the flowing and friendly trine as opposed to the confrontational, awkward quality of square.

Chakr Astrology Meditation

The following form of experiential astrology is a meditation which guides you through the astrological planets and signs and their correlations with the chakra system. Please see the book cover for a depiction of this journey through the portals of cosmic energy.

Feel the Earth beneath you. Feel your roots sink down into the crystal core of the Earth. And in that nutrient-rich soil, begin to feel that crystal core slither as a serpent of light. In your mind's eye, begin to see that serpent of your consciousness slide along the red square of the root chakra, *Muladhara*. Here you vision the planet Saturn with its elegant rings, reflecting the stability of the first chakra. You are held here, you are safe and secure. In Saturn's masculine, fixed air sign of Aquarius, you idealize the appropriate systems of egalitarian governance. You concentrate ideas into practical forms. In Saturn's cardinal feminine earth sign of Capricorn, you build the structures to support the Aquarian vision. You fulfill a role which will sustain you and those of the extended human family.

With your root solid, your serpent awareness travels into the sacrum, *Swadhisthana* chakra. At this center of sexual delight, you are embraced by a succulent orange light. The fertile waters of this energy excite you. You feel a creative pulse surge through you as you behold the symbol of the diamond above the crescent moon. Here you amplify yourself in the reflection of the benefic giant Jupiter. In the feminine sign of Pisces, Jupiter bestows upon you an abundance of spiritual vision. Your artistic intuition overflows and your empathy grows. In the masculine, spiral fire energy of Sagittarius, you feel the thirst to expand your awareness into religious philosophies and foreign cultures. You receive Jupiter's marigold blessings as you step out on the hero's adventure to create the myth of your life.

Your serpent-awareness rises once again, slithering onto the seat of fire, *Manipura*, the dancing flame of the third chakra. You are absorbed into the golden ball of fire and morph into the shape of the downward facing triangle, marking your territory. Here you encounter the strength of your will in the force of Mars.

In its outer masculine form, Aries ignites you into fearless, uncompromising action. Then, the fixed water of Scorpio turns Mars inward in his feminine side. Here, passion and intensity compel a deeper expression of the life force. In Manipura-Mars, you develop a healthy ego, as your self is motivated to own and fulfill its desires.

The serpent of light's journey continues into the throbbing emerald green garden of *Anahata*, the fourth vortex of energy. Here, your heart pulses as the center of your light body, teaching you the wisdom of the air element. With your lungs, you breathe in the lessons of balance and compassionate consideration as you meet others on your journey. With the masculine, cardinal motion of Libra, Venus practices the art of partnership through patient listening. Unconditional love pours out as the infinite fountain of heart wisdom. In the fixed, feminine earth sign of Taurus, the juicy sensuality of Venus flows in eternal abundance. Your heart blossoms like springtime buds filing the air with their perfume of affectionate acceptance and nestled embrace.

The serpent spirals up from the heart to illuminate the throat chakra, *Vishuddha*. Here you perch upon the silver crescent within a white circle. You are surrounded by a sixteen petal lotus in the radiant sky blue of ether. Here, cosmic sound flows and information channels through the lips of messenger Mercury. In the mutable masculine air sign of Gemini, divine vibration is synthesized and the storyteller emerges. Cosmic wisdom unfolds in magical language as dimensions are sung into being. In the feminine, spiral earth sign of Virgo, Mercury refines all the lower chakras into their purified essence, allowing them to cultivate a path of humble service. In Virgo, you honor the web of life by inviting a sacred dialogue between all creatures of Gaia.

The serpent reaches up from the throat into the psychic center of the third eye, *Ajna*. Here you meditate in the center of the double-petaled, indigo lotus. With single-pointed vision, you are filled with purpose and vitality as you bask in the golden glow of the Sun. The fixed fire sign of Leo allows you to harness this spiritual vision. With crystalline clarity of perception, you ascend above time and space and feel the pulse of the creative source surge through you. Absorbed in the eternal vibration of AUM, your luminous focus opens a portal of shining radiance under the guidance of the Moon goddess. Here, you receive clairvoyant vision and intuitive knowing. In the cardinal feminine waters of Cancer, your sensitivity heightens and your sixth sense awakens. In Ajna, you transcend all dualities of masculine and feminine as you integrate the heavenly lights of the Sun and Moon.

At last the serpent coils in a sacred spiral around your crown, and you are showered in *Sahasrara*, the thousand petals of universal light. The illusion of self dissolves in pure, undifferentiated awareness. In supreme stillness, no evolutionary force is required. Absolute awareness annihilates the false concepts of the knower and the known. In the unified void, bliss omniscience pulsates in enlightened perfection.

Part 3:

Archetypal Initiations – Planetary Rites of Passage

The collective unconscious is not the multiple experience of a group. Rather, it is what is deeply inherently human, the patterns and symbols deeply rooted in humankind as a whole—this is Archetype—primordial imagination.

—Carl Jung

Two things fill the mind with ever new and increasing admiration and awe, the oftener and more steadily they are reflected on: the starry heavens above me and the moral law within me."

—Immanuel Kant, *Critique of Practical Reason*

I know that I am mortal by nature and ephemeral, but when I trace at my pleasure the windings to and fro of the heavenly bodies, I no longer touch earth with my feet. I stand in the presence of Zeus himself and take my fill of ambrosia.

—Ptolemy, *Tetrabiblos*

Chapter 12
Initiatory Cycles of the Planets

"Initiation," according to mythologist Michael Meade, "is the intentional creation of circumstances that cause a person to connect more deeply to what's already inside them, and more extensively to the unseen world of the imagination." (Meade 2006).

The whole of life is a sacred act, composed of smaller, sanctified moments, jeweled diamonds on the web of life. These holy gems are the resplendent reflections of the endless initiation process. We surf this birth canal at each moment, attempting to navigate the bardo of betwixt and between. No moment is truly still.

Every planetary transit encompasses one of these golden initiations. During these planetary rites of passage, the soul, whether child or adult can attune to the "origin," the ancient patterns of the human myth. The temple within the psyche is built at these sacred moments, as the archetypal *template* is viscerally experienced in the soul. Time as a linear process is transcended, as the mysterious Other World bleeds through experiences which transform the temporal into the personally meaningful. This is the purpose in understanding the mythical map of the human odyssey we describe in this section.

As we have discussed, the planets function as evolutionary impulses in our souls. Every planet represents a particular evolutionary cycle of growth, with specific years where the planet will *return* to where it was when you inhaled your first breath of life. These return cycles inscribe a mythical map which you can follow in the experience of incarnation. This planetary map marks significant rites of passage in your precious, embodied travels in this wondrous school of life. A planetary return in your chart invites you to fully engage, explore, and integrate that planetary archetype. In fact, the planet *initiates* you into the archetypal energy of that evolutionary force.

At these threshold moments, how then should you be guided? With foreknowledge of approaching cycles and hindsight into life's primary initiations, you can prevent the shadow expressions of the planet from manifesting, and work instead to harmonize and co-create with the most luminous potential of the planetary rite of passage.

As we age, maturity allows us to perceive similar planetary initiations from a vaster field of life experience. Our spiral of awareness widens and allows for an applied synthesis of accumulated wisdom. Each experience is a gift and a teaching, each step a lesson and journey towards increasing Wholeness.

As you apply the wisdom of these cycles, you refine your perception of the whole within the parts, a process which provides you the tools to piece together the seemingly disparate, yet fundamentally interdependent vocabulary of existence.

Most notably in the United States, as well as many other industrialized nations, children and the elderly are the least consulted and honored members of society. Yet, ironically, these are the very populations closest to the sacred realm of the spirit world—the multidimensional portals of birth and death. The wisdom of these elders' experiences could be used to guide the younger generations from innocence to maturity, for the stars sing in cycles. We are asked then, to listen with open hearts and a respect for history's teachings.

Because the inner or personal planets—the Sun, Moon, Venus, Mars, and Mercury—move so fast, their returns occur almost every year. One of the more famous of these returns is called the Solar Return, which I like to write as Soular Return. This is a special chart that helps you to foreshadow the major themes of the year ahead that will affect your life trajectory—the solar radiance of your unfolding life purpose.

When studying planetary initiation cycles, we give special focus to the socializing and transpersonal psychological forces in the birthchart. These are the planets which weave the individual experience into collective consciousness, and these include the evolutionary urges of Jupiter, Saturn, Chiron, Uranus, Neptune, Pluto, and the Nodes.

The following is a complete list of planetary returns and significant angles of initiation. We will then explore the biographies of famous initiates, and give practical tools for you to understand how these evolutionary thresholds can be successfully integrated into your psyche.

Below is a collection of keywords for the social and transpersonal planetary initiators. Any transit of these planets will trigger these evolutionary forces inside of us, with the force especially catalyzed during the planetary return or quadrature (90 degree square or 180 degree opposition) angle to its birth position.

Jupiter: Expansion, growth, optimism, good fortune, abundance, elevation, growth, progress, honor, magnitude, success, higher education, cultured thought, excess, extravagance, inflation

Saturn: Conservatism, restraint, limitation, heaviness, order, pressure, caution, realism, pessimism, status quo, discipline, convention, maturity, older generation

Chiron: Shaman, wounded healer, mentor, teacher, artistic craftsman, alchemy sacrifice, service, wisdom, unfairness, chronic conditions

Uranus: Sudden change, impulse for freedom, radical energy, creative epiphany, divine mind, intuition, rebellion, breakthrough, individuation, people's movements, eccentricity, originality, inventiveness, youth, defiance of authority, intellectual brilliance, innovation, lightning, electricity

Neptune: Spirituality, dreams, myths, unification, compassion, ego-dissolution, image, humanitarianism, idealism, romanticism, vision, transcendence, mysticism, illusion, fog, altered states of consciousness, psychoactive plants, pharmaceuticals, madness, depression

Pluto: Transformation, instinct, cathartic, empowerment, catalyzing, regenerating, cycle of death and rebirth, evolutionary, volcanic, overwhelming, intensity, resistance, control, dominance, depth, underworld, mysterious, occult, esoteric

Nodes: Past-life identities, habits of soul, innate gifts. Soul's quest, path of illumination and spiritual fulfillment

Sacred Life Cycles:
Your Mythical Map. Your Archetypal Initiations

Let us briefly explore what we may call the "dance of the spheres," hearkening back to Pythagoras' popular idea of the heavenly harmonies, the "music of the spheres."

The full cycle of Uranus around the sky and one's birthchart encompasses the breadth of a human life, 84 years. According to United Nations reports, in 2006, the average age for death tops off around 82 in countries such as Japan, Hong Kong, Iceland, and Switzerland. 84 is a product of the sacred numbers 12 and 7, and there are indeed seven full Jupiter cycles (12 years long) in one Uranus cycle. The 84 year cycle is also roughly composed of three full Saturn cycles (29.5 years). If we go further out from Uranus, we find that a Neptune orbit is exactly twice the duration (165 years) of a Uranus orbit, while a Pluto cycle of 250 years is exactly three times the length of the Uranus period.

It is these perfect, harmonic correspondences of the planetary orbits which humbled the great mystics, sages, and priestesses of ancient days. It awakened in them an awareness of a divine design. The cosmos was perceived as a poetic majesty as the heavens were received in the all their elegant grandeur. The sky was a symphony, imbued with significance to those who could hear the orchestar compose the archetypal theater.

The song of the Source pulses through you. The chorus of gods vibrates through you. What do they want for you? Here is their medicine and meditation, their invitation to you to celebrate the wonder of your incarnation.

INNOCENCE Phase

> 2   *Mars Return*:

You are terrible. You are two. You are Mars. You have found your will. You have unleashed the ferocious wail and whine of the Third Chakra. You empower yourself through passion and emotion.

> 4-5   *Ceres Return*:

Mama abandons, but returns. You are thrown from the nest and welcomed back. You learn to cry in front of strangers. You learn what nourishes and what does not. You care for dolls and stuffed animals and conceive great fantastic worlds where you are the Great Mother archetype.

AWARENESS Phase

> 7   *Saturn waxing square Saturn*:

You learn to write your name. You begin to read on your own, silent. You hear voices within yourself and from the outside world. Whose do you trust? You have your first responsibilities with homework. You differentiate yourself from others at school. You choose friendships and activities which then structure your vision of reality.

> 11-12   *1st Jupiter Return*:

You are able to care for yourself, you are even capable of caring for your little siblings. You begin babysitting, mowing lawns, earning money, and you find that one teacher that inspires you, that respects you. You wish to align yourself with something greater—you compete in sports or you cheer for your favorite team, you join an afterschool program, or you begin to voraciously read adventure and fantasy stories.

> 14-15 *Saturn opposite Saturn*:

If they have authority over you—parent, teacher, classmate, teammate—you rebel. You structure your consciousness in direct opposition to those who try and discipline you. You are the youth and the future. You learn to distrust those who claim some right to make rules you must follow. You may learn to cheat to get by, to go along with the program, to swim in the system, because even in your rebellion, you must still conform: you align yourself with a social label, and if you choose not to, you may be called a loner. But Saturnian solitude is your necessary friend, helping you to develop your own value system. You alter your consciousness with music, drugs, alcohol—you are trying to access your inner authority. Allow each experience to mature your soul.

Since Saturn rules the bones and skin, you experience the joys of acne, and learn the harsh lessons of patience. Your skateboarding, snowboarding, and all other sports also offer you ample opportunities to break bones.

You are now permitted to drive and must be shaped by the regulations of the law.

APPRENTICE Phase

18   *Jupiter opposite Jupiter:*

Your beliefs about reality our tested, your faith is challenged as you feel the call to grow beyond the world you have grown accustomed to. A course of study or a foreign philosophy facilitates your spiritual awakening.

19   *1st Lunar Nodal Return:*

A destined encounter, a significant teacher, a sexual awakening, a powerful relationship, an epiphanous depression, treasured information—experiences of profound proportions enter your life and change your perspectives and your path forever. You awaken to both the habits and the potentials within your soul.

20-22   *Uranus Square Uranus, waxing:*

Free at last! Free at last! Your parents are crude and boring oafs. You may patronize them, since you are the cutting edge now. You risk it all. You volunteer your independence or you get kicked in to it by the parental units. You embrace chaos, you endanger yourself, and you pull the Fool card. Perhaps you quit junior college or your enslaved job, you travel for the first time, you live on your own, or you move in with your lover—you do whatever allows you to assert your freedom.

21-22   *Saturn Waning Square:*

And yet, you must direct all that electric Uranian energy into some new form. Something must contain your independence. Who and what will you align yourself with? A crisis in consciousness ensues as you question who will be your comrades and what you will commit yourself to during your 20's? Is it time to "author" your own life, is it time to take on a spiritual name?

23-24   *2nd Jupiter Return:*

You feel the call pulsing through every cell—you must grow—and the invitation to expand throbs from every possible horizon. Is it a child that you birth, or do you birth yourself into the world, traveling and living abroad, and absorbing the ideas, philosophies, religions, mythologies, and cosmologies from places spanning time and space. You let go of limiting beliefs and any material things which prevent your faith and optimism from ascending. Perhaps you take on a spiritual name, perhaps you meet a guru, as Jupiter bestows his blessing in proportion to your ability to receive.

27   *Lunar Return:*

You light a candle to your soul. You cradle into fetal position. Issues with your mother surface. What was your birth like? Your ancestors, who were they? Why were you given your birth name? Intimations of past lives pour through. Your emotional body rebirths itself through whatever sign and house your moon fall in. In your increased sensitivity, your unfulfilled needs seek healing. Tears call you home. You dig for roots, community, and the connections that will nourish the depths of your being. Nurture yourself and be compassionate with the flow of your emotions

27-28   *1st Lunar Nodal Opposition:*

The Fates ripen and unhinge your soul. Karmic retribution creeps through. You sense the path of growth and the lure back to old ground. But you cannot root in this old story. You must listen to a deeper wisdom and invite in the unfamiliar. Anchor to the known, but tether your lasso to excitement of the opposite unknown.

28-30   *Saturn Return:*

The games of youth dissolve as fears of responsibility surface. The taskmaster of Time has reckoned- The house position of Saturn demands your absolute attention and your heart's undivided in-tension. The world seeks to sculpt you into your role, and you cower under the weight of stone, brick, mortar, as your consciousness is chiseled. How do you lay you foundation? What role shall we heave upon you? You must lay in your roots and play the part you choose—your profession, home, relationships, your role as a parent. No more blame now, as you "author" your own life. And what karma yoga, what path of action will you become the disciple of?

35-36   *3rd Jupiter Return:*

A teacher, a philosophy, or travels abroad feed your soul the medicine of expansion, and the song of inspiration. Create space and allow the vision of your heart's desire to guide you. Broadcast, publicize, and amplify your message to the world.

35-36 *Saturn Waxing Square Saturn:*

You question decisions made at the Saturn Return. You must reflect and adjust. How crooked or straight is the path have you taken?

This unique overlapping of the Jupiter and Saturn initiations allows you to awaken to an inspired teaching and take strategic steps towards your spiritual growth. Communicate your vision to everyone you know and co-operate with the cosmos in actualizing an enduring foundation in the material world. Those around you con-spire to help you build supportive structures to practically implement your vision. You can achieve great success, reward, honor, and respect if you work hard at following your bliss.

REGENERATIVE THRESHOLD Phase

36-38 *Pluto square Pluto*

The volcanic shadow erupts as repressed or traumatized aspects of yourself boil to the surface. Emotions flail in the lava of inner turmoil. You battle like some Olympian god for power, and you question who may betray you. Jealousy, manipulation, and control rear their ugly heads. You are invited to dance with your shadow through regenerative psychological work and journeys that confront your soul—shamanic work, past-life regression, psychotherapy, tantra, rebirthing, breathwork, and any kind of catharsis which allows you to cleanse, release, and renew.

38 *2nd Lunar Nodal Return*

Dancing with destiny, your soul can take evolutionary leaps forward as you attune to your path of spiritual illumination. Significant soul-contacts manifest in your life and mirror back to you your soul's potential as your intrinsic gifts greatly affect those around you. Reflect on the correspondence of events during your last nodal return, when you were 19.

40-42 *Uranus opposite Uranus:*

Emergency, emerge and see! The electric winds of change rush in. The future is urgently upon you now. On their wings, the sirens' songs of youth seduce you. You discard the old, outworn, stagnant structures—is it the job, the marriage, the home, or even your version of your own "identity?" Restless, you unchain yourself in Promethean rebellion from all unnecessary responsibilities. Is this revolution of your identity traumatizing or liberating? Is this crisis or opportunity? It's all in your perspective. Break the bonds, transcend the limits. Let go and surge forward into your authentic freedom, your self-actualization. Look to age 21 as your mentor and guide in how to proceed and what warnings to heed.

42-43 *Neptune square Neptune*

Behold, your spiritual longings for divine union and profound ecstasy have arisen. If you have curtained your creativity, you must now immerse yourself in your imagination. The unrealistic ideals of youth have faded and disappointment may dawn. Be not deceived, nor allow your boundaries to be easily permeated by dishonest, untrustworthy, or inept people. Words, excuses, explanations all dissolve as confusion and contradiction demand you to slow down. Enjoy the kiss of the mist on your face, and make no hasty decisions. Be strategic with your magnetism to drugs and alcohol as you are already more sensitive to the vibrations you swim in. A new, more pragmatic hope emanates from within some deep well as your inner life blossoms. Let the ego take a break through myth, poetry, film, meditation, and inspiring literature as the visionary dreamer and magical mystic awakens. It is time to forget time, and paint a song on the breeze. It is a time to hover on clouds, to detach from certainty, to listen to the whisper of the dream.

CRAFTSMAN Phase

43-44 *Saturn opposition*

The wild Uranian opposition and the mystifying Neptune square are now tempered. The exciting experiences, the spiritual revelations, the new dreams all ask to now be given form. Goals can be accomplished if you break through the blockages and allow rising frustrations to motivate you to re-adjust your foundation to build stable structures towards success.

47	*2nd Lunar Nodal Opposition*
48	*4th Jupiter Return*
49-50	*Chiron return, Saturn trine Saturn*

You feel yourself compelled to heal old wounds. As you confront your life's great traumas and trials, you understand earlier experiences of pain from a more holistic perspective. You recognize that those very events of this lifetime or others which may have been the most challenging can now serve as your greatest gifts in your ability to teach, mentor, or guide others.

51-52	*Saturn waning square Saturn*
54	*2nd Lunar Return; Saturn sextile Saturn*
55-56	*Uranus trine Uranus; Neptune trine Neptune*

Spirit renews as the true self blossoms through you. No longer encumbered by the fantasies, fears, and demands of youth, an invigorating freedom pulses through you as you transform to your ideal self image. Your unique abilities can now be honored, as old talents re-surface and mature under the guidance of a healthy emotional and mental framework. Parenting tasks minimize so that your creativity can soar to inspiring heights of the imagination. It is time to dream the vision of final years.

57	*3rd Lunar Nodal Return*

MASTERY – ELDER Phase

57-60 *2nd Saturn return*

In the mirror, you scour at the wrinkle, the gray hair. You remember the mirror of 15, acne and those early signs of Saturn. Bones and joints require continuous care as Saturn initiates you into the role of elder in the community. How have you cultivated gifts and matured your talents over the last thirty years. What wisdom can you share with others? Even as regrets and resentments may arise, recognize that experience is necessary to gain wisdom. Now you can begin to strategize a retirement that anchors you into a productive and peaceful final third of life.

60	*5th Jupiter Return*
	Birth Lunar Phase Return

63-64	*Uranus waning square Uranus*
66	*3rd Lunar Nodal Opposition*
67	*Saturn waxing square Saturn*
71-72	*6th Jupiter Return*
73-4	*Saturn opposite Saturn*
76	*4th Lunar Nodal Return*
81	*Saturn waning square Saturn*

WIZARDRY Phase

82-84   *Neptune opposite Neptune, Uranus Return, 7th Jupiter Return*
The great myth of your life has unfolded. It is time to review, reflect, to send gratitude and forgiveness. You wonder if your whole life was in fact a dream, as memories are painted across your consciousness in an impressionistic mirage. A profound reversal takes place as the events of your life which seemed to sparkle with so much importance, now don't seem to glitter with such gold. But matters which once seemed unfortunate are now perceived in a blinding spiritual light of purpose and blessing. You question your unique contribution to the whole of life. How did you fare on the hero's journey of your incarnation?

With humility and honorable pride, you can recognize that there was no failure, only opportunities to evolve, to weave a sacred web with others, or to disconnect from the ego's desires. You can offer overflowing fountains of wisdom to others through memoir, storytelling, and wise counsel as you now comprehend the spiritual unity of all life. You feel most kindred with the innocence of the infant. The illuminated mystic can awaken within and prepare you to meet your maker.

85	*4th Lunar Nodal Opposition*
86-90	*3rd Saturn Return*

Chapter 13
Famous Examples of Planetary Initiations

Jupiter Return: 11-12, 23-24, 35-6, 47-8, 59-60, 71-72, 83-84

Success and recognition, optimism and opportunity are the hallmarks of the Jupiter return, occurring every twelve years.

Many travel around the world during this cycle of growth, inspired by the exotic flavors of foreign lands and the treasures of deeply spiritual cultures.

No example of Jupiter's expansive and limitless potential is quite as potent as Barack Obama. He took the oath of office as the first African American U.S. president at the age of 48, within a week of his exact Jupiter return. His Jupiter is in the sign of idealism and "hope," Aquarius, and he ran his whole campaign on the optimistic, Jupiterian mantra of "Yes, we can," and the one word slogan of "Hope."

In the media, the Jupiter cycle often opens us to our big break and increased popularity. Actor Johnny Depp began his role on the 1980's hit *21 Jump Street* during his second Jupiter Return, making him into a reluctant teen idol, and launching a massively successful acting career. Actor Matthew Broderick played a rather "jovial" character in his most famous role as Ferris in *Ferris Bueller's Day Off*. The limitless possibilities of life, the fortune and luck, the popularity of Ferris Bueller as a character, all signify the grand and benevolent Jupiterian energy in Broderick's life at the time. John Travolta was catapulted into pop consciousness through two films that came in his 23rd and 24th birthday, right at the second Jupiter return, *Saturday Night Fever* and *Grease*. Musicals, such as Grease, have a grandiose, Jupiterian flair to them and the extreme style and extravagant tastes of disco in *Saturday Night Fever* recall Jupiter's boisterous energy as well. In the film, Tony Manero, played by Travolta, became the king (Jupiter/Zeus) of the discotheque. Even the hand moves of disco seem to emulate the archer of Jupiter's ruling sign Sagittarius.

At his third Jupiter return, writer Daniel Pinchbeck published *Breaking Open the Head: A Psychedelic Journey into the Heart of Contemporary Shamanism*. In the book, Pinchbeck described his Jupiterian travels abroad to participate in healing ceremonies with plant medicines in the Amazon jungle, in West Africa, and his expansive adventures at the Burning Man festival. Jupiter rules all foreign and exotic terrains, so publishing about these travels during this cycle correlates perfectly. After the publishing of this book in 2002, Pinchbeck was featured on the radio show Coast to Coast AM. Both publishing and broadcasting are ruled by Jupiter. Lastly, integral philosopher Ken Wilber published *The Spectrum of Consciousness*, at his second Jupiter return at the age of 24, synthesizing much of the world's spiritual systems into a holistic tapestry of the process of self-reflective awareness. Jupiter is concerned with Wilber's topics—the worlds religious and philosophical systems.

Saturn Return: 28-30, 58-60, 88-90

In his book, *Cosmos and Psyche*, archetypal astrologer Richard Tarnas writes, "In examining many hundreds of individual biographies I regularly observed that the succeeding three decades—the persons' thirties, forties, and fifties—could have been decisively shaped by the structural transformations that took place during the first Saturn return transit between the ages of twenty-eight and thirty" (2006, 121). Many artists, philosophers, musicians, and other cultural creatives deliver their works to the public sphere for the first time, essentially defining their personalities and becoming recognized, in what Tarnas calls, a "biographical crystallization." In was during his first Saturn Return, for example, that Beethoven composed his first symphony and gave his first public concert.

Writer Jack Kerouac completed his most famous work *On the Road*, at 29. Within weeks of Oprah's 30th birthday, the first airing of the Oprah Winfrey show occurred, engraving her personality into the mainstream culture. Frederick Engels was 28 and Carl Marx 30 when they published *The Communist Manifesto*. Steven Spielberg produced and directed two of his most famous films, hallmarks in the history of cinema, filled with the taboo and edgy themes that would prevail throughout his career. *Jaws* and *Close Encounters of the Third Kind*, released in 1977 and 1978, served as a template for Spielberg's career and cemented him as a Hollywood icon.

Besides playing the pivotal role in the development of our career, the Saturn Return gives a sense of gravity to our life and our relationships as we reflect on the conditioning of family, social class, education, and religion. Life-changing and life-shaping decisions, often involving endings, occur with the Saturn return as one matures their perspectives on what is considered tangible and real.

Actress Angelina Jolie divorced her husband Billy Bob Thornton during her Saturn return, stating "It took me by surprise, too, because overnight, we totally changed. I think one day we had just nothing in common. And it's scary but...I think it can happen when you get involved and you don't know yourself yet." By the end of her Saturn return, the stories circulated of her involvement with Brad Pitt, with whom she now shares a family. It was also during these critical Saturn return years that Jolie's humanitarian work overseas hit its peak, as she traveled on field missions to meet with refugees from places such as Sudan, Afghanistan, and Thailand. Saturn helped to give her focus and a cause to work diligently for.

Often, a personal crisis ensues with Saturn cycles, involving an encounter with mortality. During his first Saturn return, at the age of 29, spiritual teacher

Eckhart Tolle, experienced a total breakdown that led to a spiritual epiphany he describes as an "inner transformation." He woke up in the middle of the night with a bout of serious depression so painful he no longer wanted to live. He then asked himself, in his words:

> Who is the 'I' that cannot live with the self? What is the self? I felt drawn into a void. I didn't know at the time that what really happened was the mind-made self, with its heaviness, its problems, that lives between the unsatisfying past and the fearful future, collapse. It dissolved. The next morning I woke up, and everything was so peaceful. The peace was there because there was no self. Just a sense of presence or 'beingness'…. (Scobie, 2003)

Intense depression, the heaviness of the past, the fears of future responsibilities—all mark the existential contraction which can occur with the Saturn return. But simultaneously, one can build resilience and maturation in the process and develop an enduring philosophical perspective. For Tolle, the revelations from his Saturn return breakdown led him to a path as a spiritual teacher culminating one full Saturn cycle later, at his second Saturn return, when he published his second book *A New Earth*, which spent nearly a year on the New York Times Bestseller list. At the close of his Saturn return, Oprah Winfrey then partnered with Tolle for a series of instructional webinars.

Pluto square Pluto: 36-38

At the age of 38, during his Pluto square Pluto and his Nodal Return, Larry Harvey joined with friends on the beaches of San Francisco in 1986. With an effigy to a past love, they burned through all of the Plutonian emotions of jealousy, possessiveness, obsession, and manipulation—they burned through the Shadow they confronted in the cleansing flames. And so began Burning Man. Twenty years later, 50,000 people join together annually for a week of Plutonian catharsis, regeneration, and transformation by creating and destroying epic pieces of inspiring artwork with fire. Appropriately, Harvey's Pluto is in Leo, a fixed fire sign—the archetype of the performer, artist, and playful, solar child. His North Node, the energy of his Nodal Return, is in the sign of Taurus - the dancer, the musician, the builder, and the appreciator of all sensual and aesthetic experiences.

Uranus Opposition: 40-42

When we think of the infamous phrase, "midlife crisis," we are really referring to a collection of archetypal forces and evolutionary urges which stack up on themselves beginning around the age of 37 and continuing to about 44, peaking in intensity with the Uranus opposition between the ages of 40-42.

We can consider this the "full moon" moment of the personal Uranus transit cycle. The Uranian urge is to unchain ourselves from any status quo that has stagnated us. By the nature of the opposition, we sometimes feel drawn to pull a "180" on our life up to that point. Freedom becomes of paramount importance, eclipsing the needs of family, work, or any other responsibilities which don't directly help to liberate us from our own limiting definitions of who we are. An irritation in the soul impatiently delivers a wake-up call to those areas of our lives in which we have not been authentically ourselves. So we seek to recover the promise of our youth. We are magnetized towards more risky behavior, invoking the archetype of Uranus' tarot card, The Fool. We embrace accelerated change, and sudden, emancipatory revelations are possible if we allow our intuition to guide us at this time towards a path of self-actualization. This is the peak opportunity for our unique genius to break through, the unhindered and unrestricted Promethean impulse to rebel, revolt, innovate, and achieve creatively.

The pinnacle works of great scientists, inventors, psychologists, philosophers, and artists often occur during this cycle. Galileo, Descartes, and Newton all culminated their revolutionary works during their Uranus opposition, works that literally shifted the paradigms of our perspectives on reality.

The man who discovered Uranus, William Herschel, actually did so during his Uranus opposition in 1781. Remarkably, he died at the age of 84, just as Uranus completed its full rotation around his chart.

Friedrich Nietzsche wrote his seminal work, *Thus Spoke Zarathustra* during his Uranus opposition. In this work, he described the "Ubermensche"—a Promethean figure associated with Uranian urges. The Ubermensche is the overman seeking to incessantly overcome himself.

Sigmund Freud's Uranus opposition occurred between 1895-1897, a period during which he was flooded with revelatory discoveries which eventually seeded psychoanalysis. During this time he began writing *The Interpretation of Dreams* and stated, "Insight such as this falls to one's lot but once in a lifetime.

For psychologist, Carl Jung, the years 1914-1917 comprised his Uranus opposition, a time in his life he claimed to be the most crucial in his career. It was during this period when Jung delved most deeply into his own self-analysis, arriving at his concepts of the collective unconscious, the process of individuation, the Self, and the inner objectivity of psychic reality.

Importantly, both Jung and Freud lived to the fulfillment of their Uranus return. Freud died just shortly after his, but before this was able to complete his definitive summary of psychoanalytic theory, *An Outline of Psychoanalysis*. Jung contemplated the totality of his life, the self-actualized existence, in his final book, *Memories, Dreams, and Reflections*, written at his Uranus return, the year before he died. In both cases, the final works of these great innovators demonstrated the integration of their lives' revolutionary work, a testament to the potential each of us have to honor the authentically lived individual life with the aid of Uranus.

Rebellion and individual rights are also key Uranian themes, highlighted in the Uranus opposition of Rosa Parks and Betty Friedan. In an act of Uranian defiance, Parks refused to leave her seat on the bus in Montgomery, Alabama and helped to catalyze the civil rights movement. In 1962, Betty Friedan published *The Feminine Mystique* during her Uranus opposition, helping to launch the modern feminist movement.

As his Uranus return which began at age 40, writer Daniel Pinchbeck published one of the most influential cultural studies of the new millennium, *2012: The Return of Quetzalcoatl*, in which he investigated a global transformation of consciousness resulting in a new perception of time and space. The edgy subjects of crop circles, aliens, and psychedelics all eloquently portray common Uranian themes of the radical experiences that challenge our versions of reality and the possibilities of transcendent mentalities communicating to and through humans.

The overarching topic of prophecy in Pinchbeck's book is also highly Uranian as it involves the access to the higher mind and how cultures and individuals will receive enlightened flashes of intuitive insight, as if Prometheus is passing the torch down from the heavens directly into the vessel of the human mind.

Shortly after the publication of the book, Pinchbeck began an online publication called Reality Sandwich, in which he invokes the Uranian cycle's desire for innovation and breakthrough creativity, seeking to offer "a new paradigm for a planetary culture." Immediately following this, Pinchbeck also helped to formulate Evolver.net, an online profile group for Uranian individuals, such as, visionaries, artists, writers, and others interested in exploring the various fields of consciousness through discussion groups, blogs, and sustainable commerce.

Lastly, the mystical Jewish Kabbalah was never taught until one was the age of 40, the same time when the Uranus opposition begins. The Kabbalah is an esoteric system of profound wisdom teachings, relating the connection between the eternal and mysterious Creator and the mortal and finite universe. In presenting teachings concerned not only with ontology and cosmology, but also methods to attain spiritual realization through this understanding, Kabbalah is directly linked to the transmissions of the higher mind represented by Uranus.

Chiron Return: 49-50

The Chiron Return is our opportunity to shift our personal stories of wounding, to understand them in a greater context of meaning, and to assist others through a process of mentorship. We can step into the higher octave of our life purpose during this critical passage.

Earlier we mentioned Eckhart Tolle's powerful Saturn return initiation. It is at Tolle's Chiron return, at 50, when he published *The Power of Now*, which made him an instant teacher and guide to those seeking transformation in their lives. When Tolle speaks, he almost sounds how one would imagine Chiron, the wise centaur, would sound—with a serious, commanding tone, but also an ironic chuckle.

If we do not answer the invitation at the Chiron return to heal our wounds, we can sometimes go deeper into the wound, and inflict it fatally ourselves. This was the case with Michael Jackson, who died within months of his exact Chiron return. His Chiron was in the fourth house of family and upbringing, signifying the pressures and intensity from his father to groom a pop-star at such a young age. His desires to create Neverland and to surround himself with youth spoke of unhealed childhood wounds.

Astrology of the Avatars: Planetary Initiations of Religious Icons

Some people argue against the validity of Christ's existence, while some will argue over the dates for specific events in the life of Siddhartha the Buddha or the Prophet Muhammad. But in the majority of the stories that exist, the time-tables for these great religious leaders are astrologically aligned with the specific planetary initiations of which we have been speaking. Behind the veil of these avatars' biographical lives lies a mythical fact resonant with certain key archetypal themes we all experience at the same critical junctures in our lives.

One of the most famous stories of the Gospels involves the young Jesus teaching in the synagogue at the tender age of twelve. Apparently, his parents Joseph and Mary thought that Jesus was accompanying them after the Feast of Passover, when in actuality he stayed behind to converse, study, and teach with the rabbis in the synagogue. Jupiter is the "guru," the teacher, the source of faith and religious inspiration. Hence, at this age, Jesus studied and conversed with the religious community of the time.

As Jesus completed his Saturn return at age 30, he stepped out into the world to begin his mission of teaching and healing. It was this portion of Jesus' life which the majority of his biography centers around. Also, in reading the Torah, we find that the Jewish teachers would never begin their rabbinical teaching until the age of 30.

At the age of 29, Prince Siddhartha left his palace in order to meet his subjects. Despite his father's effort to remove the sick, aged, and suffering from the public view, Siddhartha encountered mortality through a variety of Saturnian images—an old man, a diseased person, a decaying corpse, and an ascetic. His charioteer Channa delivered him the harsh Saturnian reality check that eventually all people would grow old, get sick, and die. Deeply disturbed by these revelations, Siddhartha abandoned the conditions of his royal life altogether and became an ascetic.

At the age of 35, Siddhartha sat under the Bodhi tree, vowing to not arise until he found the Truth. After 49 days, Siddhartha became the Buddha, the "awakened one" attaining enlightenment about the nature of suffering, its causes, and the steps necessary to eliminate it. When two merchants found the Buddha shortly after his enlightenment, he joined them and began his teaching.

Between the ages of 35 and 36, two planetary initiations overlap, that of the Saturn square to itself, and Jupiter's return to its natal position. With the combination of Jupiter and Saturn, one can learn how to give form and structure to philosophical and religious ideas that can have an enduring effect and extensive reach.

In addition, it is revealing to investigate the concept of the 49th day, when the Buddha attained enlightenment. If we think of the 49th day on a fractal level and allow one day to be equated with one year, we arrive at the 49th year of life. One one level, the 49th year follows the activation of the teacher and expansive wisdom of the fourth Jupiter cycle at 48. Additionally, the 49th year is another Saturn cycle, the waning square signifying a crisis in consciousness. And most importantly, age 49 marks the crucial activation of the higher life purpose, the triggering of the mentor and guide archetype at the Chiron return.

Lastly, the prophet Muhammad lived a relatively normal existence as a merchant and shepherd until his Uranus opposition. At the age of 40, he began receiving revelations in a cave where he went for meditation and reflection. In brilliant flashes of illumination, the divine mind was said to speak through the Angel Gabriel to Muhammad, overwhelming him with religious insight. Three years after this, after his Uranus opposition ended, Muhammad started preaching these revelations publicly.

Chapter 14
Planetary Cycles:
Timemap, Path of Compassion, and Evolved Communication

Each of these rites of passages opens a window into your incarnating soul's evolutionary lessons. These are collective, universal occurrences that modify our spiritual awareness. The human story unfurls as a song of glory, as a myth of magic and meaning in the sacred act of initiation.

Investigating the nature of these evolutionary initiations provides you with a profound tool of empathy and understanding. Simply by knowing these evolutionary lessons intrinsic to various stages of life, you become able to relate more compassionately with your fellow beings. You can gaze directly into the spiritual needs invoked by a planetary initiation as it relates to the lives of your parents, your children, your friends, your lovers, and those who might challenge you in life.

One of the first questions I often ask people is their age. Instead of being rude, this question actually opens the door into this empathic pathway. With this information, I can understand in what initiation they currently find themselves, as well as what passage they have just traveled through or will soon enter. Then I can guide our conversation around the archetypal themes represented by the particular planets involved. If we can learn to allow these "timemaps" to inform our social interactions, we can then all become emissaries of the gods, assistants on the journey of awakening for our fellow human travelers.

By implementing the wisdom of these universal cycles in your life then, you can understand and empathize with the cycles of your loved ones. You can see how best to support their rites of passage, to assist in their initiatory processes, and most importantly, to be able to ask for appropriate compassion and guidance during your own cycles.

helping Spirits, Threshold Moments

When we begin to see the links, *through time*, between repeating evolutionary themes, we can even learn who may be the best mentor for one going through an earlier cycle. For instance, a person who is around 24 or 36 could be an ideal guide for an 11-12 year old, as each is being initiated through a Jupiter cycle. There will be a natural resonance as the themes of expansion, foreign culture and philosophy, vaster horizons of awareness, and inspired learning will be highlighted. Likewise, everyone who is roughly seven years apart in age, will be experiencing a similar Saturn initiation. Concerns about grounding, discipline, one's role in the world, and the maturing of one's path of integrity will be experienced by all undergoing a Saturn cycle. Imagine how the second Saturn return initiate at ages 58-60 could apply their wisdom by advising the first Saturn return initiate. Elders could share their wisdom by reflecting on their own journey through the first cycle—including regrets or disappointments, how they achieved success through a commitment to hard work, and the need to abandon certain lifestyle practices in order to master others. And even if one is not experiencing the same cycle, just through understanding the purpose of another's planetary initiation passage, we can each play the role of helping spirit at another's threshold transition.

Life Review

Ultimately, study of planetary initiations lends itself to cyclical "life review." In his profound book, *A Year to Live*, long time hospice provider and practicing Buddhist Stephen Levine calls the Life Review a "healing contemplation," which both allows us to honor our individual existence and also to let it go. "Part of truly preparing for death is the eventual letting go of our story line and looking back on our life with equanimity and a sense of completion." (Levine 1997, 76-80) Imagine how much meaning these planetary rites of passage can provide for one who is dying. Imagine the healing potential of placing an entire life into the cosmic context of archetypal initiations. When we do, memory opens a pathway to mending the chaos of our lives and understanding the spiritual framework universally experienced in the human journey. This process helps us to complete the unfinished stories.

In retrospect, you can look back to previous initiation cycles to understand the evolutionary drives which were guiding you at that time. This "temporal distance" can help to uncloud and heal your perspectives, as the present moment is so often limited by our ego-reactions. Through this astrological means of reflection, you can be instructed more clearly as you project your life into the future. You can prepare for the planetary wave about to crest in your life, instead of being dragged into the undertow, ignorant of just what the hell is going on and how best to survive and thrive. This timemap can assist you in understanding the intention of a particular initiation and how best to harmonize with the planetary force or forces at play.

When to Do the Life Review

Amends feed the heart and quiet the mind.

—Stephen Levine

The mind creates the abyss and the heart crosses it.

—Nisargadatta

To study your life is to honor the educational nature of embodiment. An astrological lens into the ebb and flow of your life lessons helps you to fine-tune your perceptions in order to appreciate the nuanced instructions of the planetary teacher.

The whole life can be perceived as a sacred teaching delivering you to the holy moment of the life review—when the soul at last has an opportunity to exist in grateful reflection and humble introspection. But you need not wait until your final breaths to receive the gift of the life review and the cosmic instruction on your journey through your planetary rites of passage. There are teachings and practices in many traditions to help prepare for this "final rite of passage." For example, many Tibetan Buddhists practice the "transference of consciousness," called Phowa, each night before they go to bed, in preparation for the eventual experience of death.

You might ask: When should I do these life reviews? One of the most appropriate times of the year to do a life review is during the Sun's passage through your fourth house. The fourth house is the deep well of your being, the soul-vision of your personal mythos. Thus, the Sun's journey through here for thirty days connects you with a very ancient part of your soul. Also, when the Sun journeys through your twelfth house, you are connected to the cosmos at large. During this month, your consciousness is naturally attuned to reflection, contemplation, archetypes, and myth, and you are preparing to rebirth in some sense once the Sun crosses your Ascendant. The life review can be an important tool for the next year's conscious evolution. Lastly, the birthday Solar Return is always a powerful time for both retrospective and future analysis, as your vitality is renewed each year at this sacred time.

To begin a life review process, you can create a special journal to study your rites of passage. You might label it Planetary Initiations or Sacred Life Cycles.

Begin by allowing a dialogue to surface between you and each of the planetary rites of passage we have mentioned above. You can use photographs, old journals, previous e-mails, and the power of memory and meditation to venture back through your initiation cycles. With these tools, look back at your life so far and see how you harmonized with these rites of passage. What cycles are just ahead of you? How can you apply the wisdom of the previous rite of passage toward the spiritual promise of the next initiation?

In your process of life review, in that delicate dance with memory, you meet with old friends and lovers. Thus, many powerful emotions will likely arise.

But remember that reflection does not need to lead to reaction, especially as you invoke the witness of your higher self. The goal is to be mindful as you exercise this self-transparency. This will allow you to finish conversations with forgiveness, resolve relationships with gratitude, and honor your own process of evolution.

Naturally, it will be helpful to compare your own rites of passage with those of loved ones in order to understand how similar initiation cycles are experienced. In this way, you can perceive the various textures of the planetary archetypes in their many modes of manifestation.

In this process, resentments and disappointments may arise, either directed towards yourself or others. Perhaps you tried to fight that initiation and do the opposite, perhaps your lover or parent did not support that initiation at all. These more difficult reflections afford you an opportunity for healing through forgiveness and compassion. Each of us, works only with the tools of consciousness we have cultivated until a certain moment, and we are constantly conditioned by our environments. This is important to remember as difficult memories arise. As Steven Levine writes, the life review is a "regathering of awareness to illuminate the past with a new mercy." (Levine 78)

As you reflect on each planetary initiation, the goal is to bless the event that came into your life at that time. Consider it a gift from that planetary archetype. A part of your soul desired to awaken through the specific events and individuals who arose into your consciousness in those threshold moments. Who showed up at that time and how were they angelic messengers for you, planetary emissaries sent to assist your initiations? And also, how have you held vigil and kept prayer at other's rites of passage? Send loving gratitude to these circumstances, these people, and to yourself for the willingness to answer the call of spirit.

What archetypal flavor did that planet present to you and how did you respond? Did you spit out or did you savor that dish? Did you go on a planetary fast and try to push that evolutionary plate away, claiming "no thanks, I'm not ready for this." Or did you ask for seconds, demand dessert, and drink in the medicine of that initiation?

In looking ahead, you can ask when that planetary force will knock again. How are you prepared? How does studying your life experiences from this perspective teach you the nature of that universal evolutionary urge breathing through you? Who do you know who is entering the cycle from which you have just come? How can you offer them counsel and perspective? Who do you know who has recently journeyed through the rite of passage you will soon enter? What can they teach you? Knowing the approaching planet's energy, what kinds of questions can you direct towards them? Can you mentor someone going through a similar planetary cycle, an earlier Jupiter, Saturn, or Uranus cycle perhaps? If you are 40-42, who's showing up around 21? How is Uranus initiating you both? If you are 58-60, how can you work with someone 28-30? What would you have wanted to know at their age?

You see that one who is 72 can relate to one who is 11-12, or 23-24 as they both experience their Jupiter Return. Age, in this perspective, is transformed. The same flavor of experiences can emerge across the ages. Age, however, provides the accumulation of experiences which can allow for more wisdom to be integrated, and hopefully a more conscious experience of that planetary initiation.

The earliest planetary initiations involve innocence, naiveté, and purity in the expression of that planetary energy. The later cycles tend to take on a more serious and contemplative tone, as your ability to maturely respond to the initiations and your capacity to contribute positively to the collective is evaluated.

In this process, the goal is to become ancient quickly, to be ready to start again, to will the initiatory experience that connects you back to the original templates and the primordial mind.

The spread of Alzheimer's wasn't happening 80 years ago. There is no separation between what's happening in the brain and what's happening in the culture. In our obsession with the future, we are losing our ability to allow the past to inform and guide us. If applied appropriately, the utilization of planetary initiation cycles will naturally create an increased capacity for intergenerational dialogues, allowing the innocence of youth and the wisdom of age to guide us just as powerfully as those in the middle third of their lives. Imagine the counsels we could have if those undergoing certain initiations speak on behalf of the planet to assist others during that life cycle.

"Humans," as Michael Meade says, "are the agents of epiphany," when their intention is given to the moment and their attention is given to "the real," the world behind forms (2006). These moments are the eruptions of apocalypse, a word which means, "to lift the veil." When we unveil the apparently normal, and perceive the archetypal patterns beneath, a numinous experience occurs. The mundane is transcended, the sacred beheld, the divine design unleashed in epiphany. The majesty of the human myth unfolds. Honoring our glorious story is essential, since, "When we lose mythic sense, nothing makes sense." (Meade 2006).

Points to Remember in Studying Planetary Initiations

When investigating our rites of passage, you should remember two very important points. First, whether in reflection upon the past or preparation for the future, you should remember that no planetary initiation is an island, since many transits overlap. For example, just because you are about to enter an inspiring and expansive Jupiter cycle, remember that you may also have two or three overwhelming and intense Pluto transits occurring simultaneously. Or when Uranus is telling you to break free and liberate yourself, remember that Saturn may also be transiting your Sun or Moon, bringing incredible weight, pressure, and responsibility into your life.

All of these transits are evolutionary triggers and initiatory experiences. What we have done in this section is allow you to see the evolutionary skeleton of life through the consistent, recurring planetary cycles. This is an archetypal map of the human psyche unfolding in space and time.

Secondly, when studying your planetary returns, or oppositions, it is important to remember not only the house that planet occupies in your birthchart, but also the area of life that planet rules. That house will be significantly affected in your life. As you study previous rites of passage or prepare for incoming initiations, this point is helpful to consider to more specifically understand the purpose of a particular initiation.

For instance, Saturn rules my ninth house of philosophy, cosmology, broadcasting, and foreign travel. It also rules my tenth house of vocation and career. During my Saturn return, I traveled to study and absorb the astrological cosmology and techniques. I chose to become a professional astrologer who would both travel to teach as well as publish books on or referencing the astrological language. Also, my Saturn is in the fourth house of roots and home. Over the duration of my Saturn return, I moved consistently trying to find my home, finally arriving at my current location in Colorado at the tail end of my Saturn Return. Thus, knowing the house that your planetary cycle rules and the house where the planet is located in your birthchart helps you to specify the textures of your initiation. Refer to the earlier section on the planets for keys into sign rulership.

Chapter 15
harmonic Synchronization

With the life-map of planetary initiations, and the attributes listed in the StArchetypal Theater section, you are equipped to fully harmonize with incoming rites of passage. I would like to give some examples of how you could add the archetypal ingredients to willfully invite these planetary initiations as an act of sympathetic magic, so that your intentions and consciousness can mirror the evolutionary passage which approaches. The goal is for you to create these rites yourself. These are suggestions to inspire you to synthesize your own archetypal verse into a harmonic tapestry of personal meaning.

Sympathetic Magic with Planetary Initiations

Relocation Astrology and Rites of Passage

As a relocation astrologer, I recommend places that will support the evolutionary initiations individuals are undergoing at that time. Sometimes, I will suggest that people travel to a location on the earth where the energy of their current planetary initiator is the strongest. Both astrologer and client must be responsible in this practice, for we must consider the condition of that planet in your birthchart to decipher just how much we wish to invoke that energy even more. If you seek to fully embrace the initiation cycle, traveling to a resonant planetary line can be a powerful catalyst towards fulfilling your rite of passage. On the other hand, we may wish to avoid that line completely because the planet in your birthchart is giving you enough strife as it is. This is why I recommend each person receive at least a few relocation astrology readings in their life. It is helpful to have one's radar attuned to these lines so that you can best harmonize with your cycles.

Jupiter Return: 11-12, 23-24, 35-6, 47-8, 59-60, 71-72, 83-84

As you approach a Jupiter return, it is important to create space, to envision what you truly want so that Jupiter may bestow you his blessings. It is an ideal time to plan travels abroad. Where will in-spire you? Literally, which place calls you as a pilgrim, where can your faith grow, and your spirit vitalize? If you cannot travel abroad, consider what have you always wanted to learn and study? Where can you take classes and feel yourself expand the horizons of your awareness?

Find an oak tree to revere. Laugh as you prance around it in huge bounds and leaps to gypsy and fusion music. Light some sandalwood incense, carry a sacred piece of turquoise with you, meditate with the Jupiter collage and perform the Jupiter mantra during this cycle.

Perhaps you can make a special weekly date on Thursday night, Jupiter's night, to indulge in foreign cuisine with optimistic friends. In all matters, remember to trust your intuition.

Uranus Square or Opposition: 20-22, 40-42, 62-64

The Fool card in the Tarot deck shall be your guide as you invite your most unique forms of self-expression to come out and play. Allow yourself to be as weird and eccentric as possible, and don't expect anyone to "get it." You will not seem "normal," to those who know you, for this is your time to invoke the Mad Hatter and Mad Scientist. You are re-inventing yourself, and that's why your sudden outbursts and unexpected behavior confuses others and often yourself.

Be crazy enough to be fully YOU, as you discover your unique contribution to the planet. Study alien abductions and string theory while listening to jazz, discordant music, or electronic breakbeats. You may find yourself equally as drawn to the circus, the strip club, the psychedelic festival, or the new texts on artificial intelligence and neuroscience. Free your mind and the child inside. Be fascinated, be shocking, become more authentically your individual being.

Chiron Return: 49-50

Where you can step into the higher octave of your life purpose? What wounds do you still carry? Where is their source? Allow yourself during this cycle to seek out counsel from many different modalities of healing—regression therapy, hypnotherapy, astrology, EFT (Emotional Freedom Technique), bodywork.

Allow the feelings of alienation, the orphaned parts of yourself, to emerge into the light. Seek out mentors like Yoda, and all you trust in the healing profession. As you do this, you will recognize where your own healing gifts lie, or how to better apply them in an act of sacred service to humanity and the earth.

Pluto Square Pluto: 36-38

This is your opportunity to call in your higher witness as you watch all your resistances to surrender rear their ugly heads. Where are you "invisible" to yourself, unconscious of your motivations and surprised by the intensity of your reactions? This is your clue into the soul-transforming work required during this powerful cycle. Study the works of great psychotherapists and psychoanalysts—Freud, Jung,

Edinger, Hillman, Grof. But remember that you must go beyond mental analysis. Pluto demands a visceral and volcanic catharsis. Seek out a trusted healer to guide you through breathwork, past life regression, rebirthing, plant medicine ceremonies, as you explore the Tantric practices of transmutation from around the world. For you are on an alchemical journey during this cycle and are shifting the vibration of every one of your cells.

You can channel the dark emotions that begin to surface in you by listening to more intense music and watching films that frighten you or focus on overpowering extremes of emotional experience. Study the process of the caterpillar morphing into the butterfly and how the snake sheds its skin. Spend some time in caves or cemeteries and allow yourself to contemplate your death as you study various cultures' perceptions of that great passage into the Beyond. This is an ideal time to practice the life-review and make peace with all who have traveled with you during this life.

Also, be gentle on yourself during this regenerative cycle, as you often only perceive the gritty and negative aspects of life. Remember to take a break—from blame, from guilt, and from all the intensity of such deep soul-work.

Neptune Square Neptune: 42-44

Give yourself permission to spend full weekends listening to classical music and film scores, while immersing in novels and poetry—where fantasy and narrative imagination send your consciousness sailing into other dimensions. Bring your journal, sketchbook, camera, or guitar to your island paradise and allow the muse to move through you, in uncensored, spontaneous stream-of-consciousness. Cultivate a relationship with the endless expanse of the ocean. Savor the delicacies of the sea, scuba dive, and sway with the tide.

Allow memory and dreams to surface and guide you into your soul's connection with the web of life. As much as you can, let go of material concerns and expect little from others. Donate your time and energy to serving the less fortunate, and allow your spirit to blossom.

Begin a daily meditation practice. Trust that guides are singing through synchronicity as all logic seems to dissolve away. Mystic and mythic texts will reflect the truth your heart longs to behold, a truth which transcends ego and remembers its source.

Nodal Return and Reversal: 19, 27, 38, 47, 57, 72

Compose your life so that you surround yourself with the people, situations, and places which allow you to feed upon the archetypal flavors of the North Node, while sharing the South Node gifts you intrinsically possess. Give special attention the house and sign of the nodes, and to any planets squaring the nodes. These planets are evolutionary gatekeepers, poised at the threshold of your soul's ability to merge its past and future into a unified whole. The nodal cycles are your time to witness the tendency to fall back on familiar habits or attachments, while also being magnetized towards your soul's most illuminated path of growth. Past life regression, evolutionary astrology, hypnotherapy, and other modalities which allow you direct access into your soul's journey will be highly revealing and instructive during this initiation.

The Lunar Return, Nodal Reversal, and Saturn Return are described at length below.

The Great Passage through the Midlife Portal, 27-30

Lunar Return and Nodal Reversal

Many of us question whether the Saturn Return actually begins at 27. At the age of 27, we enter a threshold initiation in our lifetimes. Our emotions can overwhelm us, our souls can seem to drown in confusion. We seem to wander in a chaotic bardo, we wonder if we have already begun the dreaded Saturn Return.

In actuality, the tender internal landscape of the Moon is curling us into fetal positions during our Lunar Return, just as the Moon's Nodes reverse from their natal placement, sending the soul into upheaval.

During this critical juncture your reactive self seems to dominate as situations may threaten your understanding of your place in the world. Although it can sense an evolution in the unknown North Node, the soul often longs to return to its familiar and habitual territory of the South Node. The desire to anchor in something which feels secure, as our emotions swirl in uncertainty, is very appealing. But as we try to return to familiar ground, we seem to flail in quicksand instead. Experiences and relationships may suck us into old wounds and painful stories. Allow yourself to begin to integrate the story of the nodes, sharing the inborn talents of your South Node while inviting those experiences which will illuminate the goals of your North Node.

It is important to study and understand the textures of your natal Moon at this time. What does your lunar child need to feel safe? How do you seek contentment and emotional nourishment in your life? Whatever planets challenge your security in dynamic aspect to the Moon will be highlighted in the experiences of your life at this time. You embark on an inner odyssey at this time, with the potential to explore the rich depths of your primal needs. Your sensitivities heighten and your dreams may reveal unconscious longings seeking soil to root in. You question your sense of "home," your relationship with your family and your mother in particular. You may become acutely aware of what did not nourish you growing up, and so you will likely feel compelled to literally move, seeking to find roots that give you the nutrients you long for. You must be careful not to react with blame or intolerable scrutiny towards yourself or family members during this delicate time. It is an ideal passage to practice rebirthing and other means of understanding your birth trauma. You will naturally feel compelled to seek out the history of your ancestry and you may benefit from visiting the geographical roots of your family of origin.

You also seek to find and benefit from a spiritual lineage which feels like home.

This passage is the emotional preparation for the disciplined maturity and hard work of the approaching Saturn Return.

Surviving Saturn Return

Two of the most powerful and important initiations of our life involve Grandfather Time, known as "Kronos" to the Greeks, from which we get "chronology." We call it the Saturn return at the ages of 28-30 and 58-60. I want to give special focus to this cycle since it bookends the critical passage through midlife. Our decisions around these Saturn return cycles often feel heavier than at any other time in our life and so require focus, intention, and right effort.

Let us further investigate how Saturn's seven-year square to itself has legendary status in our everyday lore.

First, we have the idea of "seven years bad luck" if one breaks a mirror. Centuries ago many believed that a person's image in water or in a mirror was a reflection of that person's soul. The Romans believed that a person's health and fortune changed every seven years. Hence, to break a mirror was to damage the soul for the minimum of seven years. This is an interesting metaphor for the power of true perception. Saturn invites us to "get real" and gain clarity about our work here on Earth, as well as the roles we play.

Likely, certain classes of the Romans were well aware of Saturn's seven year square to itself. The connotations to the renewal of health after seven years also pertain to the fact that every cell in our body is renewed after seven years. In a sense, we are regenerated completely in our physical frame (Saturn rules the bones and skins) after seven years. We are also aware of the common conversion of one "dog year" to seven human years.

Lastly, all of us have heard of the "seven year itch." It refers to an irritation in relationships which takes place after seven years. According to some statistics, seven years is the average duration for marriages in North America. With Saturn, you are required to commit and endure. After seven years, you must decide whether you want to continue to lay new foundations. Many couples naturally feel this cycle. Often, the pressures and challenges of renewing their love overwhelm the couple, and they choose to end their marriages at Saturn's passage.

As Grandfather Time, each Saturn transit can feel like a burden placed on us by the laws of space and time. With Saturn, you get serious, you feel gravity weigh you down through your bones. You can be overwhelmed with a heavy pressure which will not lift. You are chastised by a stern inner voice, demanding that you achieve something, yet you feel constrained and limited by the gravitas of space and time.

Saturn is the evolutionary urge within us to author our own lives through commitment to a role in the world. Saturn demands that we contribute something to society as a whole. The first Saturn return signifies that critical decision-making time, when we lay out the trajectory of our midlife work. We begin to realize that we cannot continue to do everything we want to do if we want to ultimately master an area or provide something of importance to the world.

During this initiation, you benefit from solitude, from spaces that allow a deeper contemplation of your value system. You must mature your identity and solidify it in a way that both offers something practical to the greater whole as well as consistently invites you to work hard towards its further development.

This process requires concentration, careful consideration, and intense focus. You must overcome fears in the area of life where Saturn resides. This house will be a major realm of discipline during your Saturn return, and for the majority of your life. In this house, you can build stamina and security in steady accomplishment as you age. Initially frustrating and filled with disappointment, this is an area that you can eventually master through patience and sincere effort.

Even with his sickle held high, there is something ironically comforting to Saturn: Saturn is obvious. You are confronted with Saturnian energy constantly, often by authorities, the government, parents, or your friends who all repeatedly ask you to outwardly define yourself to them. Questions about your job, your home, your family, you relationship—all these questions seek to reinforce how you choose to identify yourself during the first Saturn return. We feel such pressure at this time because Saturn's cold and serious voice reminds us that we can no longer scatter our energies into every experimental playground of life as we did during much of our 20's.

Stepping up to the next level of maturity, you also realize that you can and must choose your alliances of identity—no longer can you blame your parents, your education, your religious upbringing, your social class, etc. You must step up and become responsible to life—able to respond to life's demands and to contribute constructively to the culture in which you live.

Think of the exquisite structure of Saturn's rings. To look at Saturn is to behold beauty. But true beauty is the achievement of a refined form, through time. Thus, your soul's various roles must be cultivated through disciplined effort. At the first Saturn return, you begin to sculpt your life. You chisel away what will not be required for that art piece of your adulthood.

At the second Saturn Return between 58-60, you must evaluate honestly the decisions you made around your first Saturn Return. What were the results of the commitments you chose—your family, your job, your place of residence, your value systems? This is a coming clean process. Just as in the first Saturn Return, you may feel disappointment or regret for decisions made, as well as pride and achievement for the paths chosen. You must ask yourself what you learned in the roles that you played—relationships, career, children are perceived more clearly, stripped to their greater meaning in the mythology of your life. This reflective process then compels you to ask how you can best begin to use the gifts you developed during your first Saturn Return to teach and guide others.

This is often an age when one takes on the role of grandparent or wise elder in the community. It can be a time of incredible self-ownership, when one becomes an authority, respected for the life they have authored during the previous thirty years.

Harmonizing with Saturn

When you undergo any Saturn transit—it can be the oppositions at 15 or 42, or the squares, the Saturn returns, or Saturn transiting one of your personal planets—you can use various techniques from the archetypal recipe book to accomplish your Saturnian mission.

For instance, you can meditate with the image of Saturn and chant the Sanskrit mantra *Om hreem shreem shanischarya namah.* Or visualize the root chakra, Muladhara, its square shape, with the glyph of Saturn in the middle, while dancing to very rhythmic, bassy, structured music.

Do a shamanic journey to the turtle or the alligator and ask them to teach you about their medicines of patience, endurance, and stamina.

Wear more black clothing.

Study the Tarot card of the Devil while praying to the Angel Kassiel for steady discipline and solid, reliable structures.

Visit the dentist and make sure to floss your teeth, while receiving regular chiropractic work. Bring more calcium rich foods, such as kale into your diet.

Practice the following affirmations:

I AM Integrity.
I manifest my authentic self.
I author my own life.

These are just a few of the many possibilities for integrating the psychological and evolutionary forces of Saturn into your life during his powerful initiations.

Evolutionary Parenting: Assisting a Child's Rites of Passage

With awareness of the mythical map of the human experience, a parent is naturally drawn towards applying this wisdom towards the education of their children. How can you best support your children's journeys through their rites of passage? What support systems and structures should you provide to assist their initiation?

Mars Return: 1.5-2.5 yrs

Mars, the fiery planet of action, is the first major planetary return cycle, at the age of two. These "terrible twos" are attempts in the child's soul to develop the third chakra or will center. The child begins to understand how to satiate her desires through emotional outbursts and gestural cues. Study the position of Mars by sign, house, and aspect in the child's chart to further understand the desire nature of the young soul. If she has Mars in Leo, this age may be a time to put a toy xylophone in her hand or to play dress up to allow the performer to shine. A Mars in Cancer may need a special doll or blankey when she is upset. She may be drawn towards games of "house" or her energies can be focused towards helping in the kitchen. The activities discovered at this time will then become a channel for her to express their desires in a healthy way.

Ceres Return: 4-5 yrs

If we go back further, the Ceres return between ages four and five offers us our first glimpse into how best to nourish this child's energy. As the grain goddess and archetypal mother, Ceres asks us how we can bring our children's souls into their richest expression and most abundant existence. Ultimately, Ceres' initiation can compel us towards pursuing a more individualized education for our children, suited to the particular needs of a child. The various textures of a young spirit's evolutionary intent are elucidated in rich detail in the birth chart and this first Ceres return is an ideal time to invite the planetary wisdom to guide the type of education and child-rearing this unique soul requires.

Saturn square Saturn: 6.5-7.5 yrs

Once parents and educators begin to apply the wisdom of the birthchart towards an appropriate educational model, the child will then be tested in his first experiences of social identity at 6-7 years of age, the first Saturn square. He is now beginning to realize who he is and is not. He begins to make choices of affiliation— friendships, certain subjects he likes to study, games he prefers to play. In essence, he is beginning to structure his consciousness. Look to the house where Saturn is located and to the house where Saturn is squaring the natal Saturn to discover what activities will help to form a foundation of initial identity for the child.

Jupiter Return and Saturn Opposition: 11-15

Returning to the Sacred - The Child as Hero

Anthropologists and ethnologists have long recorded the rites of passage performed in indigenous and tribal traditions.

Many of these correspond specifically to the Jupiter and Saturn initiations from ages 12-15. As the socializing urges, Jupiter and Saturn both connect the individual to larger roles she will play in the fabric of the society. In indigenous cultures, these initiations mark threshold "points of no return," where the child must step into a more mature stage of consciousness and begin contributing to her society.

In the United States and other Western cultures, most children never fully complete this initiation cycle, instead sustaining an eternal child complex of dependency and perpetual adolescence. In indigenous cultures and certain spiritual traditions, very clearly defined entrances and exits for these rites of passage existed, helping children to move from one stage to the next, in order to efficiently begin to awaken to their purpose and positively affect their culture.

Although not intended by the child, this vast chasm between childhood and maturity creates many narcissistic complexes that often never resolve themselves. There is a significant lack of ceremony and ritual to honor rites of passages for young people in modern Western society. Graduation can hardly account for the intrinsic desires in the soul to unfold its mythical self into the material world. Thus, a child's need for ceremony dissolves into the numb and passive experience of watching weekly football games or other sporting events or attending certain concerts. At time, the child may participate in sports themselves or join a group of musicians, but the ritual and sacred component is completely stripped from these events.

Another effect of the lack of participatory rites of passage involves a subsequent psychological projection and transference of archetypal energies onto the child's activities. For instance, many children between the ages of eight and eighteen are enamored with violence through movies, sports, and video games, yet few have experienced violent or life-threatening situations. The magnetic attraction towards violence is completely normal in understanding the archetypal forces at play in the child's psyche. But, since Western society has appropriated virtually no healthy containers for the ritual experience of one's mortality, children must project this psychic need onto movie and videogame characters and sports "heroes."

What would happen if the child became the hero himself, undergoing an initiatory test that matured him into almost mythical status, someone he respects and someone who is admired by the community?

To answer this question, let us compare the Western dilemma to the Aboriginal culture of Australia. Here, a young boy must experience the suffering of circumcision and seclusion from the community and family in order to die to himself. He is reborn afterwards into a system of reciprocal responsibility. At this point, it is not possible to project the death-urge onto others: the boy has conquered it himself and completely transformed, humbled, and empowered his sense of identity. His ability to participate in religious ceremony, to marry, and to be socially accepted is predicated upon his abilities to undergo the pressures of these Saturnian tasks, involving pain, separation, and a struggle with one's own mortal nature.

However, he is given the Jupiter faith of the Dreamtime to inspire him through the difficult journey into adulthood. He becomes familiar with the accounts of the Golden Age of Aboriginal mythology. The stories illuminate the fundamental unified cosmology of the Aborigines—the relationship between past, present, and future, the distinction between the sacred and the profane, the mysteries of life and death, the ordering of social relationships, the consequences of social actions, and the rites of passage throughout the phases of one's life.

In Western culture, a child's time in solitude is not about maturing the soul. Rather, it is usually done as a form of punishment. Hence, a complex is created whereby a child's sense of normalcy must involve constant engagement with others, shaping his or her behavior to fit the mold of the parents, teachers, or friends whom they hang out with. There is no space to develop the inborn wisdom of solitary reflection, absolutely essential during Saturn's initiation at 14-15. Nor can the child integrate something akin to the aboriginal test of "sacred separation" from the community. Instead of prayers during the child's trials of solitude, the child is only aware that his parents are angry and he is being punishment. Hence, "aloneness" equates with punishment and disapproval, a powerful and disturbing template for the relationship challenges which dominate the social world today.

In addition, physical education and arts are the first things to be cut from schools in times of budget crisis, the two areas which should be given the most attention, especially with a more sacred context. Archetypal drama and mythical dance are just two of the many possibilities of physical movement which connects children to a more primal and spiritual reality.

In Jewish cultures, the Jupiter-Saturn cycle relates to the Bar and Bat Mitzvah—the arduous path of study and memorization of the Torah and the acceptance and knowledge of the Jewish faith between the ages of 12 and 13. The child works with the rabbinic elders, family members, and friends to understand the teachings of the Torah, expanding his identity in Jupiterian fashion to the extended community of the faith. But also, the child is encouraged to think about the significance of the teachings to his own life. This invites Saturnian reflection on the adult responsibilities soon to be owned after the ceremony.

Traditionally in India, Jupiter was the significator of children, and this may be directly related to the cross-cultural fact that around the time of the first Jupiter Return at twelve years old, a girl begins menstruating, and is now able to conceive a child. In Navajo culture, these planetary initiations mark the Kinaalda, referencing a girl's first menstruation. Etymologically, the roots of this word may be traced back to the Alaskan days of the Athapaskans, where the phrase kin ya shidah, or sitting alone, was first used. (Popovic)

This etymology helps us to understand the Saturnian urges so present during this cycle of life as well. Solitude, contemplation, and serious reflection about one's maturing processes are fundamental to the Saturnian initiation.

How vastly different is this tradition than our common practices around a girl's first menstruation in western culture? Often, a girl feels ashamed at this time. Perhaps she will not tell her mother, but will resolve to what certain magazines say or the stories of her friends. There is very little respect or honoring of the child during this cycle, and undoubtedly contributes to shame, disgust, or complex and confusing feelings around her genitalia and her early experiences of sexuality, which serve to form a negative template for future experiences of sexuality and femininity.

But with the consciousness that both Jupiter and Saturn are instructing her into new social roles, the girl can learn how to work with these cycles in ways which feel honoring to her.

The ability to conceive children represents the Jupiterian urge to expand and grow one's identity. However, the responsibilities of the Saturn opposition cycle remind the girl that pregnancy will bring pressures, hardship, limitation, constriction and severe discipline in her life. Hence, she must learn to mature her interactions with the opposite sex and develop a healthy relationship with her own desires.

The Vision Quest

For both girls and boys, the Saturn opposition is an absolutely necessary time for personal empowerment in solitude. In essence, this is the ideal cycle for a vision quest. In some Native American cultures, the vision quest is utilized as a tool for maturing the spirit of the young initiate. A spiritual journey alone in the wilderness, the vision quest also includes fasting, entirely appropriate for the harsh Saturnian lessons of struggle through limitation.

In most vision quests, community friends and family tend a fire in prayer and hold vigil for the initiate. By passing time alone, yet being prayed for by the extended social network (Jupiter and Saturn), the child knows that his path of maturity is supported by those who have gone before him, those who will then benefit from his determination and persistence through solitary hardship. The child also has the opportunity to build his or her faith in the earth herself, to begin to listen to the signs and messages from the birds, the wind, and the inner authority.

The vision quest, like the Navajo Kinaalda, both last for four days, and the symbolic numerology of four relates to the stability, foundation, and strength of endurance represented by Saturn.

The close proximity of the Jupiter and Saturn initiations between 11-15 helps us to understand the opposite but interdependent urges of the two planets: to amplify and enlarge one's identity and influence in the culture (Jupiter) through a commitment towards responsible action towards all (Saturn).

If an inspiring teacher and spiritual pathway can enter the young person's life at the Jupiter return, the child can build the necessary faith and trust to then engage a wilderness initiation of maturity at the Saturn opposition. For parents and teachers, knowing the specific conditions of Jupiter and Saturn in the birthchart, by sign, house, and aspect can be an invaluable tool in designing an appropriate rite of passage. For instance, a child with Saturn in the sixth house may best journey through his initiation by performing weekly acts of service to the community, a path of selfless, bhakti yoga. With Saturn in the ninth house, a semester studying abroad, especially somewhere where the child may have little knowledge or other friends on the journey, may be exactly the kind of initiation to best evolve the soul.

Most importantly, the Jupiter and Saturn rites of passage afford a unique opportunity for a blossoming soul to begin to author his or her own life, discovering a depth of wisdom rising from within, not some inapplicable knowledge forced from outside. As the young adult attunes to the inner authority, there is little need to rebel against outer authority figures, such as parents, teachers, and law enforcement. The child has matured into a young adult, conscious now of the center within, aware of the power of the inner life.

A young teen's discontent with academic learning, desire to alter their consciousness, longing to affiliate with a group (often resolving into joining certain gangs) and search for his own personal myths, all reflect the dual urges of Jupiter and Saturn that must be honored. If not exercised consciously, Jupiter and Saturn's evolutionary urges will distort at this time—Jupiter will tend towards extravagance and extremes, and the Saturn opposition child will tend to rebel at all cost and to experience bouts of depression and resentment. The same themes that could have been confronted and dealt with at this age then must be repressed, only to surface again at later initiations from the same planets—the Jupiter opposition at 18, the nodal return at 19, the Saturn and Uranus square at 21, the Jupiter return at 23, and the Saturn return between 28-30. All of these later cycles can be more consciously experienced, not simply reacted to, as the earlier initiations are more deeply integrated. This occurs in many adults who do not honor the earlier initiations, such as one who experiences their second Saturn return still needing to deal with the issues of their first Saturn return.

A Generation's Needs

Children born since 1990 have been born with the transpersonal forces of the outer planets all in the final signs of the zodiac, also transpersonal in nature. The outer planets describe the archetypal motivations of each generation. Hence, these children are naturally drawn towards mythology, cosmology, alien civilizations, psychic powers, and spirituality. In both Western and Eastern cultures, the youth of today have grown up in a highly mythologized media—one need only to look at media like Harry Potter, Lord of the Rings, Percy Jackson, Clash of the Titans, the infinite number of superhero movies, Japanese animation, and the popularity of video games, especially role-playing games. Hence, it is often much easier for these children to accept the gods, goddesses, and nature spirits than even their parents. This is particularly true due to the prevalence of the Roman, Greek, Nordic, Celtic, and Persian deities and their analogues in the mainstream culture.

Due to these facts, we should feel no hesitation to introduce the gods Jupiter and Saturn into their lexicon at these times of their initiations. The cross-cultural stories of Zeus, Indra, Thor and others can all be studied as part of the Jupiterian rite of passage, as can the stories of Kronos and Saturn. Lessons can be gleaned and applied to the individual child's life. With this practice, a child's life is perceived much more mythically, not just filled with random and challenging emotions, not simply chaos and confusion, but actually a sacred reflection of universal, archetypal forces. This is an incredibly empowered perspective for a soul maturing into its next stage of evolution. It is up to elder generations to institute archetypal awareness and astrological rites of passage as a natural part of educating the next generation, who will guide the Earth towards her further evolution.

Jupiter Opposition leading to Nodal Return

The ten year period from the first Jupiter return to the Uranus and Saturn square at age 21 provides the emotional, social, educational, and spiritual template for the rest of the child's life. Towards the latter part of this cycle, the ages 18-20 challenge the young adult in very specific ways which modern culture has not honored. As Jupiter opposes itself, for about a year, one's understanding of the world seeks to be broadened. One's faith may be tested as the world does not reflect experiences and relationships in harmonic accord with the young adult's belief systems. Therefore, his or her spirituality and philosophy is tested. And all of this occurs just before the Nodes return to the place they were at one's birth.

The Nodal return is a very important time when young adults can receive powerful insights into their souls' birth vision. Often, the young adult's intrinsic gifts manifest quite strongly, and they feel called to illuminate their potential.

Naturally, this is the time when we finish high school and thrill at the idea of going off to university. And though university or college may be an exciting time, the ensuing freedom can often feel daunting. Often, the young adult's specific goals and talents have not been cultivated in the high school educational system. Thus, many young adult are confused and overwhelmed by the options before them. Insecurity arises as how best to invest their time, money, and energy.

I remember being 18 and 19, in my first two years of university. I knew I had many talents, but had little life experience. Choosing a major felt like an overwhelming and impossible pressure. How did I know what I wanted to study until I was studying it? I also despised having to take pre-requisites, classes that I had no interest in but were necessary for a certain course of study.

It is important to remember that the combination of the Jupiter opposition and the Nodal return provide for an ideal opportunity to travel in order to discover one's gifts, as well as the vast possibilities life has to offer.

The Jupiter opposition is already demanding an expanded perspective on reality. Meanwhile, with the Nodal return, the soul is ripe to experience that which will inspire its evolution. Knowing the specifics of the nodal placements in the chart, the young adult can tailor travel and volunteer work to awaken the longings seeking actualization in the soul. Global experience, more than any book, affords a surplus of opportunity to mature, humble, and empower the young adult.

Today, our world is accelerating at rates where we cannot afford for the next generation to waste their energies in activities and education which they do not give one hundred percent of their heart's energy towards. Revolutionary education must at all times support students devoting their efforts to the pursuit of their passions, even if the course of study involves, for example, travel through the multicultural world of the global classroom.

The confusion that can arise at this time can often be amended with the objective voice of a trusted counselor. It is my feeling that the 18-21 year old time frame is the ideal window for young adults to begin to grasp the shapes and contours of their natal birth vision, the codex of their souls. This is a crucial threshold. Their souls are ready for languages which will elucidate the path towards their own self-discovery. In studying their birthcharts, these young souls will find the map they have been seeking, a map leading directly to the treasures within themselves.

This critical juncture continues into the Uranus square between 20-22, when the young adult seeks to authentically live an individual path. Epiphanous revelations can occur at this time, moments of awakening and genius spilling through, if there is a consciousness prepared to handle it. In most cases, the urges for liberation or freedom will compel young adults at this stage to rebel against whatever they are doing, often leading them to quit school, break off relationships, leave home, intoxicate heavily, or feel a total disconnect from their families. It is important to remember that while they might seem uncertain of what to do next, the revolutionary impulse of Uranus is actually awakening their unique self seeking expression in the world. Again, travel allows for opportunities for freedom to explore the fullness of one's being.

Yet, immediately, the waning Saturn square appears, presenting a crisis in consciousness: How do I author my own life, but not be confined by my decisions? Young adults can feel a lot of pressure at this time as they have worked so hard for freedom, but then feel the intense weight of deciding how to unfold their life. They begin to realize that, if they are going to choose their own way, they can no longer blame their parents or education or friends. It is time to align themselves with the groups, schools, places, philosophies, and work which support their maximum individual self-expression. How many of us, during this delicate transition, could have benefited from a few deep astrological readings from a compassionate mentor? Instead of becoming paralyzed by the range of choices, astrological insight at this age can bring clarity and confidence to the gifts seeking development at that time, while understanding potential pathways that young souls can take to strategize the decade that lies ahead. Instead of the 20's appearing as a chaotic rollercoaster of uncertainty, the birthchart can help young adults guide their own ships to fulfilling experiences, enriching relationships, and inspiring studies that feel evolutionary on every step of their journeys.

Art of Partnership: Planetary Initiations in Relationships

As a member of the Pluto in Libra generation, I am compelled to help transform the archetype of partnership. We are a generation (1970-1984), many who grew up in divorced environments, who are seeking to build sustainable and empowering partnerships which do not confine or suppress our individuality, represented by the Aries polarity. One insight into relationships we can all remember is that they also must conform to the laws of planetary cycles.

All relationships, including lovers, friendships, business partnerships, and families will undergo the evolutionary initiations of the planets. We can apply the same mythical storyline to our relationships as we did above to our individual lives.

We already mentioned above, the "seven year itch," related to Saturn. If we look to when a relationship between two people begins, seven years following this, Saturn will square itself and challenge the relationship with some kind of obstacle that compels the couple to question whether they should continue to build a structure with each other or tear the existing structure down. By the sixth to seventh year of a relationship, the areas of discontent and disconnect within the relationship are usually quite conscious in both people. Therefore, this is an ideal time to seek counsel, especially the detailed astrological analysis which can elucidate each individual's cycles as well as the transits and progressions to the composite energy of the couple. Hopefully, this mutual willingness for cosmic assistance will prevent any hurtful activity that could be the very cause of a future break-up. Instead, the two people can decide to engage with increasing commitment or to maturely leave in honor and gratitude for the journey they have traveled together.

Mars and The 2-Year Itch

The seven year itch however, is now more commonly a two year itch, thanks to the Mars cycle. According to certain statistics, one in twelve couples heads for the divorce courts after two years. Through observation, you will probably recognize the large numbers of friends who date someone for 1.5-2.5 years and then the relationship ends, sometimes abruptly or with fire in the belly.

Roughly around the two year mark, we become more consumed by the Martian themes of aggression, conflict, confrontation, friction, opposing will, and desires for freedom, just as we notice in a child during their "terrible twos." Each individual may become more territorial at this time, with ensuing power struggles. The ego tends to rear itself more prominently as our will-chakra's personal needs supersede the sharing and listening of the heart-chakra.

For a relationship to survive the Mars return, it must be infused with new life force. The flame of vitality needed can be discovered in many areas of life—a new physical expression to the relationship is an ideal way to channel the fire of Mars. Exciting, adventurous travel that pushes the couple to their edges can be a powerful tool during this cycle. The couple can also begin a certain shared exercise program which demands more physical exertion—biking, rock climbing, rafting, or hiking, for example.

And one of the most exciting areas to conjure Mars is through sexuality. Beginning a regular tantric practice and invoking techniques of sexual magic at this time can invigorate the couple and rekindle their passion for each other. In addition, arguments or power struggles can be transmuted in the sexual act and raised to a higher vibration.

Handfasting and the Solar Relationship

As we all know, the Sun, our sacred star and life-giver, journeys through the horoscope over the course of a year. As the horoscope is a complete picture of the twelve-step archetypal odyssey, the Sun illuminates a house or realm of archetypal experience every 30 days. In a year's time, our sacred star will radiate its life through each realm of the twelve-step journey of the soul.

My father once communicated the wisdom that all relationships should experience at least a year together, to "know the cycle of the seasons." Without recognizing it, my father had channeled the wisdom of the Solar cycle, a cycle honored in a relationship tradition of the Celtic and Pagan path.

Handfasting was practiced widely, most noticeably in the British Isles, for hundreds of years. It is common in pagan traditions around the world today. Although it varies in its details, in general, the ceremony is officiated by a minister, priest, priestess, shaman, or elder. The couple states their vows in front of their spiritual community of friends and family. They literally tie their hands together with a cord to symbolize the shared journey they will embark upon together. The two hands bound together form the symbol of infinity. After one year, the couple returns before the community once again and state their intentions. At this point, they are invited to commit to their beloved for another solar cycle, to commit to each other for the rest of their earthly existence, or to do a "handparting," a ceremony which will unbind the couple from each other, and allow them to honor their journey together, while recognizing the need to move forward in separate directions.

The handfasting model may be the most appropriate model for our modern relationships, where we seek a certain level of commitment and stability without the feeling of life-long confinement. Here, there is a respectable compassion and understanding for the various life missions we are on, and whether they overlap with another's. This model also helps us to honor the various soul contracts we have with other beings. Often, we feel that we have powerful work to do with others, perhaps exploring or resolving some partnership energy, yet our relationship agreements may not allow the space to engage in this important soul-healing and spirit-weaving.

The hand fasting model also follows the natural movement of the Sun and Venus, the goddess of love, in their year-long journey through the sky. Recognizing that Venus-Aphrodite takes one year to charm every aspect of our life, to adorn each house with her grace, beauty, and affection, this fact should be a significant clue as to the natural cycles of love, which must be renewed on a yearly basis for the Goddess to continue to bestow her blessings.

Balancing Your Personal and Relational Rites of Passage

Successful relationships must also honor the individual life trajectory of each person. So as you journey through your planetary initiations, you must observe how these align or conflict with your partner's. For instance, if you are 23 and your partner is 28-30, you will each be experiencing fundamentally different planetary initiations. Your expansive spirit, your Jupiterian desire to grow and learn and travel will likely feel constricted by the Saturnian forces demanding discipline and serious decision-making in your partner. These Saturnian forces require responsibility and may make your partner feel emotionally heavy, embittered, or resentful—feelings which may be easily projected onto you. Or your partner may want to "tie the knot," invoking the Saturnian desire for commitment and grounded responsibility. How will this feel to that Jupiterian spirit, seeking unbounded freedom to explore?

During planetary rites of passage, you will naturally be drawn to people and relationships resonant with that planetary initiation. For instance, during a

Jupiter initiation, the attraction to a guru, teacher, spiritual path, foreign travel, or higher education is very strong during this time and may in fact supersede a love-relationship in importance. Jupiter, as the juicy, generous, gaseous giant, needs a lot of space to bestow its fortunes. At these cycles, Jupiter will require that your relationship be expansive and full of opportunities to learn and feel inspired. If this is not the case, the relationship will need to end in order to make space for this benevolent energy to arrive.

Most relationships and marriages are shaken as one or both partners enter the Uranus opposition. Since the need here is for ultimate freedom, the reclamation of youthful vigor is often projected out into an attraction towards younger people and a lifestyle which even temporarily, invokes more risk, reckless abandon, and individual self-development. The need for authentic self-expression is paramount. Uranus will demand that whatever is stagnant in a relationship be either re-invigorated or discarded for a fresh perspective which brings both excitement and liberation to the individual.

Of course, we would need volumes of books to cover all the delicate dynamics of partnership astrology, but we should remember that one's individual initiations, one's planetary transits, are just as important to honor as the synastry, or connections, between two people's charts. This point helps us to humbly honor that disorienting feeling that arises when we know this might be the right relationship, but the inappropriate time. It is my hope that you will allow the birthchart to be your map, and an astrological mentor to be your guide, in the shapeshift dance of relationship.

A Planetary Initiation Self-Portrait

In my own life, I have witnessed how profoundly these planetary rites of passage have shaped me. Each step on the journey has increased my perception of my life as a grand opera of mythic proportions.

I will share a little here to allow the symbolism to pour through. At the tender age of two, I slipped on a whiffle ball and broke the largest bone in my body, my left femur. As mentioned above, Mars first returns to its natal place at the age of two and Mars signifies all accidents and surgeries. Interestingly, Mars is conjunct Saturn in my birthchart. Saturn rules the bones. Hence, I had a Mars accident and surgery on the Saturn bones just as Mars returned to transit both Mars and Saturn.

Between the ages of six and seven, I had to wear a retainer in my mouth, a very bizarre contraption that had a key to lock it in place to the roof of my mouth. This retainer's function was to stop the growth of my upper teeth. Six to seven years of age marks the delicate passage into our first Saturn square, a time of beginning to identify ourselves independently out in the world. It is interesting how so many orthodontic appointments begin around this age, since Saturn governs the teeth.

At the age of twelve, I began studying the Korean martial art, Tae Kwon Do. My teacher fulfilled the Jupiter archetype, as an inspiring and powerful force in my life at that time of Jupiter return. In Jupiterian fashion, my social circle and faith in my abilities expanded with my classes, as well as my spiritual horizons, as bits of eastern spirituality seeped into our practice. Within two-and-a-half years, I achieved a black belt fairly unprecedented at the school up until that point. My journey had been quite Saturnian—two-three times a week of practice and never missing a test to the next belt degree. So I was rewarded by Saturn for my hard work just as Saturn began to oppose itself at the age of fourteen.

At that time, an appointment with the pediatrician took an unexpected turn. He discovered that my hips were misaligned, due to the fact that my left leg, which I had broken when I was two, had grown back one-and-a-half inches longer than the right leg. We would have to do surgery to cut out that extra inch-and-a-half of bone.

As Saturn came to oppose my natal Saturn, it also opposed my natal Mars, and so the combination of surgery (Mars) on the bones (Saturn) occurred. I was unable to walk for an entire summer, and for more than a month could not even send a signal down my left leg to my toes. Confined to a bed for three months, the Saturnian lessons of limitation, frustration, melancholy, disappointment, and the physical body itself forced me to mature my character. Each day I had to discipline myself to stretch, attempt to move my leg, and eventually learn to walk again. For a few months after I returned to school, I walked with crutches and then a cane, invoking the image of the Saturnian grandfather elder.

What I consider to be the most profound initiation of my life occurred just two years later at the age of seventeen. I believe the event that occurred was from the planetary agent of Chiron, the shaman and wounded healer of the chart. But the spiritual ramifications of the event had much more to do with the planet Jupiter.

On a spiritual retreat in the Santa Cruz mountains for my senior year of high school, I experienced sharp, stabbing pains in my chest, while unable to catch my breath. This lasted for hours, which felt like eternities. At times, I left my body and entered a bardo realm. My higher self communicated messages to me to prepare me for death. My prayers deepened in that moment of greatest spiritual testing as I experienced the shock of absolute uncertainty. After being rushed to the hospital, x-rays revealed that my right lung had spontaneously collapsed.

Over the following ten days, I was visited by what seemed to be every being who knew me—school teachers, priests, relatives, current and former girlfriends, and my parents, who occupied my bedside 24/7. Over the ensuing months, as Jupiter opposed itself, as he traveled the eighth house of death, rebirth, and psychological regeneration, I felt like each person who visited me was an angel, a messenger of a transcendent love and pure faith which no experience less extreme could have offered me. My faith was renewed and transfigured in the reflection of myself as a child of love in the faces of those I knew.

Jupiter also delivered to me the first experience of true synchronicity that I acknowledged as six weeks after my first lung collapse, I experienced my other lung collapse while I was in the doctor's office, receiving my check-up. Although I suffered horrible pain and loss of breath once again, I simultaneously felt my spirit uplift and amplify into dimensions beyond my comprehension at the recognition of the perfection of the timing.

At the return of the Lunar Nodes at age 19, I suffered much loneliness and mild depression at university, uncertain of why I was friendless and what I hoped to do with a creative writing major when I felt I had little life experience to write about. In a writing class, I met a fellow student from Scotland who shared with me his experiences of traveling and working abroad on a kibbutz in Israel. This synchronistic encounter changed my life destiny forever.

The next year, just as my Uranus square to Uranus began, I left a private university which I had a scholarship to attend, in order to travel and volunteer in Israel and Egypt. I consider this to be the most critical decision in my life, when I fully stepped in to my authentic individuality, by liberating myself from the status quo academic environment and the expectations of family. Uranus demanded that I rebel against the normal path and instead embrace the unknown. I felt simultaneous excitement and trepidation, traveling alone for the first time. Yet, I told myself that once I stepped off of the plane halfway around the world, I essentially would win my own life, because I had chosen it—quite the Uranian revelation.

Travel, freedom, and self-discovery dominated the two year Uranus square. In this trip, I met Europeans and Israelis who initiated me as a global citizen. The crucial moment of my second real cognition of synchronicity occurred during this trip, due to following my intuition under the guidance of Uranus's higher mind.

I had attempted to find a kibbutz, a sort of sustainable community common in Israel. When two weeks of phone calls failed to yield an opportunity to volunteer, I allowed myself for the first time to feel, completely throughout the whole of my being, the totality of disappointment, the feeling of having failed to accomplish what I had intended to do. I then listened to an inner guidance which told me to hop on the bus to Cairo to go and visit the pyramids. On the bus, I met two travelers from England whom I stayed with in the craziness of Cairo. During our days together, I discovered they were vacationing from their volunteering on a kibbutz. They called their supervisor and asked if I could return with them to help out. She said yes, and so a week later I found myself back in Israel, surrounded by Europeans and Israelis doing everything from working in an oil barrel factory, to delivering baby chicks, to harvesting avocados.

This experience then continued into the next summer, when I traveled to Europe, mostly alone, visiting friends, volunteering, studying Spanish, and essentially following the winds of Uranian freedom wherever they took me. These included my first real journeys with marijuana and psychedelics, and wild and crazy adventures such as paragliding and bungee jumping off the highest gondola in the world in the Alps.

Towards the end of this Uranus square, I began attending raves and found a whole new tribe of eccentric, unique, exciting friendships. But also, in Uranian fashion, these friends entered and quickly exited my life.

As Saturn came in to square itself, a conservative voice, including my parents', compelled me to return to school. With Saturn's pressure and insistence to structure my life, I felt myself drawn to accomplish something academically and finish what I had started. However, I was now infused with my deeper Uranian discoveries of my authentic self. So I vowed to finish school by designing my own major—Communication and Self-Conception.

The second Jupiter return between twenty-three and twenty-four, I felt the call to finally embrace nature, absent in my life until that point. I joined an intensive five-week backcountry trip which would also give me some school credit. Here, we hiked daily in complete isolation from the world, while diving deeply into nature philosophy and religion. My senses awakened as never before, as the Jupiterian truth of existence in its boundless, manifold expressions, the voluptuous curvature of Being, revealed itself in canyon wall and desert sand. Jupiter inspired my sense of faith and my spiritual connection to the web of life. Jupiter, as the god of storms, even visited five days in a row in the costume of the awesome grandeur of a flash flood.

And nothing could have been more expansive to my identity than the reception of my name, VerDarLuz, in the heart of a mystical aspen forest. Breaking the word down into its Spanish components, ver means "to see," dar "to give," and luz "light." Verde means "green," signifying the bounty and beauty of nature and the heart chakra, while verdad means "truth." Since that momentous gift of my name, I am constantly reminded of my work here in this life each time I translate my name for those who ask. Like Jupiter, the description of my name always restores my faith and my connection to Spirit.

Within a month of this trip, I embarked on an odyssey to the annual Burning Man festival for the first time. It is hard to imagine an event more akin to the expansive growth potential of a Jupiter return than Burning Man. Creative inspiration surrounded me in the extremes of the environment, the hedonistic indulgences, and the extravagant play and loving optimism of the Burners. (Jupiter rules Sagittarius, a spiral fire sign, and it is quite intriguing the number of fire-spinners who have a large dose of Sagittarius or a prominent Jupiter in their chart.)

Jupiter, the bestower of blessings, loves to enhance the synchronicity quotient, which seemed to overwhelm me from every corner of the Burning Man playa, including telling my friends I would stay out a little longer and visit one other stage. It was at this crucial moment when I encountered a being who would become one of the deepest loves of my life, a woman whom I almost left Burning Man to follow. Since Jupiter rules my house of partnership, it was entirely appropriate that during my Jupiter return cycle, I should find such an exquisite love, and of course, that we would be in states far removed from each other, requiring Jupiterian travels to reconnect again.

In this same Jupiter return year, I began composing my thesis on different perceptions of time and space, and how they affect the concept of the "self." I also began strategizing my indefinite travels through Asia. I sold all of my belongings and prepared for the journey that would change my life forever.

We now arrive at where we began this book, the portal into the midlife passage described in the Introduction, beginning with 27's Lunar Return and Nodal Reversal, and culminating in the Saturn Return of 28-30.

I thank you for exploring my personal planetary rites of passage with me. In Part 3, we have outlined the archetypal structure of the human life as it unfolds one planetary cycle initiation after another. It is my hope that you are inspired to practice this life review and to work with an astrological mentor as you journey through this process of sacred self-reflection and preparation for the cycles ahead.

Conclusion and Invitation

In his audio series on initiation, mythologist Michael Meade states that "the job of myth is to shape the world into meaning. [And] meaning is about being able to create a story that matures the collective vision of humanity" (Meade 2006).

In our journey together through the StArchetypal Theater, you have awakened to your sacred script, your unique contribution to the evolving story of humanity. Only you can fufill the spiritual need of the universe reflected in your birthchart. The planets invite you and initiate you as the hero, out on center stage. You are the protagonist, and your stage is filled with your supporting cast—with the cluster of souls who con-spire to make this the best prayerformance you could all imagine together.

With the astrological Codex of the Soul, your map and mirror will guide you as you travel ever deeper into your core center and towards your ascended return. Your birthchart is not a static picture—rather, it is a pulsing frequency, a dynamic dance within you, a poem for you to proclaim to the world. This is only the beginning. For as you apply this language more as a living spiritual practice, you will sing the Song of You as a brilliant Sun, and you will revel in the Full Moon celebration of your Being and the wonderland journey of your Becoming.

As my favorite Sesame Street character, game show host Guy Smiley would say- "This is Yourrrrr Life!" So Live it. Love It. And Illuminate it with the magic, mystery, and message of the heavens.

Sing your Stars
Dance your Destiny

And may all beings experience real love, compassion, joy,
understanding, wisdom, and bliss.
May my practice benefit all beings.

Above the cloud with its shadow is the star with its light. Above all things reverence thyself.

—Pythagoras

The Emerald Tablet of Hermes

In truth, without deceit, certain, and most veritable.

That which is Below corresponds to that which is Above, and that which is Above corresponds to that which is Below, to accomplish the miracles of the One Thing. And just as all things have come from this One Thing, through the meditation of One Mind so do all created things originate from this One Thing, through Transformation.

Its father is the Sun; its mother the Moon. The Wind carries it in its belly; its nurse is the Earth. It is the origin of All, the consecration of the Universe; its inherent Strength is perfected, if it is turned into Earth.

Separate the Earth from Fire, the Subtle from the Gross, gently and with great Ingenuity. IT rises from Earth to heaven and descends again to Earth, thereby combining within Itself the powers of both the Above and the Below.

Thus will you obtain the Glory of the Whole Universe. All Obscurity will be clear to you. This is the greatest Force of all powers, because it overcomes every Subtle thing and penetrates every Solid thing.

In this way was the Universe created. From this comes many wondrous Applications, because this is the Pattern.

Therefore am I called Thrice Greatest Hermes, having all three parts of the wisdom of the Whole Universe.
Herein have I completely explained the Operation of the Sun.

Appendix

Astrologers Cheat Sheet

PLANETS				
☉	Sun	Self-expression, will, assertion	♅ Uranus	Change, liberation, rebellion
☽	Moon	Response, intuition, feeling	♆ Neptune	Nebulousness, illusion, imagination
☿	Mercury	Communication, thought, movement	♇ Pluto	Renewal, deepening, transformation
♀	Venus	Harmony, love, beauty	⚷ Chiron	Wounding, healing, re-integration
♂	Mars	Energy, impulse, aggression		
♃	Jupiter	Expansion, achievement, excess	☊ N. Node	Joining (relationship)
♄	Saturn	Limitation, structure, containment	☋ S. Node	Separating (relationship)

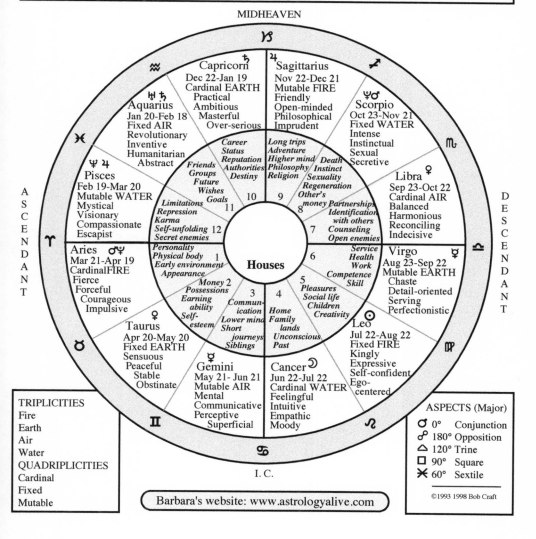

MIDHEAVEN

Capricorn — Dec 22-Jan 19, Cardinal EARTH, Practical, Ambitious, Masterful, Over-serious

Sagittarius — Nov 22-Dec 21, Mutable FIRE, Friendly, Open-minded, Philosophical, Imprudent

Aquarius — Jan 20-Feb 18, Fixed AIR, Revolutionary, Inventive, Humanitarian, Abstract

Scorpio — Oct 23-Nov 21, Fixed WATER, Intense, Instinctual, Sexual, Secretive

Pisces — Feb 19-Mar 20, Mutable WATER, Mystical, Visionary, Compassionate, Escapist

Libra — Sep 23-Oct 22, Cardinal AIR, Balanced, Harmonious, Reconciling, Indecisive

Aries — Mar 21-Apr 19, Cardinal FIRE, Fierce, Forceful, Courageous, Impulsive

Virgo — Aug 23-Sep 22, Mutable EARTH, Chaste, Detail-oriented, Serving, Perfectionistic

Taurus — Apr 20-May 20, Fixed EARTH, Sensuous, Peaceful, Stable, Obstinate

Leo — Jul 22-Aug 22, Fixed FIRE, Kingly, Expressive, Self-confident, Ego-centered

Gemini — May 21-Jun 21, Mutable AIR, Mental, Communicative, Perceptive, Superficial

Cancer — Jun 22-Jul 22, Cardinal WATER, Feelingful, Intuitive, Empathic, Moody

ASCENDANT — DESCENDANT

I. C.

Houses:
- 1 — Personality, Physical body, Early environment, Appearance
- 2 — Money, Possessions, Earning ability, Self-esteem
- 3 — Communication, Lower mind, Short journeys, Siblings
- 4 — Home, Family, lands, Unconscious, Past
- 5 — Pleasures, Social life, Children, Creativity
- 6 — Service, Health, Work, Competence, Skill
- 7 — Identification with others, Counseling, Open enemies
- 8 — Death, Instinct, Sexuality, Regeneration, Other's money, Partnerships
- 9 — Long trips, Adventure, Higher mind, Philosophy, Religion
- 10 — Career, Status, Reputation, Authorities, Destiny
- 11 — Friends, Groups, Future, Wishes, Goals
- 12 — Limitations, Repression, Karma, Self-unfolding, Secret enemies

TRIPLICITIES: Fire, Earth, Air, Water

QUADRIPLICITIES: Cardinal, Fixed, Mutable

ASPECTS (Major)
- ☌ 0° Conjunction
- ☍ 180° Opposition
- △ 120° Trine
- □ 90° Square
- ✳ 60° Sextile

Barbara's website: www.astrologyalive.com

©1993 1998 Bob Craft

Bibliography

BOOKS

Bobrick, Benson. *The Fated Sky: Astrology in History.* New York: Simon and Schuster, 2005.

De Fouw, Hart and Robert Svoboda. *Light on Life: An Introduction to the Astrology of India.* London: Penguin, 1996.

Fabricius, Johannes. *Alchemy: The Medieval Alchemists and Their Royal Art.* London: Diamond Books, 1976.

George, Demetra with Douglas Bloch. *Asteroid Goddesses: The Mythology, Psychology, and Astrology of the Reemerging Feminine.* San Diego: ACS Publications, 1986.

Hauck, Dennis William. *The Emerald Tablet: Alchemy for Personal Transformation.* New York: Penguin Compass, 1999.

Lawlor, Robert. *Sacred Geometry: Philosophy and Practice.* London: Thames and Hudson, 1982.

Levine, Stephen. *A Year to Live: How to Live This Year as If It Were Your Last.* New York: Bell Tower, 1997.

Miller, Anistatia R. and Brown, Jared M.. *The Complete Astrological Handbook for the Twenty-First Century.* New York: Schocken, 1999.

Myss, Caroline. *Sacred Contracts: Awakening Your Divine Potential.* New York: Harmony Books, 2001.

Newton, Michael, Ph.D. *Journey of Souls: Case Studies of Life Between Lives.* St. Paul: Llewellyn, 1998.

Paterson, Helena. *The Handbook of Celtic Astrology: The 13-Sign Lunar Zodiac of the Ancient Druids.* St. Paul: Llewellyn, 1998.

Phipps, Kelly Lee. *Celestial Renaissance: A Revolution of Astrology.* Kearney, NE: Morris Publishing, 1997.

Rinpoche, Sogyal. *The Tibetan Book of Living and Dying.* San Francisco: HarperSanFrancisco, 1992.

Santoro, Franco. *Astroshamanism, Book 2: The Voyage Through the Zodiac.* Findhorn: Findhorn Press, 2003.

Schermer, Barbara. *Astrology Alive: A Guide to Experiential Astrology and the Healing Arts.* Freedom, CA: The Crossing Press, 1998.

Suhrawardi. *The Shape of Light. Interpreted by Shaykh Tosun Bayrak.* Louisville, KY: Fons Vitae, 1998.

Starck, Marcia. *Healing with Astrology*. Freedom, CA: The Crossing Press, 1997.

Sullivan, Erin. *The Astrology of Midlife and Aging*. New York: Penguin, 2005.

Tarnas, Richard. *Cosmos and Psyche: Intimations of a New World View*. New York: Viking, 2006.

Virtue, Doreen, Ph.D. *Archangels and Ascended Masters*. Carlsbad, CA: Hay House, 2003.

Whitfield, Peter. *The Mapping of the Heavens*. Rohnert Park, CA: Pomegranate Artbooks, 1995.

Yeshe, Lama Thubten. *The Bliss of Inner Fire: Heart Practice of the Six Yogas of Naropa*. Boston: Wisdom Publications, 1998.

Zoller, Robert. *The Arabic Parts in Astrology: A Lost Key to Prediction*. Rochester, VT: Inner Traditions International, 1989.

MAGAZINE

Challen, John. "The Expansive Mirror of the Asteroids: An Unexpected Adventure." *The Mountain Astrologer*, Feb/Mar, 2007.

Keepin, William, Ph.D. "Astrology and the New Physics: Integrating Sacred and Secular Sciences." *The Mountain Astrologer*, Oct/Nov, 2009.

Kollerstrom, Nick. "Milestones of Genius: The Uranus Cycle in Isaac Newton's Life." *The Mountain Astrologer*, April/May, 2001.

Tarriktar, Tem and Kate Sholly. "Oprah Winfrey and Eckhart Tolle: Creative Collaborators." *The Mountain Astrologer*, June/July, 2008.

INTERNET

Brady, Bernadette. "Fixed Stars, Why Bother?" 2004. http://www.skyscript.co.uk/bb1.html

Dean, Geoffrey and Arthur Mather. "Sun sign columns: History, validity, and an armchair invitation." 1996. http://www.rudolfhsmit.nl/s-hist2.htm

European Space Agency. "New study reveals twice as many asteroids as previously believed." April 4, 2002. http://www.spaceref.com/news/viewpr.html?pid=7925

Forrest, Steven. "Evolutionary Astrology and Storytelling." Audio Interview. 2009. http://engagedheart.com/astrology

Plato, The Republic, Book X. http://classics.mit.edu/Plato/republic.11.x.html

Popovic, Mislav. "Kinaalda." http://traditionscustoms.com/coming-of-age/kinaalda

Schermer, Barbara. "Midlife Transits: An Introduction." 2005. http://www.astrologyalive.com/Midlife06.html

Schwartz, Jacob. "The Significance of Asteroids." 1995. http://www.astrologyalive.com/Asteroid.html

Scobie, Claire. "Why now is bliss," Telegraph Magazine, September 29, 2003. http://www.theage.com.au/articles/2003/09/28/1064687666674.html

Tierney, Bil. "Dreams for Sale: Neptune Transits." 1999. http://innerself.com/html/astrology/transits/neptune-transits.html

TELEVISON

The Universe, Season 1, Episodes 1-11.

FILM

Joseph, Peter. *Zeitgeist: The Movie.* 2007.

Phipps, Kelly Lee. *Return of the Magi: A Documentary Film About Authentic Astrology.* 2008.

AUDIO

George, Demetra. "Asteroids," The Blast Astrology Conference, 2007.

-----------. "The Thema Mundi," United Astrology Conference, 2008.

McKenna, Terence. "Eros and Eschaton," 1994.

Meade, Michael. "Initiation And The Soul: The Sacred and The Profane" [Disc 1], Mosaic Multicultural Association, 2006.

Phipps, Kelly Lee. "The Sacred Language of Astrology" Audio Astrology Course, 2003.

Lightning Source UK Ltd.
Milton Keynes UK
UKHW041434010419
340280UK00002B/533/P

Cat Therapy

Feline First Aid to
Lift the Spirits

Charlie Ellis

summersdale

CAT THERAPY

Copyright © Summersdale Publishers Ltd, 2016

Photographs © Shutterstock

All rights reserved.

No part of this book may be reproduced by any means, nor transmitted, nor translated into a machine language, without the written permission of the publishers.

Condition of Sale
This book is sold subject to the condition that it shall not, by way of trade or otherwise, be lent, resold, hired out or otherwise circulated in any form of binding or cover other than that in which it is published and without a similar condition including this condition being imposed on the subsequent purchaser.

Summersdale Publishers Ltd
46 West Street
Chichester
West Sussex
PO19 1RP
UK

www.summersdale.com

Printed and bound in China

ISBN: 978-1-84953-951-7

Substantial discounts on bulk quantities of Summersdale books are available to corporations, professional associations and other organisations. For details contact Nicky Douglas by telephone: +44 (0) 1243 756902, fax: +44 (0) 1243 786300 or email: nicky@summersdale.com.

To..

From......................................

When you're special to a cat,
you're special indeed.
Lester B. Pearson

For 10 minutes, at the beginning and end of every day, take some time to just sit, reflect and relax with your cat. Enjoy the calming feeling that this brings.

You can't look at a sleeping cat and feel tense.
Jane Pauley

Pet owners have been found to have higher levels of self-esteem and confidence than those without pets.

There are two means
of refuge from the misery
of life – music and cats.
Albert Schweitzer

Your choice of pet says a lot about your personality. Outgoing types often find themselves with a playful puss while quieter sorts tend to own pets with a calmer temperament.

If there were to be a universal sound depicting peace, I would surely vote for the purr.

Barbara L. Diamond

On occasion, envy can dominate our minds. Stop comparing yourself to others and work on being the best version of yourself. In short, be the person your cat thinks you are.

In nine lifetimes, you'll never know as much about your cat as your cat knows about you.

Michel de Montaigne

When you connect with your pet, oxytocin, the hormone that relieves stress and anxiety, is released, helping to reduce blood pressure and lower cortisol levels. Even if you feel run off your feet, take a moment to focus on yourself and your pet. Whether grooming or playing with them, the connection will soothe you.

Never wear anything that panics the cat.

P. J. O'Rourke

Interacting with animals relaxes the part of the brain associated with self-consciousness and social anxiety, but if you find yourself held back by the fear of most social situations, then you might consider Cognitive Behavioural Therapy. Learning to confront your fears can be amazingly empowering.

There are few things in life more heart-warming than to be welcomed by a cat.

Tay Hohoff

There is nothing stronger than the unspoken bond between pet and owner.

A meow massages the heart.

Stuart McMillan

Cat owners score very highly when it comes to how trust worthy they are and how much they trust other people. The love and trust that develops between a cat and its owner over time may well be the key to greater warmth and openness with others.

Animals are such agreeable friends – they ask no questions, they pass no criticisms.

George Eliot

Helping others makes us feel better about ourselves. Buy your cat a toy or treat and enjoy the obvious pleasure they take in it.

The ideal of calm exists in a sitting cat.

Jules Renard

A cat's purr produces vibrations ranging from 25 to 140 Hz, which provide us with a variety of health benefits, including: increased bone strength, a decreased risk of a stroke, lower blood pressure, and a boost for the immune system. Even damaged muscles and ligaments can heal faster.

You will always be lucky
if you know how to make
friends with strange cats.

Proverb

When you're out and about, pause to appreciate your surroundings, really seeing the things you take for granted every day. You'll be surprised by how much you've missed before. If you're inside, then place a photograph of nature or something that makes you smile in a place where you spend much of your time. Look at it often and allow yourself to relax.

Who hath a better friend than a cat?

William Hardwin

Have some fun with your feline friend. Playing with your pet is not only fun, it can raise your serotonin and dopamine levels, which are chemicals in your brain associated with happiness and calm.

I pet her and she pays
me back in purrs.
Terri Guillemets

Pets can provide a calming and happy influence on our lives. They encourage us to slow down our day, and provide us with moments of quiet reflection.

I have studied many philosophers and many cats. The wisdom of cats is infinitely superior.

Hippolyte Taine

Rhythmic petting or grooming can be comforting to your cat, and you. Concentrate on the texture of their soft fur, the warmth they radiate, and their deep breaths.

**Time spent with cats
is never wasted.**
Sigmund Freud

Another benefit of the chemical oxytocin, released when you interact with your cat, is that it is likely to make you more kind and empathetic over time.

I really love animals.
My cat is my little soulmate.
He's not just a cat,
he's my friend.

Tracey Emin

If you're feeling down, talking to your cat can help lift the burden off your shoulders. They're great listeners, they won't judge you and they'll still love you tomorrow.

Who among us hasn't envied a cat's ability to ignore the cares of daily life and to relax completely?

Karen Brademeyer

Cat owners are less likely to suffer from cardiovascular disease, as they tend to have lower triglyceride and cholesterol levels than those without. You can help to keep your heart healthy by paying attention to your diet, exercise and doing some simple mindfulness practice every day. Savour the everyday things, giving yourself time to really notice these lovely moments and life becomes full of small pleasures.

It is impossible to keep a straight face in the presence of one or more kittens.

Cynthia E. Varnado

The Center for Sleep Medicine at the Mayo Clinic in Arizona conducted a study into pet owners' sleep habits. Fifty-six per cent of the participants shared their bed or bedroom with a cat or dog. Forty-one per cent said having their pets in bed actually helps them sleep better and that having their pet in the bed relaxed them and made them feel safe and secure.

Wherever a cat sits, there shall happiness be first.

Stanley Spencer

If you're feeling a little overwhelmed but have trouble remembering to incorporate mindfulness into your day, place little notes around your home that will act as prompts for you to 'breathe', 'remember' and 'be mindful'.

Until one has loved an animal, a part of one's soul remains unawakened.

Anatole France

When your cat is sleeping, focus on trying to match its deep breathing. This will instil a wonderful sense of peacefulness and tranquillity.

A beating heart and an angel's soul, covered in fur.

Lexie Saige on cats

When you're feeling lonely, interacting with your cat can help to alleviate the feeling of solitude. Often a pet is very intuitive and will seek you out when you're feeling down.

When they are among us,
cats are angels.

George Sand

Following your cat's lead and taking a midday nap can help improve your overall mood, memory, productivity, alertness and creativity.

Cats are magical...
the more you pet them
the longer you both live.

Anonymous

Your cat can distract you and keep you present, taking your thoughts off the issues that are troubling you. When you are fully in the moment, you are not worrying about the past or the future. It's just you and your cat.

If you're interested in finding out more
about our books, find us on Facebook
at **Summersdale Publishers** and follow
us on Twitter at **@Summersdale**.

www.summersdale.com